*" Back in the 1950s, when my brothers Carl, Dennis and I were singing three-part harmonies in our bedroom in Hawthorne, California, there were three brothers in England learning to do the same thing … I love the Bee Gees and whenever one of their songs comes on the radio I definitely stop what I'm doing and listen.*

*The magic of the Bee Gees is in their songwriting and their lyrics … but the real secret is, they're a family, they're brothers. There's nothing more important than spiritual love in music and the Bee Gees have been giving us that spiritual love for 30 years. "*

BRIAN WILSON, ROCK AND ROLL HALL OF FAME INDUCTION CEREMONY, 1997

*" We are in fact the enigma with the stigma. "*

BARRY GIBB, ROCK AND ROLL HALL OF FAME INDUCTION CEREMONY, 1997

# prologue

Her name was Susan. At least I think it was Susan—this was, after all, 1977, way, way in the past. I was 16, a western Sydney kid in the standard uniform of Miller western shirt and desert boots. Grey Levis. Straggly hair. I had just one claim to cool—an expanding collection of Bob Dylan albums. Apart from that, you could safely file me under typical suburban dag, lacking in style, worldliness and anything resembling a clue.

Living in the 'burbs back then was tough enough, but Susan—I'm sure it was Susan, the more I think about it—decided, inadvertently, to complicate my teenage life. And it was all the fault of the Gibb brothers. Let me be perfectly clear: I was an old school Bee Gees fan. I had been raised on their classic 1960s hits and such later fare as 'Lonely Days' and 'Mr Natural' and I loved them all, equally. But lately, things had changed for the Bee Gees. And I was a bit uneasy with the shift.

I may have been a callow kid, but I did know one cold, hard fact: disco sucked. I had a T-shirt stating just that, which I'd wear like a badge of honour to all the usual school dances and under-age gigs—where, of course, disco music featured prominently. And why did disco suck? In my mind, it was probably as much to do with the look as the music—what suburban kid wanted to risk strutting around in a body shirt, open to the waist, teamed with nut-crunching trousers, gold chains and platform shoes, risking physical harm and endless ridicule? We wore jeans. We wore boots. We played footy. We listened to rock'n'roll.

Disco sucked, OK?

Anyway, none of this mattered to Susan. We were currently at the 'getting familiar' stage of our relationship. As these relationships would usually run their course after around a month, we must have been about a week in, the point where I'd do anything, hopefully, to rid myself of my damned virginity. Well, nearly anything.

Susan's birthday was a few days away.

'What would you like?' I asked her, as I fumbled with jean button and/or bra strap, perhaps both.

'Well, you know,' she said, sitting up, 'I'd really like a copy of the *Saturday Night Fever* album.'

Shit. *Really?*

I stopped doing what I was attempting to do. Of all the albums, all the freaking soundtracks, why this one? Not Neil Young or Bob Dylan or Lou Reed or Bowie—no, no, no—not even the Angels or Dragon, bands I could have coped with. Nope. My object of desire wanted a disco record. And not any disco record; this was the biggest disco statement this side of John Travolta. Bigger than his flares. Bigger than a mirror ball. Huge. Unavoidable. Everywhere. But not anywhere near me, thanks all the same.

So what to do? My mind started ticking over. If I didn't cough up the cash (which, fortunately, was one problem I didn't have because I had a job), I had no hope of closing the deal with my girlfriend *du jour*. But if I did buy the record—or, worse still, was spotted by anyone in the act of buying the record—the ridicule would be long, painful and endless. Soul destroying public humiliation. A disco record? What was I, a traitor to rock'n'roll?

All this hung heavily on my mind as I loitered like a stalker outside my local record store. To buy or not to buy? She did seem awfully enthusiastic about the record, I thought, and who knows what kind of carnal mayhem buying it might bring on.

Suddenly, a brainwave.

Twenty minutes later, after doing several laps of the store, pausing a few times at the soundtrack section before finally making my move, I walked back into the sunshine. The two black vinyl platters that comprised the *Saturday Night Fever* soundtrack were tucked under my arm. Inside a brown paper bag. Perfect.

What did I know at 16? Not much, as it turned out. For one thing, buying the record didn't get me laid. For another, the music on the album, especially the dazzling collection of Bee Gees songs, either crooned by the group or written for others—'Jive Talkin', 'You Should Be Dancing' and the rest of them—were as good as any songs created in an era that doesn't get its just musical dues. (I blame the body shirts and the perms; *that* shit hasn't aged very well.) But the Bee Gees' songs were amazing, and they also marked a stunning career turnaround for the three singing siblings.

In the early 1970s, before *Saturday Night Fever*, the Gibbs were as good as done, just another bunch of faded, jaded former pop stars, playing any gigs that came their way and cutting good records that were universally ignored. Yet by the mid-to-late 1970s they were kings of the world—for the second time, having already risen to the top with some exquisite pop in the 1960s. Who else could say that? To make it to the top once was almost beyond belief—but twice? Not a chance.

Fast forward 30-odd years and my two kids are watching the animated flick *Despicable Me*. Towards the end of a movie that provided me with as many laughs as my kids, there's a scene where villain-turned-nice-guy Gru is invited onto the dance floor to bust a move. He shakes his head: No, not me. His minions and others insist, but he resists, just as I did time and time again during my uncomfortable teens. So what song is it that eventually pulls Gru onto the floor—and unleashes his inner Travolta? The Bee Gees' 'You Should Be Dancing', of course. And whose music do you think my kids insist on adding to their iPods, even before the final credits roll? *Come on, who do you think?*

Flares and body shirts have aged badly, but great music never dies.

act

# beginnings

# 1

Hugh Gibb wasn't destined to be a pop star. For one thing, he was born out of time and place, in working-class Manchester, England, on 15 January 1916, the third child of seven born to Hugh and Edith Gibb (nee Yardley). The stars of Hugh's younger years were Americans Glenn Miller and Jimmy Dorsey, big band leaders, grown-up entertainers. And crooner Frank Sinatra, of course, who was about as close to a pop star—at least in terms of teen appeal—as the era produced. Hugh, however, had music in his blood but was too humble a character to hog the spotlight, unlike the four sons he would father.

The mild-mannered Hugh Gibb was a misfit, the family oddball who wasn't especially interested in pursuing a regular, responsible job, despite the urging of the rest of his clan. All Hugh ever wanted to do was to play the drums, while his siblings took 'sensible' jobs: older brother William was an engineering clerk; sister Hilda, eight years older than Hugh, worked as a typist.

While Hitler's war machine was goose-stepping all over Europe, the Hughie Gibb Orchestra, with Hugh keeping the beat, made a reasonable living playing the Mecca ballroom circuit in the north of England. Sometimes they'd cross the border into Scotland, where Hugh's father (also named Hugh) had been born in 1892.

Hugh's role as an entertainer excluded him from active service, although he did voluntary work in Metro's Gun Shop, a supplier of searchlights for the war effort. And as his son Maurice would say, Hugh 'did the soundtrack to World War II' in various ballrooms and theatres. As far as his audience (and the government) was concerned, Hugh and the orchestra were providing an essential service, a necessary escape from the sense of doom that lingered like a big black cloud over the UK in the early years of World War II. Every night, the audience, heavy with servicemen and women, danced and flirted and cut loose as if it was their last night on earth, which was a horrible possibility. Still, Hugh's family lived in hope that one day he might get smart and find a proper job, punch the clock. Musicians were one step up from vagabonds and gypsies in the eyes of the steady-as-you-go Gibbs.

Hugh didn't especially care. One night in 1941, when he and the orchestra were playing yet another gig in Manchester, he spotted a striking woman on the dance floor, amidst a sea of fledgling jivers and jitterbuggers and the odd stuffy ballroom dancer. Her name, as Hugh would learn, was Barbara May Pass. She was 20; Hugh was 25.

Hugh might not have been the most handsome man in England—his hairline was retreating, ever so slightly, even then—but he was a fast mover, and in the break between songs he nudged a member of the orchestra. 'Here, you take over,' Hugh said, pointing to his drum kit. The substitute stepped in for a couple of tunes as Hugh made a beeline for Barbara on the dance floor.

That night, Hugh and Barbara found out they had a strong musical connection. Barbara was a singer in another local dance hall band; she'd taken a night off from performing to check out the Hughie Gibb Orchestra. The stars aligned and a romance formed,

11

even though it took three more years before they were married, on 27 May 1944. In Manchester, of course.

A daughter, Lesley Barbara Gibb, was born on 12 January 1945.

With the war at an end, the peripatetic stage of the Gibb family life began. Hugh and his growing family shifted wherever the life of a jobbing muso took him. First there was a move to Edinburgh, where the work was heating up. One night, they played to a couple named Gray, the future in-laws of their yet-unborn son, Barry. Then came a move back to Manchester, where the family of three lived for a time with Barbara's mother, Nora.

Baby Lesley was barely 18 months old when Barry Alan Crompton Gibb was born, on 1 September 1946 at the Jane Crookall Maternity Home in Douglas on the Isle of Man in the Irish Sea. The Gibbs had relocated once again; they were now living on the Isle, settling in the capital Douglas, where Hughie held down residencies at the Douglas Bay Hotel and the Hotel Alexandra. With a population of barely 20,000, Douglas was a world away from the bustling manufacturing centre of Manchester, where the Avro Lancaster aircraft had been churned out in serious quantities during the war, even as the Luftwaffe's bombs battered the city. Douglas by comparison was sleepy, provincial.

That didn't necessarily mean that life in the Gibb family home was dull. Hugh had a tendency to bring his work home with him, in the form of 78-RPM records, which he'd play endlessly on the family stereogram. Hugh's music worked its way into baby Barry's DNA, as it would his twin brothers soon after.

Among the platters that mattered to Hugh were those of Bing Crosby, the era's No.1 crooner, whose 1942 recording of 'White Christmas' remains the biggest-selling 'single' of all time. Hugh admired Bing's creamy G-rated ballads, his cardigans, his pipe—his all-round, silky-smooth 'Bing-ness'. Hugh would also play the massively popular recordings of his old favourite, swing bandleader Glenn Miller—'Chattanooga Choo Choo', 'Tuxedo Junction', 'Pennsylvania 6-5000' and the rest of them—until the needle wore a groove in the shellac.

But there was another act much loved by Hugh that would, over time, have a huge influence on his musical offspring. The Mills Brothers comprised Herbert, Harry, Donald and John Mills Jr, from Piqua, Ohio. They honed their vocal chops in church, before establishing themselves as major recording stars in the 1930s. They were the first African American performers to appear at a Royal Command Performance, when they harmonised for King George V and Queen Mary in 1934. Their popularity transcended race and nationality. Sometimes known as the Four Kings of Harmony, the Mills boys hit it big with such solid gold smashes as 1931's 'Tiger Rag' and 1932's 'Dinah', which was recorded with—*vive la coincidence*—Bing Crosby. Over time, the Mills Brothers would sell some 50 million records, the kind of massive numbers that the Bee Gees would one day match, even surpass.

Hugh couldn't get enough of the Mills siblings; he loved their harmonies, their golden voices—and their relentlessly polite on-stage personas. A smile never left the Mills brothers' dials; it was as if they'd been born that way. As his own sons started to forge their musical career, Hugh would constantly remind them of the Mills Brothers and their willingness to please. 'Smile,' he'd tell his sons. 'Even if it hurts.' 'I think Dad wanted us to be little white Mills brothers,' Maurice Gibb would one day say with a laugh. It was pretty close to the truth.

On 22 December 1949, Barbara gave birth to twin boys. First to arrive was Robin Hugh, who was born at 3.15 a.m. Maurice Ernest arrived 35 minutes later.

A simple newspaper notice announced their arrival: 'GIBB— December 22nd, to Barbara and Hugh Gibb, 50 St Catherine's Drive, Douglas—twin sons. (Thanks to Dr McPherson and Sister Carine.)'

The twins' personalities quickly became apparent: Maurice was the more extroverted and eager to please—a 'goody goody' in his own words—while Robin was quieter, more withdrawn, a little wary of others. When they could talk, Robin called his twin 'Moggie'; Mo referred to Robin as 'Bodding'. That was close enough. Like brother Barry, Bodding and Moggie both grew substantial sets of choppers.

Just as the hierarchy of the twins was established at birth, with the older Robin usually calling the shots, Barry immediately assumed his life-long role as boss of *both* boys, the archetypal older brother. Maurice would regularly joke that they always referred to themselves as triplets—'except something went wrong with Barry'.

Barry's slow development—he'd barely started speaking when the twins were born—may have been brought about by a domestic accident that happened when he was about 18 months old. Home alone one day with Barbara, Barry tugged at a tablecloth until the contents of the tabletop, including a piping-hot pot of tea, rained down on top of him. Barry was so badly scalded that when he was admitted to hospital, doctors gave him 20 minutes to live. Barry was in a coma for some time and spent months recovering.

Barbara believed this accident toughened Barry, made him strong, a character trait he'd retain for life. Barry Gibb was built to last; a survivor. Interestingly, Barry erased the entire experience from his memory, and whenever the subject was raised he'd defer to his mother. He didn't remember a thing. Or perhaps he chose not to.

Hugh, meanwhile, expanded his musical operations. He now ran a concession, hiring musicians to entertain passengers onboard *Thistle*, a tourist ferry that criss-crossed the harbour at the Isle of Man. Hugh didn't collect a formal wage; instead he 'passed the hat' among the passengers, collecting tips. His official job title was 'bag man'. Money was tight for the Gibbs.

Hugh also continued to play with his band at the Isle's Glen Helen Hotel. The setlist featured the usual hits of the day: 'Sweet Georgia Brown', 'I'm In the Mood for Love', 'Moonglow'. Family-friendly entertainment.


Barry wasn't the only Gibb to experience a serious childhood incident. The River Dhoo flowed east towards Douglas through the central valley of the island before connecting with the River Glass and pouring out into the sea.

The river was a favourite place, both of the Gibbs and pretty much all the neighbourhood kids. Maurice was only a few years old when he and some other children trod warily over a pathway of stones linking the river's banks. The family Pomeranian was first to slip on the slimy rocks. Maurice immediately followed, falling straight into the drink. He was swept downstream, his one-piece 'siren' suit weighing him down. His head bobbed in the water, occasionally slipping below the surface.

Unable to fish him out of the Dhoo, the others raced back to the Gibb house, shouting for Hugh, hysterical. 'Dad,' they yelled, breathless, 'quick, Moggie's in trouble.'

The Gibbs could see the Dhoo from their window; the river

flowed only six metres or so feet from the rear of their cottage. But it took some time to spot Maurice, who'd been carried around 100 metres downstream. Hugh raced into the water fully clothed and pulled him out. It was a very close call. Maurice had been in serious danger of drowning.

Barry was barely five when he was enrolled at the Braddan School in September 1951. But Barry and school were not a good fit; most days he'd burst into tears at the slightest provocation. Maybe the bond with his mother was so strong that he just couldn't deal with separation—perhaps he was just a bit of a sook. Barry was teased and taunted, picked on and pushed around. He was nicknamed Bubbles. Big sister Lesley, who also attended Braddan, was regularly forced to come to his defence—one time she even chased off a local girl who terrorised her brother.

If he had had his way, Barry would have spent his time driving around the neighbourhood with Hugh, who'd taken on an extra job delivering bread for the local bakery, while Barbara was a cleaner at the Quarterbridge Hotel. Barry loved the smell of fresh bread, so much so that he sometimes sneaked into the back of the van without Hugh knowing and hollowed out a loaf or two, devouring the warm doughy interior and leaving the outer crust. More than a few islanders couldn't work out what was going on with their daily bread. Did it always come with holes?

Music wasn't the only distraction in the Gibb household. Christmas 1952 was especially festive, because Hugh managed to scrape together enough money to buy a TV set, the first in the street. Their home fast became the local do-drop-in; seemingly every kid within walking distance gravitated to the Gibbs' front room, staring wide-eyed at this new contraption.

TV was a cultural wasteland in the early 1950s, but that hardly mattered. Barry, in particular, developed square eyes; he found it hard to drag himself away from the set. *Flower Pot Men*, an out-there kids show set in an anonymous backyard garden and featuring Little Weed and Bill and Ben the Flower Pot Men, was a particular fave.

When Barry was seven, in 1953, he watched a TV variety show. It wasn't typical children's fare, but there was one performer whom he watched, spellbound. He was a song and dance man, a relic of the old music hall days, who sang, did a little soft shoe shuffle, got the audience laughing. Barry loved this performer, even if he didn't catch his name. 'That,' he said to no one in particular, pointing at the screen, 'is what I'd like to do.'

It was no surprise, really, given the background of his parents, and the music constantly playing in their home. Why wouldn't he want to be an entertainer? When alone, Barry would sing to himself, strumming a tennis racquet, air-guitaring in time to the music he heard in his head.

When not glued to the tube, Barry played a knife game called 'split the kipper'—a lark described by one reliable source as requiring little more than 'soft ground, stout shoes, a knife and large amounts of stupidity'. The aim of the game was to throw a knife so it stuck in the ground near your opponent's feet, but Barry wasn't especially skilled with the blade. He threw wildly, hitting a friend's finger instead of the ground and almost severing his buddy's digit. Barry decided to stick with air guitar.

Despite taking on all the work he could, Hugh found it almost impossible to make ends meet on the Isle of Man. When his contract at the Hotel Alexandra wasn't renewed in 1955, the family agreed to return to the mainland, to Manchester. Lesley was ten, Barry nine, and the twins six.

Upon arrival, the family split by necessity, as they had no home. The twins, Lesley and Barbara moved in with Barbara's sister. Barry and his father lived for a time with Hugh's family. All the Gibbs then reunited at a boarding house at 161 Withington Road in Whalley Range, before settling at 51 Keppel Road in Chorlton.

Manchester was cold; bitterly cold in winter, especially. They'd wake in the morning and turn on the taps to make tea, and find that the water had frozen in the pipes. Getting out of bed was a struggle, let alone making it to school. Shorts were part of the boys' school uniform and their legs would turn to ice during their brisk walk to Manley Park Junior School.

Barry disliked Manley Park as much as he had school on the Isle of Man. But rather than cry away his problems, he now took a more pragmatic approach—he started skipping classes, sometimes entire days. He and Lesley would walk to the bus stop, watch the bus go by, and then return home and claim it had never arrived. The twins, meanwhile, found their own wayward niche: they became firebugs, junior pyromaniacs. Anything that looked vaguely flammable— paper, dry grass, wood, whatever—was fair game.

One particularly lively afternoon, this time with big brother Barry along, Robin and Maurice lit a fire behind a set of billboards and watched with both glee and fear as the whole lot caught ablaze. Thinking it best to make themselves scarce, the brothers headed off to the nearby baths for a swim, as the local fire brigade and police tore past them, sirens wailing. After their swim, Barry, all innocence and light, asked a copper what was going on. 'Some idiots lit a fire,' the officer replied, 'but don't worry, we'll get 'em.' Barry smirked, nudged Robin and Maurice, and scarpered to the safety of Keppel Road.

Duly inspired, Robin moved his firebuggery indoors, stashing away leaves and twigs inside his coat and then sparking the lot up under his bed. When caught—the billowing smoke was pretty hard to miss—he'd blame his more innocent twin. 'Moggie did it!'

'If I had been my parents,' an adult Barry admitted, 'I would have been pulling my hair out. And my father had little enough as it was.'

Before their pyromania got completely out of hand—and there *had* been a few questions posed by the local constabulary about the Gibb boys—the brothers found another, more lawful pastime: music. Barry's air-guitaring days ended not long after moving back to the mainland, when he was given a very rudimentary guitar, his first, a gift from Hugh that cost a whopping four quid. A neighbour taught Barry a few 'open' tunings, his first real steps to a musical life.

An early hero of Barry was Tommy Steele, a working-class hero, a vanilla replica of Elvis Presley. A solid-gold teen idol, Londoner Steele was everywhere in the late 1950s: on the pop charts, in movies and starring in West End musicals. The soundtrack to *The Tommy Steele Story* film reached No.1. Barry was a huge fan.

At home on Keppel Road, the brothers discovered the simple joys of harmonising: it was as natural to them as lighting fires. It may have been desperately cold, but they discovered that their parents' bedroom had a great echo, pure reverb, almost as good as a recording studio.

Hugh was in the kitchen one afternoon when he heard voices

coming from somewhere else in the house. He was confused. 'I'm sure the radio isn't on,' he thought to himself. Hugh eventually traced the source of the music: Barry, Maurice and Robin were working on their harmonies in the bedroom. Hugh was impressed; from that day onwards, he decided pretty much on the spot, he'd do whatever he could to further their musical careers. It had to be better than arson.

Singing was high on the curriculum at primary school. The Gibbs would belt out standards like 'All Things Bright and Beautiful' at school assembly, although the brothers were once banned from the choir because they improvised harmonies during the daily rendition of 'God Save the Queen'. Some songs, they discovered, were sacrosanct. Not the most popular kids (Barry had been nicknamed 'Smelly' by some wags, hardly an improvement on Bubbles), the Gibb brothers would spend a lot of time lingering by the entrance to the school, swapping inside jokes, imitations—the Goons were big favourites—and singing. Always singing.

There were a couple of hit songs of the day that played key roles in their early musical development. Maurice—now 'Mo', no longer 'Moggie'—was especially excited by the Everly Brothers' 1957 hit 'Wake Up Little Susie'.

'That's when I really felt the love,' Maurice admitted.

And there was a lot to love about the song: the harmonies, the indelible melody, a whiff of bad teen behaviour, and the fact these singing Americans were siblings. That was interesting. 'Susie' was one song the brothers would sing repeatedly in their parents' echo chamber of a bedroom.

Another big source of inspiration was 'Lollipop', a hit for British family band the Mudlarks—Jeff, Fred and Mary Mudd, no less—all the way from not-so-exotic Luton in Bedfordshire. 'Lollipop' was a hit in both America and the UK. While nowhere near as new or thrilling or sexually charged as the early rock recordings of Elvis Presley, Little Richard and their fellow trailblazers that were making waves across the western world, this doo-wop chestnut was hard to avoid. Again, it was the golden harmonies that got the Gibbs excited.

'The harmonies became instinctive for us,' Barry would one day explain, 'because we loved the oldies.'

The next logical step for the Gibbs was a public performance. Chorlton's Gaumont Theatre, located at the corner of Manchester and Nicholas Roads, was like many other post-war entertainment venues, an opulent, neo-classical joint, with a 2000-plus capacity. Its centrepiece was a huge stage fifteen metres wide and seven metres deep. In between screenings of the latest offerings of Abbott and Costello and the Three Stooges, or imported features such as 1956's *Smiley*, a sort of Australian version of *Huckleberry Finn* starring the rugged Chips Rafferty and a kid named Colin Petersen, who'd one day become a Bee Gee, local hopefuls would get up on stage and mime to the hits of the day. Tommy Steele and Elvis were ripe for the imitating. Whoever and whatever was on the charts.

Barry, Robin and Maurice were regulars at the Gaumont's matinees. After another Saturday morning watching the usual rag-tag collection of performers, they agreed: 'We can do better than this lot.' Come next Saturday—it was now just after Christmas (probably 1957, though the brothers were never clear on the date)—the Gibbs would make their public debut. They christened themselves the Rattlesnakes.

At 10 a.m. they headed off to the Gaumont with a couple of

mates in tow, clutching their prized collection of vinyl records, among them the Everly Brothers' 'Wake Up Little Susie' and Paul Anka's 'I Love You Baby'. Their plan was pretty straightforward: crank up their favourite songs and sing along, karaoke style, imagining all the time that they were in their parents' bedroom at home. What could go wrong?

Barry was in charge of the records; he also had his acoustic guitar tucked under his arm. Understandably nervous, he raced up the steps of the theatre, stumbled, tripped and dropped the box of singles, smashing them into a thousand pieces. Crap. Barry turned to look at the others, fear in his eyes. 'What do we do now?'

The show had to go on. But now they had to sing for real.

Breathing deeply and shaking like leaves, the Gibbs stepped out in front of the rowdy gathering and harmonised their way through a song they knew inside out, the Mudlarks' 'Lollipop', plus a couple of other favourites. The response wasn't as awful as they'd imagined; in fact the Gaumont's manager slipped them a shilling each and asked if they'd return next Saturday and do it all over again.

'We just did what we did at home,' Maurice recalled many years later, 'and the kids loved it.'

Robin had once boasted to a friend, 'We're going to be rich one day, we're going to form a band.' It was little more than youthful bluster. But after the Gaumont performance, the brothers were walking home when Barry turned to Robin and Maurice. 'We're going to be *really famous*, you know.'

As always, Hugh was supportive, overwhelmingly so. Apart from their appearances at the Gaumont, Hugh found them another gig, singing at a Russell Street club, for which they were paid two shillings and sixpence each. Now that was impressive. Hugh backed them on the drums, then he smuggled them out the back door after a few songs. Kids weren't allowed on licensed premises.

'We thought, my goodness, they like us,' recalled Barry. He wasn't fooled, though: he realised that part of their appeal was their age; the toothy trio were just kids. Still, a pre-teen combo singing in three-part harmony was rare. 'We were doing something no one had seen before,' Barry said.

More performances followed. Their act started to take some shape, as they harmonised their way through personal favourites and current hits, but they were stuck coming up with a name that worked. They ditched the 'Rattlesnakes', and were, briefly, Wee Johnnie Hayes and the Bluecats, Barry re-christened as Johnnie Hayes. If Tommy Steele (aka Thomas Hicks) could change his name, why couldn't he?

When not performing for an audience, Barry, Robin and Maurice would rehearse wherever they could find a suitable space. A neighbour let them use her cellar; they also found a user-friendly echo in the men's toilet at the John Lewis department store. They liked the ambience there so much, in fact, that for the rest of their musical lives, the Gibbs preferred to rehearse and record in rooms that reminded them of that toilet. They'd ask each other, 'Does it sound like John Lewis?'

Andrew Roy 'Andy' Gibb was born on 5 March 1958, the fifth and final Gibb child. Over time, Andrew would come to most physically resemble big brother Barry. He was the Gibbs' other golden boy.

Soon after Andy was born, the family was on the move again. Hugh was still struggling to keep the good ship Gibb afloat with work as hard to find on the mainland as on the Isle of Man. And while the boys had moved on from their days of arson, they were still getting into trouble. Barry was linked to the theft of a toy pedal car. When an exasperated policeman arrived at the front door to have a 'little chat', he made a suggestion to Hugh and Barbara that resonated more strongly than he could have imagined: 'There must be another country you can take these children to.'

Funnily enough, there was. When World War II ended in 1945, the Australian government introduced what was known informally as the 'Ten Pound Pom' plan, designed to bump up the population and supply labour for the country's booming industries. It was open to all British subjects. The price of entry was, funnily enough, ten quid, which subsidised the cost of travel. As an added bonus, kids travelled free. The Gibbs were among roughly one million immigrants who took advantage of this and similar schemes. Their fellow Ten Pound

Poms included the families of two future PMs – Julia Gillard and Tony Abbott – and businessman Alan Bond.

Hugh Gibb, admittedly, had been doing it tough up north, even spending time on the dole. 'Work was pretty difficult for my dad to come up with in the late '50s,' said Robin, 'and he needed a fresh start. He was still young enough to do that ... So it was kind of a natural move.'

When Hugh broke the news to the rest of the family, they were by turns excited and confused. Australia? Where the heck was that? Neither Robin nor Barry had heard of the place. Maurice, however, had some background on their home-to-be; he knew a bit about the indigenous wildlife. He expected to step off the boat and find kangaroos hopping down the city streets. Perhaps he'd caught a glimpse of *Smiley* when it screened at the Gaumont.

While kangaroos didn't frequent the cities, Australia was still a bit of a backwater in the late 1950s. Long-time Prime Minister Robert 'Bob' Menzies ran the country like Little Britain, in eternal deference to Buckingham Palace. When Queen Elizabeth II undertook a royal tour of duty in 1954, Menzies couldn't have been any gushier. 'I did but see her passing by,' he swooned in a newspaper editorial, quoting the poet Thomas Ford, 'and yet I love her till I die.'

To most Ten Pound Poms, Australia's culture and manners felt familiar, even if the climate was nothing like dark and gloomy Mother England. In 1958, smooth crooners Perry Como and Pat Boone were top of the pop charts Down Under, along with the Gibbs' favourite group, the Everly Brothers. The only thing vaguely Australian to be heard was a quaint country ditty, 'Pub With No Beer', sung by a true-blue bushie named Slim Dusty. *South Pacific* and *The Ten Commandments* were packing them in at cinemas with

Anglophilic names: the Tivoli, the Bijou, the Regent. Even the place names felt familiar: Victoria, Queensland, Adelaide, Newcastle. Cricket was the summer sport of choice. It really was Little Britain.

In Sydney, a fast-living ex-pat American promoter named Lee Gordon imported international rock'n'rollers such as Buddy Holly and the Crickets, and Jerry Lee Lewis for shows at an old boxing barn at Rushcutters Bay known as Sydney Stadium. The only local rocker to gain real prominence at these 'Big Shows' was Johnny O'Keefe, who'd soon enough play a role in the world of the Gibbs. Local content across any form of entertainment was hard to come by: all things English or American were preferred.

The Gibbs commenced their five-week journey to Oz in late July 1958, travelling in the third-class section of the *Fairsea*, taking in the Suez Canal and the Red Sea along the way. At every opportunity, Robin, Maurice and Barry – billed as 'Barry and the Twins' – would gather at one end of the boat, giving free shows for their fellow passengers, often outstaying their 'off-decks' curfew of 9 p.m. 'We had a ball,' said Maurice.

Among their fellow passengers was a British kid, Redmond 'Red' Symons, who'd one day undertake his own musical odyssey as guitarist and resident shit-stirrer in Melbourne shock-rock outfit Skyhooks. When they weren't singing, the Gibbs and Symons darted about the decks zapping passengers with water pistols.

The Gibbs reached Australia on 1 September, Barry's 12th birthday, settling in suburban Redcliffe, on Moreton Bay about 30 kilometres north-east of Brisbane. They were now in sub-tropical Queensland, where the temperature rarely dipped below the high

20s. Now this was different. The locals couldn't have known it of course, but the town's most famous residents had just arrived: Redcliffe would become known as a sacred place for the Bee Gees, home today to Bee Gees Way.

'There were passionfruits in the streets and banana trees in everybody's garden,' Robin marvelled.

In Redcliffe, water didn't freeze in the taps and kids didn't risk frostbite going to school. The boys wore khaki shorts and no shoes, and swam off the dock at Deception Bay every morning—Mo included, who'd clearly gotten over his near-drowning back on the Isle of Man. Redcliffe wasn't sophisticated—Brisbane was really not much more than a big country town—but to this family of Brits it felt like paradise. Barry was fascinated by blue-tongue lizards; he'd never seen anything like them before.

'I was a stranger in a strange land,' Barry wrote in 1999. 'We came to [Redcliffe] without any real idea of where we were going … and we found ourselves here in paradise … Johnny O'Keefe was singing "Shout" on the radio, Col Joye was singing "Bye Bye Baby" and Johnny Cash was singing "[Ballad of a] Teenage Queen".'

Anything seemed possible for the Gibbs.

Hugh found work as a 'bush photographer', shooting family portraits in some of the more far-flung Brisbane suburbs. His 8mm film camera also came in handy for home movies, often with Maurice directing. (Some of these Gibb flicks still exist today.) Hugh also did some work for the local Scarborough council. The children, still thrilled by endless days of sunshine, enrolled at Scarborough State School.

Brisbane's 4KQ was one of many Australian radio stations of the era to host a *New Faces*-type program, simply called *Talent Quest*. TV hadn't even hit Queensland yet so radio was still the dominant medium. *Talent Quest* is where the trio, now simply called the Gibb Brothers, made their bittersweet Australian debut. They didn't win, and this stung Barry, because he referred to it with regret in his 1999 letter, a big-hearted valentine to Redcliffe. But they'd soon make a far more important breakthrough at the nearby Redcliffe Speedway.

Barry and a buddy named Ken Griggs would go to Redcliffe Speedway every Saturday, not so much to watch the races—neither Barry nor his brothers really fit the Aussie sporting stereotype—but to sell soft drinks to raise a little extra cash. As he walked through the crowd, a case of drinks strapped around his shoulders, Barry noticed that there were lengthy gaps between the races, with little in the way of entertainment or other distractions. He enticed the twins to come along to the speedway; they set up a makeshift stage under the grandstand and sang whenever the roar of the cars died down for any fair length of time. Passers-by didn't know what to make of the buck-toothed twins and the gangly 12-year-old with a guitar.

One typically lively Saturday night, a driver approached 28-year-old Bill Goode, who managed the speedway, and told him there were three kids who wanted to sing at interval in what was called a 'coin drop'—the crowd would throw loose change onto the track to thank the boys for their singing as they crooned from the back of a truck. These were the same three kids, of course, who'd already been singing on their makeshift stage—but it was the first time Goode knew anything about it.

The idea sounded just fine to Goode; he was up for anything to keep the crowd occupied. Come interval time, Goode was as preoccupied as ever when he heard voices wafting up from the direction of the pits, coming through the dodgy old Tannoy speaker that passed as the speedway's PA system. Goode couldn't see the Gibbs, he had no idea of their age, and he didn't actually get to see them do their first circuit of the track, collecting coins as they went, but he was hugely impressed by what he heard.

Forty years later, performing at Redcliffe still resonated with Barry Gibb. 'The smell of the oil, the noise and the atmosphere was incredible.'

Bill Goode leapt into action. 'Where did you find these kids?' he asked the driver who'd first suggested the idea. The driver told Goode that they were locals who lived close to the Speedway.

Goode knocked at the door of the Gibbs' house in Oxley Avenue. 'Are you the kids I heard singing the other night?' he asked the boys. They said they were and invited him inside.

Goode had a look around the brothers' music room. Apart from his beaten-up guitar, Barry had fashioned a rough instrument out of a tea chest and some fishing line; the twins fiddled about with a timber fruit case and a single drum. OK, so they needed some real equipment—but it was their voices that interested Goode. 'I've come down to listen to you,' Goode said, 'so that I can work out whether I think you're future talent or not.'

Barry, always the big brother and leader of the pack, stepped forward. 'What would you like to hear?' he asked. 'One of the songs we've written?'

Goode didn't expect this. They wrote songs, too? 'How many have you written?' he asked.

'Oh, about 180,' Barry replied.

Goode was gobsmacked.

The boys started to sing, and for the second time Goode was spellbound. He'd never heard voices this good. And original songs, too? Amazing.

'Barry was mature beyond his years,' Goode said in a 2013 ABC interview. '[He was] well spoken and kept the other two pretty much under control … Barry was determined, I think, to make sure they got somewhere.'

Goode called 'Swinging' Bill Gates, who worked at radio station 4BH. Goode placed ads with Gates; the DJ sometimes drove cars at Goode's speedway. 'You've got to hear these kids,' Goode told Gates. 'They're incredible.'

Gates had the same response as his friend. The pair agreed to promote the brothers as hard as they possibly could through the radio station. 'So what's their group called?' Gates asked. Good question.

The Gibbs had already worked through a few dodgy names: the Rattlesnakes, Wee Johnny Hayes and the Bluecoats. But they needed something a bit more authentic, less jokey. After a little toing and froing, Goode and Gates came up with an idea: why not the BGs? Goode, Gates and Barry Gibb all shared the initials; Barbara Gibb was yet another BG. Clearly this was a good omen. There seemed to be a hell of a lot of Bs and Gs in their world right now.

When Goode again caught up with the boys, the name was settled upon, with one slight tweak: the BGs became the Bee Gees. Perfect.

Goode met Hugh Gibb, and learned that the family was broke. Hugh was now trying his hand as a travelling salesman, flogging brooms, but without much luck.

Andy was just a baby, barely one year old. The Gibbs really needed some good fortune. Perhaps the boys' musical talent could generate some income, Hugh suggested to Goode. 'What do you think?' Goode drew up a rough contract and came onboard as the Bee Gees' first manager. Hugh agreed to start looking for pub and club gigs for the brothers, while the boys continued to perform at the speedway, sometimes bringing home as much as three quid—not a bad day's work.

Goode was hoping that the boys' music would get the right exposure on Gates' Sunday radio show, *Midday Platter Chatter*. Keith Fowle, a local producer, agreed to help the brothers in the 4BH studio, where they worked with a three-piece band. The Bee Gees cut six of Barry's original songs at 4BH; these included 'Let Me Love You', which they'd already played at the Speedway, plus 'Twenty Miles to Blueland' and 'The Echo of Your Love'.

All great in theory, but having their music heard all over Australia was harder than any of them could have imagined, and this would remain a problem until the mid-'60s.

Still, Gates played the hell out of the only pressing of the record, and talked it up to anyone who'd listen, including influential Sydney DJ Bob Rogers, who also took a shine to the Bee Gees. And with the introduction of TV to Brisbane in 1959, producers were constantly on the lookout for local, cheap talent. In March 1960, the Bee Gees made their TV debut on ABC Brisbane's *Anything Goes*. Maurice and Robin sang while standing on boxes, so the height difference between the twins and big brother Barry wasn't so pronounced.

This led to a weekly show, broadcast live on Friday nights in Brisbane, *The BGs' Half Hour*. The brothers took time off school every Friday to film the program. The Gibb brothers have never been shy when it comes to embellishing a good story, and Barry insisted that the 'Children's Welfare Department' contrived to end the show.

31

'They did not consider we were old enough to do this kind of work.' *The BGs' Half Hour* was cut back to monthly and eventually killed off altogether. Still, it was hardly the end of their early TV career—anything but. BTQ 7's Desmond Tester, an ex-pat Pom himself and one of the best-known TV personalities of the era, hyped the Bee Gees on shows he hosted such as *Cottee's Happy Hour*.

The Gibbs were one of 14 acts on the bill of another of Tester's shows, *Strictly for Moderns*, which screened in 1960. Their co-stars included singers Kerry Lyons and Jill McInnes, along with comics and dancers, while Don Burrows blew a civilised sax as a member of Joe Loufer's Swingtet. It was all frightfully earnest, early Aussie TV at its starchiest.

During a jukebox jury segment, while the small studio audience was being asked to pass judgment on the Safaris' song 'Image of a Girl', Barry, Robin and Maurice sat anxiously in the front row, looking on. They were decked out in matching outfits: zippered cardigans, pants and ties. Barry had his acoustic guitar rakishly slung over his shoulder, trying desperately to look cool. Or close to cool.

Tester then invited them on stage. Barry set himself stage right, Robin in the centre, Mo to his left. The boys looked sharp enough in their bespoke outfits and flashing their toothy smiles, as they finger-clicked their way through Barry's 'Time is Passing By', a particularly mature reflection on a relationship from a kid barely into his teens whose voice had barely broken. It was a sort-of country/sort-of pop ballad with a hint of Everly Brothers harmony. The audience responded politely. Unlike many of the others on the show, the brothers seemed reasonably assured, if frightfully serious. 'It was great experience because you were on the spot,' Barry told British talk show guru Michael Parkinson in 1981. 'Nothing was pre-recorded. You picked up your guitar and you went on and you played and you sang.'

Hugh, meanwhile, found his three sons work in local pubs and clubs, some of these venues setting new standards in dodginess. Because the boys were under-age, they'd be whisked in through a rear door—and then they'd usually confront a rowdy, boozy gathering with little idea about what to make of three squeaky cleans in matching waistcoats with the letters BG emblazoned on their lapels.

One night, Hugh found them work in a club without a roof. The brothers worked through their usual routine, which now included a bit of a comedy act, Robin delivering the punchlines and Mo sporting a tie that 'levitated'—'like an erection', according to Barry— and a setlist featuring such English novelty chestnuts as 'Does Your Chewing Gum Lose its Flavour (on the Bedpost Overnight)?' and 'My Old Man's a Dustman', along with a few Mills Brothers tunes and the odd Barry original such as 'The Echo of Your Love'.

As they sang, rain came 'pissing down', Barry recalled, and drenched the Gibbs. The few punters in the room didn't mind; they just kept drinking. Then a fight broke out, forcing the brothers to take a few steps back from the front of the stage, for fear of copping a flying chair or a random fist. All the while, teetotaller Hugh stood nearby, encouraging the boys to keep on smiling through the mayhem. Just another night in Aussie clubland.

As educations go, this apprenticeship was hard to top: what audience could possibly be more demanding than drunken, rowdy shearers and sailors?

Hugh may have tried his best to shelter the boys from the rough 'n' tumble of Queensland nightlife, but sometimes they found their own mischief. Mo insisted that he lost his virginity to a showgirl backstage somewhere in Nowheresville, Australia, at the ripe old age of nine. It was surely a bit of myth-making by Maurice—*nine?*—but it's clear they were exposed to some craziness as they played the far-flung clubs and pubs. In another discussion of these eye-opening times, Mo altered the script slightly: this time it was a stripper, he was 11, and they merely shared a dressing room, which was juicy enough for any kid.

'We had a great childhood,' smirked Mo.

Group leader Barry found romance, of sorts, with someone more his own age. In August 1960, during a gig at Brisbane's Woolloongabba Town Hall, he spotted Ann Blackmore sitting near the stage, sharing a table with her date for the night. When the brothers broke for interval, and Ann's date excused himself briefly, Barry headed straight for the pretty young girl, just as his father had done with his mother all those years ago in Manchester. 'Mind if I join you?' Barry asked, easing himself into a seat.

For the next 20 or so minutes, Barry filled Ann in on where the Bee Gees had been—and where they were headed. The two even managed a quick twirl round the dance floor before Ann's date returned and Barry got back to work.

The two were close for the next couple of years; she'd visit him and the family at their suburban home, where they'd set up a makeshift studio in a space under the house. Baby Andy would settle into Ann's lap as Barry led Mo and Robin through his latest tunes, ever the bandleader and big brother. Little did Ann Blackmore know it, but she had a front row seat to pop music history.

Just as in England, in Redcliffe, Barry and education had an uneasy relationship, so when he turned 15 in 1961, he left school and started looking for 'proper' work to bolster the meagre income generated by the band. Unfortunately, Barry's first and only non-musical gig, assisting a tailor, didn't last long. One day he forgot to hand along some money and was sacked. And that was it for Barry and regular employment. (Mo and Robin fared little better than their brother in the classroom and fudged documents so they could both quit school at 14.)

Soon after, Barry was thrown a lifeline, a handy five-year publishing deal with Belinda Music, thanks mainly to Tony Brady, a staffer who'd heard about Barry's songwriting prowess and spoke up for him. It wasn't a recording contract, but at least a publishing deal gave Barry the chance to get his songs heard—perhaps even recorded—by some key artists. At Belinda, Barry's fellow singers and songwriters included up-and-comers Lonnie Lee and Johnny Devlin, both regulars on *Six O'Clock Rock*, the ABC TV show hosted by the Wild One himself, Johnny O'Keefe, that aired nationally and was watched each week by more than a million viewers.

Barry's good fortune touched his brothers—when the family shifted to the holiday haven Surfers Paradise the trio snagged an

18-month residency at the Beachcomber Hotel, where O'Keefe and his band the Dee Jays, as well as Tenterfield piano man Peter Allen, had played.

O'Keefe saw the brothers play in Surfers and invited them to audition to perform on *Six O'Clock Rock*. The try-outs were held on Saturday mornings in an inner-city Sydney church hall, after which the successful aspirants, hand-picked by O'Keefe, would race convoy-style to the ABC Studios in Gore Hill to shoot the program. At the ABC studio, hundreds of teenagers would be jostling for admission to the live shoot.

When Barry, Mo and Robin turned up at the church hall, they took the unusual step of bringing their own musical charts. O'Keefe's band, the Dee Jays, were all jazz-trained musos, serious players. The Dee Jays, as one, raised their eyebrows when Barry handed over a sheet of paper.

Control freak O'Keefe walked over and demanded, 'What's this?'

'That's our song,' explained Barry.

O'Keefe said nothing, just handed the music back to his band. It looked as though these kids in their matching waistcoats knew what they were doing.

'Snotty-nosed brats,' mumbled one Dee Jay, as the Gibbs breezed through the audition and scored their first national TV spot.

While in Sydney, the brothers visited Hyde Park in the city centre and found that the public toilet there had great acoustics, just like the loo at the John Lewis department store back in Manchester. Robin managed to work this into his comedy routine at their next show. He joked that he and his brothers had been in Sydney, singing 'in some of the best toilets in town'.

Barry's publishing deal was a boon for the Bee Gees, but what they really craved was a recording contract, the chance to get into a studio and cut some of Barry's tunes.

Johnny O'Keefe's pop rival, Col Joye, played his part in helping them take this next step up the pop ladder. Joye, a lanky, clean-cut 20-something from Sydney's working-class south-west, was touring Queensland in 1962 with his band the Joy Boys. His songs 'Bye Bye Baby', 'Rockin' Rollin' Clementine' and 'Oh Yeah Uh Huh' had been huge national hits. Joye was also the face of Channel 9's *Bandstand*, hosted by Brian Henderson, the commercial network's bland rival to the more energetic *Six O'Clock Rock*. Johnny O'Keefe apart, no one had more pull in the Australian music industry in the early 1960s than Col Joye.

Before an evening show at Surfers Paradise, Joye and his band were rehearsing in a church hall barely 100 metres from the Gibb family home at Cambridge Avenue. The boys knew that getting their music to Joye would be incredibly helpful so they turned up at the hall. After much talk about who was going to take the lead, Barry manned-up. 'Bugger it,' he said, 'I'm going.'

The story goes that he crossed the road and started talking with a fellow outside the venue, who turned out to be Kevin Jacobsen, Joye's brother—and a Joy Boy, to boot. 'Hang on,' Jacobsen told the gangly kid. 'Col's on his way out.'

Joye proved to be as amiable in the flesh as his nice-guy public image suggested. He agreed to sit down with Barry and listen to some of his songs. Barry was gobsmacked—Col Joye wants to hear my songs! He tore across the street, grabbed Mo and Robin and together they undertook an impromptu audition for Joye, who, while not blown away by Barry's songs, was struck by their pristine harmonies. And these kids were so young. There was clearly something special here.

In another version of the same story, it was father Hugh who lobbied Joye, setting up the church hall audition. Either way, Australia's newest shining star was now aware of the singing, harmonising Gibb brothers from north of the border.

Joye gave Hugh and the boys some advice, echoing something Johnny O'Keefe had already told them: 'Move to Sydney, the Big Smoke,' Joye said. 'That's where the music business is based.' Surfers was pleasant and the work steady, but career-wise it was a bit of a dead-end.

Joye was right, of course—both *Bandstand* and *Six O'Clock Rock* were Sydney-based, as was Festival Records, Australia's biggest local record label, home to Joye and O'Keefe, among others. And there was a thriving live circuit of clubs, pubs, community centres and halls in and around Sydney that hosted concerts seven nights a week. Sometimes you even got paid for your work. Laid, too, on a good night.

Hugh Gibb had recently decided to take over the boys' career as his full-time job, and amiably parted ways with Bill Goode, who actually encouraged Hugh to step up. There's no doubt that his commitment to making his sons stars was vicariously fulfilling the musical destiny that eluded him during his playing days. Barry half-jokingly referred to this an 'extension of father's frustration'.

Regardless of the motivation, the Gibb family shifted south in early 1963, settling at Colin Street in western Sydney's Lakemba. One of the first things they did in their new home – soon known as 'Swingin' House' – was transform a garden shed into a makeshift studio-cum-rehearsal room. When not singing and/or composing, the brothers would 'play TV' in their studio, pretending to host their own tonight show. 'We have a different script every day,' Mo said, when asked about Channel Gibb, 'and we're always changing the floor plan and [moving] the sets around.'

The brothers even improvised feature films. They revealed that they'd made their own version of *The African Queen*, but played strictly for laughs, Goons-style. A horror film was next.

Robin introduced himself to his new neighbours by crashing his bike, narrowly missing a delivery van, knocking himself out. 'People passing by thought I was dead,' Robin observed. Hello, Lakemba.

Sister Lesley, meanwhile, established the first Bee Gees fan club.

The epicentre of rock'n'roll in the Harbour City was the 10,000-capacity Sydney Stadium, in the city's east, which also staged boxing and wrestling bouts. And it was still the plaything of pop and rock promoter Lee Gordon, whose all-star Big Shows packed the old tin shed. There were whispers that the well-connected Gordon had shifted his operation to Australia back in the '50s after a run-in with mobsters Stateside. Gordon was jet set, larger than life, someone who lived life as if he knew time was in short supply. He smoked dope, rubbed shoulders with hustlers and gangsters, and hosted the type of parties Sydneysiders had never witnessed before. Some say he even slept in a coffin.

Kevin Jacobsen had a word in Gordon's ear, and the promoter agreed to put the Bee Gees on the bill of Chubby Checker's January 1963 Australian tour. It was quite the rapid rise from the Beachcomber.

Checker, the hefty American made famous by the Twist dance craze, was the headliner, but it was Johnny O'Keefe, also on the bill, who worked the teenage audience into a frenzy, humping the microphone stand and thrusting his package at the crowd in a way that put a whole new spin on the term 'giving his all'. O'Keefe slayed, if not quite laid, the Stadium audience. The Gibbs, who were due on after O'Keefe and before Checker, looked on from the wings in despair: how could they follow this sexual dynamo? They were three snaggle-toothed kids in matching waistcoats. What chance did they have?

Barry protested to Lee Gordon that they'd get murdered by the JO'K-mad crowd, but surprisingly, the thoroughly G-rated Gibbs held their own, doing well enough to be invited along for the Melbourne and Brisbane dates. 'Three Brisbane brothers took a risk when they recently toured with Chubby and JO'K,' reported the *Australian Women's Weekly*, 'and came out of it with their name—the Bee Gees—made.' No small praise.

The Gibbs debuted on *Bandstand* in February 1963. *Bandstand* was hosted by Brian 'Hendo' Henderson, a square in specs and a cardie who looked more like a librarian than the hip and happening host of a pop show. Still, *Bandstand* had rated like crazy ever since its first broadcast in late-1958 and to score a spot on the show, alongside the more established Johnny Devlin and the Delltones, featuring the deep-voiced Pee Wee Wilson, was quite a coup. 'Robin, Maurice and Barry Gibbs [sic] are three brothers who started singing in 1958,' said 'Hendo' by way of introduction as the boys glared uneasily at the studio camera. 'Here they are, a great act ... the Bee Gees.'

Barry, his hair slicked back in a pompadour so sharp it could have taken out an eye, strummed an electric guitar, while the twins, in their trademark waistcoats, mugged their way through the oldie 'Alexander's Ragtime Band', a crowd-pleasing chestnut that was still in their live set in late 1963. They were virtually force-feeding the Mums and Dads of the viewing audience. They followed this with 'My Old Man's a Dustman', Robin hamming it up throughout Barry's spoken-word intro, Mo looking a bit bewildered by it all. The cheese was laid on inches thick. And the grins never left their faces; you could almost imagine Hugh just off the set, urging them to keep smiling, smiling, smiling.

This cameo and their spot on the Chubby Checker tour was enough to garner a little interest from Fred Marks, the head of Festival Records. The generous Kevin Jacobsen had also had a word to Marks about the Gibbs. But initially, the label head was uncertain about the Bee Gees, saying, 'Vocal groups don't sell.' Jacobsen knew that Marks was wrong and offered him a trade.

'I'll take one of my acts off the label,' said Jacobsen, who by now was managing a stable of artists, including Little Pattie and his brother Col, 'if you sign the Bee Gees.' Jacobsen suggested 'dropping' singer Judy Cannon, which was hardly a sacrifice, as she was in the process of leaving the country. Marks accepted the trade and the Bee Gees were signed to Leedon Records, Lee Gordon's label, whose product Festival marketed and distributed. It was a lopsided deal, commercially speaking—Festival would own the Bee Gees' rights until 2005—but it was still a record deal. And Barry hadn't yet turned 17.

Around the same time as their *Bandstand* spot, the Bee Gees gathered in Festival's recording studio in suburban Pyrmont to cut their first record for Leedon. Proving that the label wasn't messing about with their new signing, Festival's house engineer Robert Iredale was tapped to work with the brothers. The buttoned-up Iredale was every bit as square as Henderson, but he did record all of Johnny O'Keefe's big hits, including 'The Wild One'. Col Joye sat in on the session, taking a production credit, while his Joy Boys played and sang on the record.

Yet as recording debuts go, the Gibbs couldn't have taken a bigger misstep. The A-side was Barry's song 'The Battle of the Blue and Grey', the lyric based on a tale from the American Civil War, of all things. The incongruity was unavoidable: three kids barely out of school trying to channel a dead soldier from a grisly 19th-century conflict. Kudos to Barry for ambition, admittedly—a simple pop song would have done the job, but instead they settled on a sort of faux country/skiffle ramble, with shades of story-songs like Johnny Horton's 'Battle of New Orleans'.

When a reporter from the *Australian Women's Weekly* asked Barry about the lyrics of this and other songs, he revealed a strange source of inspiration. 'I get the words from romance magazines and stories my sister Lesley reads.'

'The Battle of the Blue and Grey' went nowhere on release in March 1963. The chirpy B-side, 'Three Kisses of Love', was an even tougher sell, barely-legal Barry crooning how he 'would be in paradise' after one blissful snog. If recorded today, it might raise a few eyebrows at DOCS.

Even lip-synching 'Blue and Grey' on *Bandstand* in April didn't help get the record into the charts. In a Top 40 dominated by Roy Orbison and Cliff Richard and the Four Seasons—with a global phenomenon named the Beatles just a few short screams away—the Bee Gees didn't stand a chance.

Barry was philosophical about this, and future failures. 'At least if they're flops,' he shrugged, 'they're our flops.'

His words proved to be worryingly prophetic. The singles that followed in 1963 and 1964, from the sugary teen ballad 'Take Hold of That Star', with its 'la la las' and talk of starlight and rainbows, to the equally treacly 'Turn Around and Look At Me', plus 'Peace of Mind' and 'Claustrophobia', failed to bother the charts. The only success they had was when Col Joye covered Barry's 'Starlight of Love', which brushed the national Top 30 in May 1963, but faded after a few weeks.

Barry was already starting to grow a little wary of the local music biz. When a journalist asked if there was any backstabbing in Australian music, he replied, 'That's all it is—all the time.' So, what about payola (a scam where DJs were paid to play new records, regardless of their merit): does that happen here? 'A helluva lot,' Barry replied. 'With so many groups there's got to be payola.' Barry, of course, had no hard evidence of the existence of payola, nor was there a knife protruding from his back—all he really knew was that DJs across the country didn't play his records and he resented it.

The only upside to this rough time was a backstage intro to the Mills Brothers, one of their first inspirations, when they toured Australia in August 1963.

For the first but certainly not the last time in their career, the Bee Gees needed a new musical direction. And when it came, it hit the Gibbs—and the rest of the western world—like a hurricane.

Much had changed on Planet Pop between 1963 and 1964. The Beatles, four streetwise Liverpudlians who'd recently done hard yards in the sleazy bars and strip joints of Hamburg, had struck upon a solid-gold formula, channelling everyone from rock'n'roll greats Little Richard and Chuck Berry to the hot new sounds emerging from Motown. They began pumping out No.1s with roughly the same frequency as Bee Gees failures.

The Beatles' debut single, 1962's 'Love Me Do', stirred ripples of interest, and then the hits flowed: 'Please Please Me', 'She Loves You' and 'I Want to Hold Your Hand', their first million seller in America, followed in rapid-fire succession. They'd record 17 UK No.1s during the next six years. Cash registers chimed from one end of the world to the other.

The pop climate shifted overnight. Established stars such as Paul Anka, Pat Boone and Cliff Richard were suddenly the old guard. Even Elvis Presley was looking outdated. Their stranglehold on the charts and the airwaves was over. Hair started to creep towards the collar and the straitlaced morals of the white-picket-fence '50s were swamped by a tsunami of hormonal female screams as the Beatles conquered the world. The Mom and Pop era of music, personified by Anka, Boone and Richard, was over.

When the Fab Four departed Heathrow on 7 February 1964, bound for North America and then Australia, four thousand fans, yelling their lungs raw, saw them off. Just as many fans, with even stronger voices, met them at New York's John F. Kennedy International Airport when they landed—and then thousands more braved wild storms at Sydney's Mascot Airport to witness this new pop phenom at close range. The Beatles' first Australian date was in Adelaide on 12 June 1964 (with London drummer Jimmie Nicol substituting for tonsillitis-stricken Ringo Starr), and over the next 18 days, Beatlemania took over Melbourne, Sydney and Brisbane. The teen madness that erupted wherever the Liverpudlians trod was unlike anything ever seen in Australia. Johnny O'Keefe was another of the Beatles' victims; his randy theatrics at Sydney Stadium suddenly seemed so *yesterday*.

The market was flooded with all things Beatles: pendants, photos, badges, plastic wigs and anything else merchandisers could dream up and flog, while the band held the top six positions on the 2SM chart in early April '64. They delivered eight Australian No.1s in 1964 alone. Domination of this type wouldn't be approached again until, well, the Bee Gees hit disco paydirt in the mid-1970s.

Sydney Stadium conditions were primitive—the 'old barn's' revolving stage broke down and Ringo Starr was forced to manually shift his drum kit to face different sections of the crowd after each song—but the audience response was euphoric at each show during the Beatles' three-night residency, beginning on 18 June. Faces in the Stadium crowd included the Bee Gees. Their reaction to the Beatles and their wildly-successful mix of rock, pop, rhythm and blues and hysteria was immediate and emphatic: *this* was the sound they were after. Songs about the Civil War? What were they thinking?

'We've got to do what *they're* doing,' Barry told his brothers as they caught the bus back to Bunnerong Road, Maroubra, where the family now lived. Robin and Maurice nodded in agreement. As soon as Mo got home he picked up a bass guitar and tried to master every line and melody that Paul McCartney played. But it was more than the Beatles' music that the Bee Gees wanted to embrace. The Beatles' ability to make a suit and tie look dangerous and sexy was another side of the Fab Four they needed to emulate. Their look, their sound—the Gibbs craved the works. 'We modelled ourselves on them,' Maurice admitted.

'It was unbelievable,' said Mo, when asked about the Beatles in Oz. 'The whole country was in the mood of Beatlemania. I'd never seen anything like this before.' Mo took it upon himself to hit each record and music store of inner-city Sydney, checking out Beatles records, boots, sheet music and clothes with that distinctly 'Beatles-esque' look. He was a convert—they all were.

There was also a cultural connection; the Gibbs' roots were in the north of England, in Manchester, just 50 kilometres from the Beatles' Liverpool HQ. 'That was our world,' Mo said, 'we were kids from Manchester, we were northern, like the Beatles—what were we doing [in Australia]?'

The Bee Gees weren't alone in their quest to be ersatz Beatles, of course: virtually every musical hopeful in Australia under the age of 30 ditched the squeaky-clean ballads, Brylcreem and the knock-offs of American hits. The British Invasion had begun, and such locals as the Twilights, the Easybeats, the Loved Ones, Billy Thorpe and dozens of others were influenced by its sound and look. Old stagers Col Joye and Johnny O'Keefe nervously looked over their shoulders.

The Gibbs didn't waste any time. During their first post-Beatles recording session, held in June 1964 at Festival, they laid down their own version of Lennon and McCartney's 'From Me to You'. They'd cover Beatles songs in future TV appearances, too (and in 1978 they even got to play the Beatles, in a manner of speaking, during the film adaption of their *Sgt. Pepper's Lonely Hearts Club Band* album).

'Wine and Women', the first single that the Bee Gees released post-Beatlemania, in September 1965, was a marked improvement on their earlier offerings. Admittedly, 18-year-old Barry's lyric about boozing and losing strained credulity, but the song's sea-shanty melody and the brothers' pristine harmonies made it their best release to date. It was also Robin's first lead vocal.

'Wine and Women' made the Sydney Top 20 in October 1965, this being a time when charts were city-by-city/station-by-station affairs. (Sydney alone had three Top 40 charts, one each for 2UE, 2SM and 2UW. There was no national chart as there is today, at least not until the *Go-Set* chart was introduced in late 1966.) 'Wine and Women' would have climbed considerably higher if the brothers had more pocket money; as it was, they spent something like 200 quid (A$S400) in Sydney record stores, buying every copy of 'Wine' they could find, helping to nudge it up the sales chart. Their fan club, with sister Lesley at the helm, also did whatever it could to make the song a hit. The members met one morning at Sydney Town Hall, and then, armed with a guide to which shops' sales influenced the record charts—department store Waltons, retailer Woolworths, among others—they set out to buy each and every copy in Sydney. It was the 1960s equivalent of a Bee Gees flash mob.

'Wine and Women' salvaged the brothers' career. Festival Records, less than thrilled by their string of failures, was on the verge of terminating their contract, but the song saved their bacon. It also marked the start of a new musical relationship for the boys, this time with British-born producer/arranger Bill Shepherd, who worked on this song and many future Bee Gees releases. The 38-year-old Shepherd would play a key role in developing the group's sound: he was almost as important to the band as producer George Martin was to the Beatles.

At the same time, Barry's deal with music publisher Caroline Music took an unexpected upturn. Barry was a prolific songwriter, cranking out 30 songs in 1964 alone, of which the Bee Gees recorded just six. Local stars such as Jimmy Little, country singer Reg Lindsay, Bryan Davies, Del Juliana and rocker Johnny Devlin all recorded Barry Gibb originals. Little chose Barry's 'One Road' as the follow-up to his massive hit 'Royal Telephone' and the song reached No.2 on the NSW chart in 1964, Barry's biggest placing to date.

Barry's go-to guy at Caroline, Tony Brady—who'd recorded Barry's 'Let's Stomp Australia Way'—had arranged a meeting with American crooner Wayne Newton, who was performing at the Chevron Hilton in Sydney in July 1964. Brady talked up Barry—and Newton was in the market for new material. Newton brought in both the orchestra and the pathos when he recorded Barry's 'They'll Never Know' for his April 1965 LP, *Red Roses for a Blue Lady*, arranged by Terry Melcher, who'd worked with the Beach Boys. The album was a Stateside hit.

Producer Melcher heard another of Barry's tunes, 'That's What I'll Give To You', and the song made its way to erstwhile child star Jimmy Boyd—of 'I Saw Mummy Kissing Santa Claus' legend—who cut it as a single. It was released in May 1965, and while it didn't revive Boyd's stalled career, it did prove that Barry's ever-improving songwriting had potential beyond Australia.

Back in Australia, the brothers kept chipping away, despite the occasional distraction. Barry almost lost an eye when the air gun he was fiddling with went off, and had to sport a patch for a time— hardly an ideal look for a rising pop star. Soon after, returning from a show in rural Goulburn, NSW, the Gibbs' car rolled on a dark and lonely stretch of highway. Somehow, word reached some radio stations that the boys had been killed in the crash. Bruised, yes— Barry actually cracked a rib—but dead, no, not yet.

'Wine and Women' had inched its way into the charts, and the Beatles' huge splash had given the Gibbs a sense that greater things lurked offshore for them, but their next 1965 single was a dud. Inspired by the Seekers, a wholesome Aussie four-piece who'd had massive global success with 'I'll Never Find Another You' and 'A World of Our Own', Barry came up with folky soundalike 'Follow the Wind', which mimicked the Seekers' earnest campfire strumming. The song wasn't a hit.

This latest stab at songwriting-by-numbers summed up the brothers' strange situation in the mid-1960s. As writers, they were still struggling to find a sound of their own, hardly a unique scenario for fledgling tunesmiths. Authenticity wasn't something you could learn from the radio. But the problem unique to the Bee Gees was this: to truly 'sell' a song, to give it conviction, they needed real life experience. While their teenage peers were still at school and navigating their way through all the usual rites of passage, the three brothers lived on the road, playing to adults, or hung out in the recording studio, working with adults. They existed in a bubble, trapped between youth and adulthood, while the rest of the under-20 world got on with the task of cutting loose. This isolation was reflected in their songs: Barry's ear for melody and the brothers' pristine harmonies were rapidly improving, but their lyrics seemed forced. They were kids pretending to be grown-ups, singing about 'wine and women' and the weariness they felt as they walked 'this lonely road'.

Leedon released the Bee Gees' first album in November 1965. The winner of the most bleeding obvious album title of all time, it was called *The Bee Gees Sing and Play 14 Barry Gibb Songs*. For those not in the know, the title implied that the Bee Gees and Barry Gibb were separate entities. There was one gem on the album: the first single, the wordy 'I Was a Lover, A Leader of Men'. With its slightly baroque production, scratchy guitar breaks and booming vocals, this song felt very much in synch with all things Merseyside. Much of the album, however, was padding, including older singles such as 'Claustrophobia' and 'Peace of Mind'. It only contained three new songs.

'It's a good sound,' noted one reviewer, 'but it's marred by the fact that the lyrics are hard to understand. I prefer the tracks where the Bee Gees take solos and the message is clear.' The critic did acknowledge that Barry was among the country's best songwriters. That was something.

The besuited brothers flashed big grins on the album's cover, Barry's pompadour scaling new heights. Those ever-present smiles might have hinted at yet another G-rated family trio, so squeaky clean and eager to please, but if you looked closer, their smiles seemed a little strained. It was as if they were saying: What the hell do we have to do to make things better? Exactly how many dues do we have to pay? But a change would come soon enough for the Gibbs.

The direction of the brothers' early life—in fact, the direction of much of their entire career—was often dictated by the company they kept, the connections they made. First there was Bill Goode up at Redcliffe Speedway, then Johnny O'Keefe and Col Joye encouraged their move south to Sydney. All true believers, whose advice was usually adopted by the Gibbs.

Back in Queensland, they'd met American-born music man Nat Kipner during filming of a TV show called *Teen Beat*. In 1966, Kipner was head of A&R (Artist and Repertoire) at Sydney's Spin Records, a new independent record label. Kipner was one of three major shareholders in Spin, the others being media magnate Frank Packer and successful Sydney promoter Harry M. Miller. Spin, like Leedon Records, had a manufacturing and distribution deal with the much-larger Festival Records.

Producer/arranger Bill Shepherd, who'd collaborated with the brothers on 'Wine and Women', worked on most of the early Spin releases, including singles from expat Kiwi Ray Columbus ('We Want a Beat'), wheelchair-bound soulman Jeff St John and his group the Id ('Lindy Lou') and pop-hopeful Marty Rhone, who'd later strike gold with 'Denim and Lace'. Also on the label's roster was a band called Steve and the Board, featuring Steve Kipner, the label boss's son. Steve would play his part in the lives of the Gibbs.

The Bee Gees weren't the only members of the family unhappy with their lack of progress with Leedon (and by association Festival). Father/manager Hugh could see that despite the odd flicker of recognition, the brothers seemed set to live out Barry's grim 'at least they're *our* flops' prophecy. Their first single for 1966, 'I Want Home', came and went without a sniff of public interest. Another flop.

Hugh met with Festival's Fred Marks. He wanted to get the boys

JEFF APTER

out of their Festival arrangement. He felt that the label hadn't given
them adequate support, which accounted for their string of failures.
The situation was so bleak that the boys had even started working
part-time in a car wash to earn some money. Hugh also questioned
the validity of the contract with Festival; after all, none of the Gibbs
were 18 when Hugh signed the paperwork.

Marks offered a compromise. 'What if we take them off Leedon,'
he suggested to Hugh, 'and put them on Spin?'

It was an enticing offer. Spin was having some success and Nat
Kipner seemed more likely to invest time and effort in the Bee Gees.
Driven and ambitious, Kipner had even written a song, 'I'm Gonna
Buy My Mother-in-Law a Block of Land on Mars' (no, seriously)
that was a B-side to one of Barry's songs-for-hire, 'I Will Love You',
recorded by Tony Brady. Kipner also produced Normie Rowe's No.1
hit, 'Shakin' All Over'.

Nat Kipner was keen to have the boys on his label. If they
switched to Spin, he said, they could have free use of St Clair studio,
on Queens Road in suburban Hurstville. The studio, a converted
storeroom next door to a butcher's shop, was run by engineer and big
Bee Gees fan Ossie Byrne. Like Kipner, Byrne had served in World
War II, in New Guinea, where he lost an eye. He thought it hilarious
to pop out his glass eye and shock first-time visitors to the studio.
St Clair was a popular spot, too; many of Festival's acts preferred to
record there than at the label's Pyrmont HQ. The going rate was five
quid an hour and Byrne served free sandwiches, biscuits and tea. It
was an artist-friendly kind of place.

Hugh duly agreed to the change of labels. It would prove to be
a wise move—St Clair would become a sort of sonic laboratory for
the Bee Gees, who'd spend endless hours there, working mainly at

52

night. They couldn't believe their luck: what other fledgling act was given free access to a recording studio? In fact, the only other act on Spin that had such access to St Clair was Steve and the Board. Being the boss's son had its advantages. 'My Dad accommodated us,' Steve Kipner said in 2012, 'and we took advantage. Only the Bee Gees [also] had what seemed to be unlimited time in the studio.'

Kipner and Maurice became close friends; their relationship would develop even further in the ensuing years.

During the Bee Gees' first marathon session at St Clair, in May 1966, they laid down a staggering 12 new songs, even trying out an early Maurice composition, 'Where Are You', along with a handful of songs Robin had co-written with Barry. Steve Kipner added vocals, the sandy-haired Colin Petersen—the kid from *Smiley*, who'd befriended Mo at a gig in Sydney, played drums, while Nat Kipner produced the session. It was a genuine team effort. Who needed the fancy new four-track facility at Festival when they could get such good *free* sounds in St Clair? The Gibbs would record 30 songs at St Clair during 1966, not a bad year's work.

The brothers experimented, too, double tracking vocals on 'I Don't Know Why I Bother With Myself', while Maurice revealed how far he'd progressed as a bass guitarist on 'Monday's Rain'. Step by faltering step, they were coming to grasp and exploit the possibilities of a good recording studio. St Clair was no Abbey Road, the recording home of the Beatles, but it wasn't a bad place for the Bee Gees to learn their trade. It was probably a more suitable place for the twins, too, who had a tendency to run riot when they weren't needed in the vocal booth. That kind of behaviour just wasn't tolerated at Festival HQ.

These dozen songs were packaged on a proposed LP with the

working title of *Monday's Rain*. Nat Kipner gushed about the Gibbs in his draft liner notes: 'As instrumentalists they have mastered practically every instrument in the book. As harmonists and vocalists they are ... the foremost in this country.'

Perhaps they were, but when the song 'Monday's Rain' failed to set the singles charts on fire, the album was put on hold. Only one DJ, John Royce at Melbourne's 3KZ, gave the single any real airplay. Other stations said the Bee Gees were trying (too hard, perhaps) to imitate the Beatles and decided against playing the record.

A groundswell of disapproval rose, with teen mag *Everybody's* defending the group. 'The Bee Gees' new disc "Monday's Rain" has been barred by every radio station in Sydney on the grounds that [they] are not original enough!' the publication harrumphed in July 1966. 'Surely they're joking! The Bee Gees for heaven's sake write their own material. And you can count people like that on one hand.'

Adelaide station 5KA crowned Barry's 'I Was a Lover' the 'best Australian composition of the year' but it still wasn't enough to win the 'Monday's Rain' single decent airplay. The Gibbs were told to return to St Clair and try, yet again, to conjure up that one special song that would break their dry streak.

At the same time, Mo, Robin and Barry had been having some heavy-hearted dinner table conversations with the rest of the family. Australia had provided a good climate and a first-rate musical education, but for their career to take flight they needed to start again, to shake off the stigma of their embarrassing run of flops. England was the home of the Beatles and the Rolling Stones and the Who and the Kinks and all the other great bands of the day, each a massive influence on the Bee Gees. Maybe the Gibbs' luck would change if they returned to the UK and immersed themselves in this vibrant pop culture. Perhaps they'd be better appreciated in England, too.

As early as 1965, in a routine Q&A for *Everybody's*, the brothers had made their intentions pretty clear. In between the usual confessions—Barry liked 'easy-going people', Robin was keen on go-karting, they were all turned off by 'unreliable and insincere people'—their shared group ambition, 'to tour England together', was unambiguous. The Bee Gees' offshore intentions made for good copy; *Everybody's* ran several mentions of the brothers' UK aspirations, as did the *Sunday Telegraph*. The Gibbs mightn't have been able to get radio airplay for their songs, but they had no trouble rating a mention in the press.

Yet Hugh and Barbara were unsure. They saw this proposed move as a backwards step, a journey into the past. They even threatened to hide the boys' passports if they raised the subject again. Thwarted, but far from resigned to defeat, the Bee Gees headed back to the St Clair studio in June 1966. There they would record a song which would reflect the influence of the Beatles more than anything they'd ever recorded and when released change their fortunes in the process. Yet this song almost wasn't cut by the band at all.

During one of their all-nighters at St Clair, Maurice started plinking out a simple melody on the piano—in fact it was a pianola, a player piano, but with the music roll removed. Barry liked what he heard and a sketch emerged, an aching-hearted piece: 'Spicks and Specks'. But even when they had the song ready to go, Barry thought, given their recent run of failures, now something like 10 singles on the trot, they might be better served if someone else recorded it.

Dinah Lee was an expat Kiwi finding her way in the Sydney music scene, having crossed the Tasman in 1964. She'd appeared on Johnny O'Keefe's new TV show, *Sing Sing Sing*, and had become a *Bandstand* regular. Easy on the eyes, the petite Lee was christened 'Miss Mod'. She'd recorded a few hits by the time she met the Gibbs, including a No.1 entitled 'Don't You Know Yockomo'. Barry offered Lee 'Spicks and Specks' as her next single, but then Kipner and Byrne intervened. 'Are you sure?' they asked him.

Both men knew a great pop song when they heard one—and had no doubt that 'Spicks and Specks' could be huge. It had everything a great 1960s pop tune required: an overwhelming sense of pathos, an addictive hook, melody. It really could be the Bee Gees' breakthrough, especially with one of Barry's soaring vocals. Kipner and Byrne got their way and a time was set aside for the Bee Gees to cut the song.

The recording was ample proof of what magic could be conjured up at St Clair, and for next to nothing. The budget for 'Spicks and Specks', a track that as recently as 2015 was both signature song and title of a popular ABC TV show, and rated one of *the* great Australian recordings, was all of $50. The only 'indulgence' was a small horn section, recruited from a pub in Coogee. And that was pretty much it. They also cut a B-side, 'I Am the World', with 16-year-old Robin's fluttering falsetto in full cry. At home, the family laughingly referred to his vocal style as 'the quavering Arab', but it worked well here.

'Spicks and Specks' was released as a single in September 1966, around the same time as new sides from the Beatles ('Yellow Submarine'/'Eleanor Rigby'), the Lovin' Spoonful ('Summer in the City') and locals Johnny Young ('Step Back'), the Twilights ('Needle in a Haystack') and the Loved Ones ('Ever Lovin' Man'). Not a bad month for pop—and 'Spicks and Specks' was a perfect fit, a great, timeless anthem-in-waiting.

Interestingly, the *Sunday Telegraph*'s Carol Rodgers was more impressed by the flipside, Robin's 'I Am the World'. To her, it was 'by far the best record of the week', every bit as 'dramatic' as 'Spicks and Specks'. Rodgers also noted that the record's lush sound was a world away from the raw sound of most of Nat Kipner's productions.

Lanky Sydney radio DJ John Laws, who along with such peers as Bob Rogers and Melbourne's Stan Rofe, pretty much dictated what records were played on air—and duly became hits—would not believe 'Spicks' was a Kipner production. So much so, in fact, he said he'd eat the record if someone could prove that Kipner produced it. To his credit, Laws, when presented with the evidence, ate his words—and bit a chunk out of the 45 rpm record—on air.

'Spicks and Specks' took its own sweet time climbing the local charts. The newly created *Go-Set* National Top 40 logged it at No.37 on 19 October, wedged between the Beach Boys' 'God Only Knows' and the Rolling Stones' 'Mother's Little Helper'. It climbed to No.18 the following week, just behind the Monkees' 'Last Train to Clarksville'. By early November, 'Spicks and Specks' entered the Top 10 at No.5. This was truly a red letter week for Australian pop music—Johnny Young was at No.1, Judy Stone was in second place with her cover of 'Born a Woman', followed by the Twilights' 'Needle' and then the Gibbs. Four Aussies in the Top 5. The next week they were joined by the Easybeats with their tearaway rocker 'Sorry'.

'Spicks and Specks' didn't reach the top of the *Go-Set* Top 40, but remained in the chart for the rest of 1966. They'd finally broken through. The success of 'Spicks and Specks' was boosted by a goofy, Goons-worthy promo video, one of the first made in Australia, financed by Spin, which was shot at Bankstown Airport in Sydney's suburban west. Barry sported aviator shades while a young Denise Drysdale, then a go-go dancer on TV, 'acted' in the clip. As actors, the Gibbs sure were great harmonisers.

One of their last shows for 1966 was at the Mattara concert in rural Newcastle, staged at the Civic Park, hosted by local station 2KO. 'Spicks and Specks' was out but not yet a hit. The Bee Gees headlined a long bill that included rocker Jade Hurley and Marty Rhone, pulling a crowd of around 20,000 screaming teens. The first real signs of fan madness were on display as eager fans tried to drag Barry off stage. A member of local band the Second Thoughts recalled that no one seemed to mind that the brothers were a 'bit smelly', having spent much of their recent time living in caravans and on the cheap. The Gibbs played most of their set live with the backing of the Second Thoughts, who'd also recorded with Nat Kipner at St Clair, working through a set that started with them covering the Rolling Stones' 'Not Fade Away', the Righteous Brothers' 'Unchained Melody', the Beatles' 'Yellow Submarine' and a Peter, Paul and Mary medley, before ending with a short bracket of originals including 'Wine and Women' and 'Spicks and Specks'. 'You won't know these last few,' Barry told the guys in the Second Thoughts, 'but it's OK. Just jump around and pretend to play.' Barry felt he was on safe ground, because Hugh was off-stage, cueing up recordings of the songs on a turntable, which would be played through the primitive sound system while the Bee Gees mimed. But things didn't quite play out as they hoped—halfway through 'Spicks and Specks', the big finale, the record stuck in the groove, repeating the chorus over and over while Barry, Mo and Robin flailed around on stage, trying to bluff their way through. Backstage, Hugh dashed to the turntable but pushed the stylus so hard that the needle skipped right across the vinyl to the end groove, only drawing more attention to the fact they were lip-synching.

The Bee Gees played a lot of shows during their years in Australia, but never departed a stage quicker than they did that night in Newcastle.

By now, the brothers had no doubt that trying to take on the world while based in Australia was a near-impossible task. 'You had to really leave Australia,' said Robin, '[and] either go to the UK or America to go any further. We knew, by the time we left, that we could only go so far—and then we had to get out.' They began packing their bags and booking passage.

Big brother Barry seemed to be the one most hurt by their repeated failures in Oz. He carped then that Australia 'was unfair to us right to the end'. Over time, Barry would modify his tough take on Australia and come to accept that few pop music apprenticeships could beat what they'd been through over the past eight years. And for the rest of the their lives, the brothers flip-flopped between calling Australia and England 'home'. They never seemed quite sure.

As a cheeky farewell gesture, the brothers hit the menswear section of the Myer department store, running up a hefty bill—an unpaid bill, too, at least until their return in 1971.

Nor was it only the Bee Gees who were determined to get the heck out of Australia; within the next year, the Easybeats and the Twilights would be London-bound. Soon after, the Masters Apprentices would also try their luck in London, likewise members of the Loved Ones. It was a rock'n'roll exodus.

But before the Gibbs' relocation, big brother Barry had some business closer to home. A couple of years earlier, he'd begun dating Maureen Bates, a petite blonde, who was secretary of the Bee Gees fan club. They were married in the Holy Trinity Church in the Sydney suburb of Kingsford on 22 August. Barry was 10 days short of his 20th birthday; Maureen was also 19. The relationship wasn't built to last, but she was alongside Barry when Hugh and Barbara finally accepted that a return to England would be good for the boys' career.

Within days of his marriage, Barry's publishing deal with Caroline lapsed. It had been an incredibly prolific five years of songwriting for the elder Gibb, but the band could only claim the steadily rising 'Spicks and Specks' as its one true hit. From now on, Barry wrote songs for Abigail Music, a company formed by Hugh Gibb and Norman Whiteley, who'd known Hugh since the days he kept the beat on the Manchester ballroom circuit and was now living in Sydney.

If song titles were any indication of Barry's mindset, he was now writing from the heart. Among the 40 or so songs he composed during an incredibly productive 1966 were such statements of intent as 'House of Lords', 'Exit Stage Right' and 'I'll Know What To Do', which all seemed to point towards a future beyond Oz. In late November, Barry, Robin and Mo recorded at St Clair for the last time, cutting four originals, 'Gilbert Green', 'Deeply Deeply Me', 'Mrs Gillespie's Refrigerator' and 'I Can't See Nobody'—the latter a song Barry and Robin wrote after the Bee Gees shared a dressing room with a stripper.

On 25 November, Hugh packaged up an acetate disk of the first three songs, along with a copy of the recently released *Spicks and Specks* LP, and posted them to NEMS in England, the firm owned by Beatles' manager Brian Epstein and his family. The Bee Gees' world was about to be turned upside down.

As pop powerhouses went, there was none more dynamic than Britain's NEMS in late 1966. Shorthand for North End Music Stores, the Epstein family business dated back to the early 20th century when Isaac Epstein, Brian Epstein's grandfather, expanded the family's Liverpool furniture store to sell musical instruments and myriad household knick-knacks. Paul McCartney's mother once bought a piano there. After a spell at the Royal Academy of Dramatic Art, Brian was put in charge of the record department. The Beatles, his first management clients, were all NEMS customers. By the time Epstein hired expat Aussie impresario Robert Stigwood to run the company in 1966, he was managing the biggest-selling and most influential pop group on the planet and NEMS was a household name.

Few people would play a more crucial role in the rise (and

fall and rise) of the Bee Gees than Stigwood, known to many as 'Stiggy'. Born in Adelaide in 1934, Stigwood settled in London in his early 20s. There, he ran a theatrical agency with businessman Stephen Komlosy; they were considered mavericks by the theatrical establishment, a quality Stigwood wore like a badge of honour when he moved into the pop business.

The flamboyant, sandy-haired and tanned Australian was out and proud, too, which helped when dealing with the so-called Pink Mafia that controlled the English music business in the 1950s and 1960s. Stiggy spoke in a sonorous tone reminiscent of Alfred Hitchcock, yet came across as more Noel Coward, using a quaint mix of the colloquial and formal. Making a tough business decision—a firing, for instance—would be referred to as carrying out a 'foul deed'; Stigwood didn't have meetings, he had a 'chin wag'. He liked to call himself 'an old bushwhacker', some sort of Aussie yokel. But that couldn't have been further from the truth—the sharp-dressed Stigwood was one shrewd operator, a savvy businessman and *bon vivant*, who liked to work hard *and* enjoy himself. He believed in becoming close with his charges; they were his friends, not merely his clients.

Stiggy also understood the power of hype, even before the word became part of the entertainment vernacular. In pre-Bee Gees days, when he signed an Anglo-Indian singer named Simon Scott, he had plaster busts made of Scott, which he despatched to a slightly bewildered media. Over time he pumped way more money into Scott's career than the singer could ever hope to recoup. Stigwood adopted a similar approach when he took charge of a pop hopeful named Oscar, sending out fake Academy Award statuettes to the press. (Oscar, aka Paul Nicholas, would resurface in the film version of the Who's *Tommy*; the Who also worked with Stigwood.)

Stigwood had more success when he managed the career of English 'supergroup' Cream, who broke big on both sides of the Atlantic—Stigwood would continue to manage guitar great Eric Clapton for many years after Cream's demise. Clapton himself would play a role in the second coming of the Bee Gees in the mid-1970s.

By the time Stigwood linked with Epstein and NEMS, he'd been exposed to all sides of the industry: management, production, promotion, publishing. Stiggy knew the music business. Inevitably, he'd made his share of enemies: when he suggested a change of management to rock band the Small Faces, their strong-arm manager Don Arden hired a few 'heavies', bundled up Stigwood and threatened to drop him from a fourth-floor balcony. Stiggy didn't get to work with the Faces.

Although it was addressed to Brian Epstein, Stigwood intercepted the Bee Gees' audition tape in late 1966 and played it to Paul McCartney. 'I've got these Australian lads ... What do you think?' he asked the Beatle.

'Sign them,' McCartney replied. 'They're great.'

By now, the Gibb family had boarded the UK-bound SS *Fairsky*, which had departed Sydney on 3 January 1967, and was due to reach Southampton five weeks later.

Their voyage echoed their boat trip to Australia in 1958—but this time, rather than entertain guerrilla style for pennies, they sang for their supper, bed and board, paying their way by playing 20-minute sets most nights for the passengers. The Beatles' 'Yellow Submarine' was a standout of their short brackets. Hugh sat in on drums. Now older and worldlier, the brothers imbibed Benzedrine, a readily-available amphetamine, which made the long days race by. Speed was rampant in the London scene they were soon to enter.

'There were some great amphetamines,' recalled Barry in 2014.

One day on board, some Aussies told the Gibbs that 'Spicks and Specks' had finally made it to No.1 'back home'. 'Oh great!' the brothers replied, and got back to woodshedding some new songs, which occupied much of their time on board. While thrilled by the news, the Gibbs couldn't deny the irony: they'd left the country in frustration just as they'd finally broken through.

As the *Fairsky* neared Thursday Island in the Torres Strait, Hugh thought it best to drop a note to *Go-Set*, who'd just crowned 'Spicks and Specks' record of the year. 'On behalf of the Bee Gees,' Hugh wrote, 'I would like to thank you and your paper most sincerely.'

Hugh also hosed down a suggestion from some local journalists that after tasting success the Bee Gees were deserting Australia for overseas riches—and that the single's success had bankrolled their trip. Hugh made it clear that their UK venture had been in the works for 'some weeks before "Spicks and Specks" was released'.

The Gibbs gathered their bags from the *Fairsky* when they docked in Southampton and bumped straight into a pop group on the pier, dressed as the Beatles, black cloaks and all, just as they'd appeared in their recent movie *Help!* But their message for the Gibbs wasn't quite 'Welcome to the Old Dart.' 'Don't go any further,' the Beatles lookalikes told them. 'Go back to Australia. Groups are dead. Clapton lives.'

But the Bee Gees had come too far to turn tail. Anyway, how could groups be dead? What, then, would explain the continuing rise of the Beatles, the Stones, the Who, the Kinks and dozens of others? The brothers, including nine-year-old Andy, shrugged off these doomsayers and went looking for a chippie. It was good to be back.

The speed with which things happened for the Bee Gees over the next few months was the polar opposite of their experiences in Australia. There couldn't have been a better time and place for an up-and-coming pop band, albeit one whose members were already seasoned campaigners, than London in early 1967. The Who's 'Happy Jack' was scaling the UK chart, alongside the likes of the Move's 'Night of Fear', Cat Stevens' 'Matthew and Son', the Stones' controversial 'Let's Spend the Night Together', and 'Hey Joe' from electric gypsy Jimi Hendrix, his first UK breakthrough. Great, era-defining songs.

Carnaby Street was setting new trends in fashion, both good and way over the top, while the UFO Club was hosting underground darlings Pink Floyd, the Soft Machine and the Crazy World of Arthur Brown. The Beatles were about to enter Abbey Road studios to cut 'A Day in the Life', the dazzling closer to their upcoming masterpiece, *Sgt. Pepper's Lonely Hearts Club Band*. As pop culture flashpoints went, few were flashier.

Mo's friend Colin Petersen was already in London, trying to resurrect his acting career, and with his help the Gibbs found new digs, a semi-detached furnished place in Hendon, 11 kilometres from the city centre, on the Northern tube line. The family had about 200 quid to their name. As soon as they settled in, Barry and

Hugh met with Eddie Jarrett, who was managing Australians the Seekers, currently slaying the UK charts with the sweet and chirpy 'Georgy Girl'. But the word from Jarrett was not good. 'I can get the boys into the clubs,' Jarrett told Hugh, 'but that's about it.'

Live work, the old hand-to-mouth existence. It was Australia all over again, only colder. Barry and Hugh glumly returned to Hendon. *This was Swinging London?* they grizzled. Barbara, however, had some interesting news for them. The phone had been ringing all day. 'Someone called Mr Stickweed has been looking for you. And his office keeps on calling.'

Stickweed? Who the hell was Stickweed? Then the penny dropped—could it have been Stigwood? Hugh called the NEMS offices and a meeting was swiftly arranged at the Saville Theatre with the expat Aussie impresario. This was more like it.

The Gibbs might have been the stars-in-waiting, but Stigwood was the centre of attention when they met in the darkened Saville in late January. Coming off what had clearly been a big night, he was guided to a seat by his two minders, and sat there in a crumpled heap. The Gibbs, meanwhile, got ready to audition.

'I hear you write your own songs,' Stiggy croaked, barely looking up.

'That's right,' replied Barry, as he, Robin and Mo launched into their usual nightclub set. It was hard for them to tell if Stigwood was impressed—it was hard to tell if he was still alive, truth be told—but after a short time he dragged himself to his feet. 'Right,' he mumbled. 'Be in my office at five.' Then Stigwood exited, stage right, still propped up by his minders.

The Gibbs didn't know what to make of it. They stood there for a few minutes in silence. 'Do you think he liked us?' Mo asked. No one could tell for sure. (Stigwood later said that while he did enjoy what he heard, he couldn't express it at the time. 'I was in a little agony.')

That afternoon, they got down to business. On entering the NEMS building, the brothers bumped into Ringo Starr, going about his superstar day. Three sets of eyes popped out of their heads. A Beatle! Holy shit.

Stiggy intercepted the starstruck brothers and they sat down in his office to talk. 'I like what I hear,' he said. 'Can we do business?'

The offer he put on the table was pretty straightforward, at least in 1960s music biz terms. The arrangement would run for the next five years: Stiggy would be their manager, music publisher and record label rolled into one. The brothers would be on a 25 quid weekly retainer. For a paltry £1000, Stigwood bought their publishing, of which he'd retain 51 per cent. Dick Ashby was appointed their go-to guy at NEMS—Ashby would work with the Gibb family for the next six decades—while Stiggy tackled the bigger picture, exploring opportunities in the UK and North America, all the while stoking the hype machine. The Bee Gees were stitched up tight, but it was a deal with NEMS, the spiritual home of the Beatles. What more could they hope for?

'Oh, and one other thing,' Stigwood told the brothers. 'Carnaby Street is that way,' he said, waving his hand dismissively. 'Go and buy yourselves some proper clothes.' He slipped them a few hundred pounds. According to Barry, 'We couldn't have been any greener.'

'Robert Stigwood to us was a blessing,' Robin once said. 'He was the man. If we hadn't met Robert at that particular time, I don't know which way we could have gone.'

It was a fair call. Business-wise, the Gibbs had just inked a deal that would over time prove to be as troublesome as it was lucrative, but

Stigwood was connected and influential—and he was a true believer. He'd just signed the band that he felt could topple the Beatles and he was going to do everything he could to make them superstars.

Stigwood wasn't one for deep confessionals, but when he did speak of his relationship with the Bee Gees, he'd say everything they did together was based upon 'open debate'. 'Which I would normally win,' he clarified, with a slightly sinister chuckle.

The first order of business for Stigwood and his new charges was to get some attention for 'Spicks and Specks'. With the support of Roland Rennie at Polydor records, a UK record deal was also put in place for the brothers. Stiggy funded a month's work of exposure on 'pirate' station Radio Caroline, which operated from a ship just off the English coast, airing music not on the playlist of the steady-as-she-goes BBC. But despite the big push, 'Spicks and Specks' flopped.

Undeterred, Stigwood set the brothers to work on a demo recording, comprising nothing but Bee Gees originals. No more Peter, Paul and Mary covers or 'Alexander's Bloody Ragtime Band' for the Gibbs. Demo done, and now with a 'proper' band in place, with the inclusion of drummer Colin Petersen, and Vince Melouney, another expat Aussie and a former member of Billy Thorpe's Aztecs, on guitar, the Bee Gees headed into London's IBC studios for their first UK recording sessions, which stretched from early March to mid April 1967. Petersen and Melouney had worked with the Gibbs in Australia, so they were as good as family, an important factor in an outfit as insular as the Bee Gees. And IBC studios had good recent form—Cream had worked there, as had the Jimi Hendrix Experience. It was also the Beatles go-to studio before they shifted base to Abbey Road. Surely some of this success might rub off on the Gibbs.

They cut around 20 tracks during their stay at IBC; among the standouts was the oddly-titled 'New York Mining Disaster 1941', a Barry and Robin co-write. During the recording sessions, there had been an electrical blackout at IBC and everyone—band, studio staff—was forced into the basement, where they stood around in the dark, by the elevator shaft, wondering what to do next. The brothers did, however, have the foresight to bring along their guitars.

As they sat there idly, waiting for power to be restored, they asked each other: 'What if it was this dark all the time?' 'How would you deal with that kind of deprivation?' Barry started to quietly sing, and they were amazed to discover the basement had a rich, natural echo—not unlike being trapped in a mine, all things considered. A song was born. 'We just made it up,' Barry told British talk show host Michael Parkinson in 1981, when talk turned to 'New York Mining Disaster 1941'. 'We wondered what it would be like, in the dark, unable to see each other.'

With the addition of a stately arrangement from Bill Shepherd, 'New York' had pathos to spare; it was the type of dramatically-charged ballad that would sit comfortably alongside the music of the Walker Brothers, currently topping the UK charts with their epic, aching, black-as-night 'Sun Ain't Gonna Shine (Anymore)'.

Barry's 'To Love Somebody' was the other key song from these trailblazing early sessions. For a man who'd constantly have to fend off accusations of faking emotion—sometimes with good reason—Barry sang his lion-sized heart out during 'To Love Somebody'. It felt very, very real, although in lighter moments the brothers sometimes sang the song with a very different lyric: 'Don't ever piss off your wife/You'll lose your penis,' they'd chuckle, 'You'll lose your penis/The way I lost mine.' *That* version never left the studio.

Just like 'Mining Disaster', 'To Love Somebody' came with a

peculiar back story. The brothers often daydreamed about writing songs for their heroes: 'What would we write for Elvis?' they'd ask each other. 'What about the Beatles?' If they were going to become songwriters-for-hire—and Adam Faith, Billy J. Kramer and Gerry (and the Pacemakers) Marsden all recorded Gibb songs in 1967—why not set their sights high? At the time of their IBC sessions, American singer Otis Redding was big, first via his breakout single 'Sweet Soul Music', which hit the UK Top 10 in early 1967, and later in the year on the strength of a sweaty, soulful appearance at the Monterey Pop Festival—a rare black face in a sea of white. Redding had eclipsed such peers as James Brown and Marvin Gaye to become soulman No.1. 'Let's write a great record for Otis Redding,' Barry suggested to Robin, and they got to work. They had only made a small inroad in the UK, but already the ambitious Gibbs had America in their sights.

'To crack America was the ultimate dream,' said Maurice. 'The streets were paved with gold—they had five TV channels, not just two like in England.'

Sadly, Redding would die in a plane crash later in 1967 so never had the chance to put his own spin on 'To Love Somebody', although Janis Joplin, Rod Stewart and Nina Simone would later cover the song. For all that, the Bee Gees' original was the best version, thanks to the emotional power of Barry's singing and Bill Shepherd's rich, lush, everything-but-the-kitchen-sink production. First and foremost, this was a Bee Gees song, perhaps Barry's best-ever vocal. The man's heart was *bleeding*.

Interestingly, there was another inspiration for the song. A few days before his 33rd birthday on 16 April, Stigwood pulled Barry aside while the brothers were working at IBC. 'Barry, would you write a birthday song for me?' he asked confidentially. 'Something along the lines of Sam & Dave, or the Rascals—what do you think?'

Ever-obliging Barry got to work, even if the heart-way-out-on-his-sleeve lyric might have raised a few eyebrows if the Stiggy connection was more widely known. 'Personally, it was for Robert,' Barry said many years later. 'I don't think [mine] was a homosexual affection'—a fair call, given Barry's fondness for the ladies—'but [my] tremendous admiration for the man's gifts and abilities.'

'New York Mining Disaster 1941', the opening taste of the not-so-originally titled *Bee Gees 1st* LP, dropped on 14 April. Robin sang the lead and the backing vocals, while Barry chimed in with a low harmony on the first two verses. It was a perfect union of voices. There was some confusion, however, within the UK media: could this be the Beatles recording under another name? The Fab Four had recently announced their retirement from live performances, and were seeking new frontiers, so anything was possible. There were whispers that 'Bee Gees' was code for 'Beatles Group'. Clearly, these ripples spread, because some time later George Harrison pulled Mo aside at a party. 'I bought "New York Mining Disaster",' he told a hugely flattered Maurice, 'because it sounded so much like us.' Mo blushed and insisted that any resemblance was unintentional. Harrison told him not to worry; he liked what they were doing. No damage done.

It was a lively time, the week of the release of 'Mining Disaster'. Team Sinatra, Frank and daughter Nancy, were atop the UK charts with their playful 'Something Stupid', while Sandie Shaw, the Monkees and Manfred Mann all charted high. The Beatles' brilliant pairing of 'Strawberry Fields Forever' and 'Penny Lane'—now *there* was a 'double A' single—was hovering near the Top 10, along with

Jimi Hendrix's 'Purple Haze'. It was yet another Golden Age for the British charts.

As always, the Bee Gees got to work, promoting 'Mining Disaster', and recording their first BBC session at London's Playhouse Theatre, before slipping over to Germany for an appearance on the TV show *Beat-Club*. The video for 'Mining Disaster', an odd mix of lurid suits, unflattering close-ups and historical footage of miners down pit, was presented to the panel at the BBC's *Saturday Club* on 22 April, and the response was uniformly positive. With this in place, the Bee Gees prepared for their debut appearance on the hugely-influential TV pop show *Top of the Pops*, scheduled for 11 May. This was a 'dream' gig, according to Barry: 'You've made it if you do *Top of the Pops*.' It'd prove to be significant, for many reasons.

Honey-blonde Marie McDonald McLaughlin Lawrie—aka Lulu—was a fellow guest on *Top of the Pops*. Lulu was at the vanguard of a new wave of successful singing waifs, along with Sandie Shaw and Dusty Springfield. Eighteen-year-old Lulu was an established star; she'd had her first hit, 'Shout', when she was 15. She'd just toured behind the Iron Curtain, playing Poland with the Hollies, and recently scaled the UK charts with her take on Neil Diamond's 'The Boat That I Row'. Her star turn in the film *To Sir, With Love* was only a few months away. Lulu was solid gold English pop royalty.

Lulu and Maurice Gibb didn't get to speak on the day of their shared TV appearance, but that didn't stop Stiggy from planting a few suggestive stories in the press—much to Lulu's chagrin. At the time, she only had panda eyes for Davy Jones, the elfin lead singer of the Monkees. They'd met while she was playing LA's Coconut Grove. The attraction between pop idol and pop star was immediate; unfortunately for Lulu, Jones was also courting his future wife,

Linda Haines, at the same time. Goodbye Monkee, hello Bee Gee.

Lulu and Mo were quickly, in Lulu's words, 'The king and queen of the world. We thought we were ... fabulous.' But Maurice's fondness for booze, which would haunt him for much of his life, had just begun, and over time would cause irreparable damage to their 'fabulous' world.

Robin, meanwhile, had taken up with Molly Hullis, Stigwood's secretary, who'd made those first fortuitous calls to the family home at Hendon. With Barry married to Maureen—although Stiggy was doing his best to keep that quiet, after the backlash John Lennon's first wife Cynthia received from broken-hearted female fans—the brothers were clearly seeking some kind of firm foundation in their ever-shifting lives.

By May 1967, the rise of 'New York Mining Disaster 1941' was well and truly under way; the song was now perched just outside the UK Top 10, at No.12. As always, the brothers were keeping good company—everyone from Jeff Beck to the Who and the Temptations were competing with the Gibbs for chart space.

The Stiggy-powered hype machine had certainly played its part in getting the Bee Gees into the charts. Besotted fans sported 'Be a BeeGee Bopper' badges on the set of *Top of the Pops*, while Stigwood told anyone who'd listen that the Bee Gees were the 'most significant new talent of 1967—the greatest "happening" since the Beatles'.

Stigwood crowed about a deal he'd just set in place in North America for the Bee Gees with ATCO, a division of Atlantic Records, label of Aretha Franklin and Otis Redding. Trumpeting it as the 'biggest record deal ever involving a new group'—though the Bee Gees were hardly new—Stigwood revealed that the deal was worth more than US$200,000, useful change for 1967, and a long way from the

150 quid a week they were making as *Bandstand* regulars only the year before. Their first US tour, a 14-city run, was booked for early June.

Stigwood's boasting unsurprisingly stirred up a little Tall Poppy syndrome in Oz, and his 'lads' really rocked the boat when they engaged mouth before brain during an early interview with the English music press. For the first but by no means last time they were asked where the Bee Gees' hearts (and passports) lay: were they British or Australian? Who could claim them as their own? Where did they belong? The group's response was surprisingly forthright—and bitter.

'We are not an Australian group and we do not like being compared to the Beatles,' they insisted. 'We never wanted to go to Australia in the first place,' said Barry, 'but I was only 12 at the time and I couldn't very well complain.'

It was a remarkably shortsighted tirade, and also proof that some heavy resentment lingered from their struggle to be heard in Australia. Their latest Oz release, 'Born a Man'/'Big Chance', had gone nowhere, which may well have tipped Barry over the edge. They did, however, still have some supporters, among them prominent Melbourne DJ Stan Rofe, who defended Barry's brain explosion. 'I honestly believe that in many ways Australian showbusiness handed out more knocks to those kids than they deserved,' Rofe said. 'For years ... from almost every corner they were laughed at, patted on the head and told to go play with their trains. Let's for the time being treat them instead as very talented "angry young men".'

Once Barry calmed down he back-pedalled quickly, as was his eager-to-please way. He was misquoted, he insisted, misunderstood. 'We all love Australia,' he stated in early June 1967, 'and get very homesick for it.' Still, it would be four years before they again performed Down Under.

By the time of the release of *Bee Gees 1st* LP—did someone forget about their Australian albums?—the Australian media seemed to have gotten over Barry's tirade. The *Australian Women's Weekly*, who'd been Bee Gees boosters since 1960, engaged overdrive when they reported on the brothers' British odyssey. 'Following in the Cuban-heeled footsteps of the Beatles is a mighty tall order, but Australian pop group the Bee Gees have already taken a couple of giant strides in that direction … In the jargon of the trade, "it's all happening" for the chirpy trio of brothers.' Barry was quoted as saying that they 'loved it out there' in Australia. It seemed that the Gibbs were Australia's favourite expats yet again.

*Bee Gees 1st*, which was released mid-July in the UK and then a few weeks later in North America, unveiled a new and fresh-sounding Bee Gees. There were baroque pop touches, lush orchestrations, even hints of psychedelia in 'Red Chair, Fade Away'—and what sounded like a Druid chant at the opening of 'Every Christian Lion Hearted Man Will Show You'. Beatles' insider Klaus Voorman designed the candy-coloured album cover, tangible evidence they were connected to the inner sanctum of Britpop. More importantly, in 'To Love Somebody', 'Holiday' and 'New York Mining Disaster 1941' the Bee Gees had three killer singles.

'In one fell swoop,' noted a reviewer, 'they became competitors with the likes of veteran rock bands such as the Hollies and the Tremeloes ... [While] the three hits were gorgeous but relatively somber, thus giving *Bee Gees 1st* a melancholy cast, much of the rest is relatively upbeat psychedelic pop.'

On 27 August 1967, as the album began its climb up the UK chart, the brothers were taking a rare break with Stigwood when an emergency call came in. Brian Epstein, the Beatles' manager and the head of NEMS, was dead. He'd taken an accidental overdose of Carbitol, a medication he used to help him sleep. Epstein, who was prone to bouts of heavy depression, was 32. As the Beatles mourned, Brian's brother Clive was appointed chairman of NEMS and a press release was issued stating that 'policies agreed between Brian Epstein and Robert Stigwood are now not practically possible'. It was agreed that NEMS and Stigwood would part ways, Stigwood, allegedly, pocketing £500,000 in the settlement.

While seemingly cast adrift, Stigwood was now actually in a position to transform the Bee Gees, his No.1 clients, into pop heavyweights, true rivals to the Beatles. He quickly established the Robert Stigwood Organisation (RSO), where he could focus exclusively on the Gibbs without 'outside' involvement.

Prior to Epstein's death, Stiggy had already been stretching the boundaries of his relationship with Epstein and NEMS. Even without a charting record in America, Stigwood insisted that he and the Gibbs hire a yacht and tour Manhattan in style during their first visit Stateside, spending up big. They also appeared in Florida, where their US label ATCO, a division of recording heavyweight Atlantic, was hosting a sales convention—*Billboard* magazine called it the biggest gathering in ATCO's history, with millions of dollars worth of business being written. It seemed that all of America wanted a piece of the Bee Gees, or at least that was Stiggy's breathless claim to the press. 'Everyone is clamouring for Bee Gees songs,' he reported from New York. Every step they took, of course, was charged to Stiggy's NEMS expense account.

Epstein's sudden death wasn't the only very public drama affecting the Gibbs in 1967. Having finally settled on what appeared to be the perfect band, with the inclusion of Petersen and Melouney, the Bee Gees' existence came under threat when the British Home Office refused to renew Petersen and Melouney's visitor's permits. They were given until mid-September to leave the country.

Devastated Bee Gees fans chained themselves to the railing outside Buckingham Palace, screaming and crying in protest. Stigwood even floated the idea of having the pair adopt Spanish or Italian citizenship to continue working in the UK. Ultimately the matter was resolved in mid-October, when the Home Office backed down and allowed the Australians to stay. 'Because,' as one press statement said at the time, 'they were earning money for Britain.' Lots of money. There were also suggestions that the well-connected Stigwood lobbied the right bureaucrats to keep Melouney and Petersen in the country, thereby keeping his band intact.

With a second hit in September's 'Massachusetts', and ongoing sales of the *1st* album, the pounds *were* rolling in. Stigwood announced that the Bee Gees had earned A$1 million since arriving only a few months earlier. While it was probably not a dollar-accurate figure, it was the kind of turnover that would have the English taxman hoping they didn't leave anytime soon. Stiggy didn't reveal how much he'd spent making all this happen, although estimates were somewhere in the vicinity of £50,000 on promo alone for 1967. But it was more than simply commerce to Stigwood; he genuinely believed in the brothers' music and cared for them like a surrogate parent. And he was a far more effective and powerful manager than Hugh Gibb could ever hope to be.

'Massachusetts' was another Bee Gees' standard with a curious genesis, a song that emerged from their first, pricey foray into the US market, a typically spare-no-expense, Stiggy-orchestrated splurge, that at least gave America the impression the Bee Gees were superstars. In between taking in New York by boat, meeting Otis Redding, partying in LA with hosts Sonny and Cher, and sharing the stage on Dick Clark's *Bandstand* with acid rockers the Doors— now there was an unlikely double bill—they tuned into everything that was 'now' and happening on American radio. Flower power was huge; Scott McKenzie's hippy-dippy 'San Francisco (Be Sure To Wear Some Flowers in Your Hair)' wafted from radios everywhere. West coast dreamers the Grateful Dead and Jefferson Airplane were flying their freak flag proudly. Barry Gibb wasn't likely to drink the acid-tainted water—he was no counter-culture rebel—but he did process the idea of tuning in/dropping out through a Bee Gees filter. Every hippie and his dog were singing about going somewhere new, Barry thought, so why not write a song about returning home? They've had their Woodstock adventure, dropped some acid, gotten laid, now they're longing for home. '['Massachusetts'] represents anybody who wants to go back to where he came from,' explained Barry. Hence, 'Massachusetts'' deeply melancholic 'going back' refrain.

Depending on whom you choose to believe, the song itself either came to the brothers during their cruise around Manhattan harbour, or later in the day, when they checked into the St Regis Hotel. The one thing beyond dispute is that they were high on America. Robin jokingly referred to it as their 'Massachusetts state of mind'—they hadn't actually ventured north of New York, but there was a certain familiarity to the state's name—and it felt right in a song. San Francisco, California, New York, they were all celebrated in song: why not Massachusetts? And who cares if they had trouble spelling it (a true story, by the way).

As soon as they previewed the song to Stigwood, he knew it was their next hit. Oddly, the Gibbs had thought about offering it to the Seekers, but Stiggy advised otherwise, telling them to record it themselves.

They spent two days doing just that in IBC Studios during August 1967 and the single was released only a month later, evidence of how quickly musical magic happened in the 1960s. And 'Massachusetts' was gorgeous, with another stellar Robin vocal, rich harmonies and a lush, going-for-baroque arrangement by Bill Shepherd. Barry firmly believed it was Shepherd's best work, and with good reason.

British radio connected with the song immediately. On BBC Radio One's first day of broadcasting, with ex 'pirate' Radio Caroline DJ Tony Blackburn at the helm, 'Massachusetts' was the second record played, directly after the Move's big hit 'Flowers in the Rain'. Several million listeners tuned in.

The Bee Gees returned to *Top of the Pops* to promote 'Massachusetts'. This time around they stood tall, looking very much like the new kings of the pop world, rather than ever-so-geeky newcomers. They were officially stars. The song reached UK No.1 in October, muscling aside the likes of 'The Letter' from the Box Tops and the Small Faces' fabulously psychedelic 'Itchycoo Park'. 'Massachusetts' was also No.1 throughout Europe—and in Australia, too, where the brothers feared they'd been forgotten.

'We were so over the moon,' Barry said of their success, 'we thought we could get away with murder. To have a No.1 ... you have no idea of how much we dreamed of this in Australia. We felt like we'd arrived.'

Newsreel footage from 1967 caught the Gibbs standing on the balcony of a hotel, looking down over an adoring, screaming teenage crowd. 'The Bee Gees,' announced the ever-so-slightly starchy voiceover, 'the most exciting sound in the world.'

While never cutting-edge or truly hip, the Gibbs' collective fashion sense started to loosen up as their popularity grew. Barry developed a thing for bolero jackets; Robin sported turtlenecks, sometimes a full-length fur coat. Mo fancied sharp pinstripes. It was a big step-up from homemade matching jackets with the BGs logo stuck to the lapel, and daggy matching smiles. Each brother, of course, grew his hair out as much as nature—or Stiggy—would allow, even if Mo was already thinning ever-so-slightly on top. Robin didn't so much grow his hair as let it explode, cascading in unruly, comb-defying clumps, swept over and sometimes into his eyes. Barry's muttonchop sidelevers gave him the look of a pop wolverine, years before Hugh Jackman hit the jackpot with a similar look.

The brothers celebrated in their own fashion: Barry slyly entertained his many female fans, much to the chagrin of his wife. 'The women became sort of—*vroom!*' he'd later admit, with some shame. 'A good time to us was a good woman.' He'd keep a gold ring in his pocket, which he'd flash when he met someone he fancied. It usually did the trick.

Mo, meanwhile, hit the sauce, which would over time drive a wedge between him and Lulu. Robin developed a taste for pills. 'Bodding' and 'Moggie' now referred to each other as 'Pilly' (Robin) and 'Pissy' (Mo). Barry, who didn't mind a herbal cigarette or two, was 'Potty'.

'There was a lot of money all of a sudden,' recalled Mo, 'and cars and girlfriends and love interests were happening. And jealousies were happening … the drinks became more, the money became more.' Mo was all of 18, but admits he suddenly felt 'grown up. I felt like I'd been through the mill.' And with good reason—the Bee Gees' overnight success had taken 10 years.

Their newfound status came with certain fringe benefits. London venue the Speakeasy—aka 'the Speak'—was the hangout for music industry A-listers, the haunt of the best bands, hottest managers (including Stiggy), agents, DJs and label movers and shakers, along with sports stars and the assorted rich and famous. As the Gibbs quickly learned, there was a simple way to tell that you had an 'in' at the Speak. At the foot of the stairs, near the entrance, was a coffin. If, on approach, the coffin revolved, it meant you were permitted entrance. And in 1967 the coffin revolved for the Gibbs. Barry couldn't believe the sight that awaited him on his first night at the Speak—members of the Stones and the Who were drinking, laughing and whooping it up. Soccer superstar and notorious party boy George Best was holding up the bar.

Pete Townshend of the Who intercepted Barry. 'Let me introduce you to John Lennon,' he said. Standing in the presence of the Beatle—who was still wearing the *Sgt. Pepper's* uniform from that day's famous cover shoot—a starstruck Barry mumbled something along the lines of 'It's a pleasure to meet you'. Lennon was looking the other way, already engaged in a conversation, but he extended his hand to Barry, who shook it vigorously. Then Lennon continued his conversation without once looking at him. 'Well,' Barry figured, 'at least I've met him.' (Barry would later correct this: 'I met John Lennon's back. I didn't meet his front.')

Mo, the most gregarious of the Gibbs, slipped more easily into Britpop's inner circle—he even bought Lennon's black-windowed Mini Cooper S and took a seat on the Fab Four's Magical Mystery Tour, the crazy bus journey that was documented in the film of the same name. Lennon introduced him to scotch and Coke, which fast became Mo's drink of choice. 'It was like a wild world for me,' he said afterwards. A little too wild, perhaps; he found drinking as natural as harmonising.

Barry's philandering, however, came to an abrupt halt during yet another *Top of the Pops* appearance, which aired on 28 September 1967. On the set, Barry met Linda Gray, a dark-haired beauty and former Miss Edinburgh. They were introduced by Jimmy Savile, then a wildly popular radio DJ, now a reviled paedophile. 'That girl is devastating,' Barry gasped, forgetting all about his marriage to Maureen.

A few days later, Barry and Stigwood left on a US promotional jaunt. In LA, Barry pulled Stiggy aside. Something, clearly, was bothering him. 'I have to go back to London,' Barry announced, looking a little dazed.

'What are you talking about?' asked Stiggy. 'There's so much to do.'

'You don't understand, Robert,' Barry replied. '*This* is the girl. I've got to go back and find her.' With that, Barry was gone, back to London and, eventually, into the arms of Gray, whom he married in September 1970, and who remains by his side today, along with their five children.

Impressively, despite their supernova rise since arriving in the UK, and their recently acquired indulgences, the brothers' work ethic rarely faltered. As 'Holiday', their latest single, hit the UK Top 20, they were already back in IBC working on their second British album. On 3 October they recorded two tracks, 'World' and 'Words', both earmarked as likely singles.

'World' was another song with a curious, counterculture-wary message. When it was released in mid-November, Barry downplayed any flower-power connotations that might be (mis)read into the lyric. 'Why do you need LSD if you're truly peaceful and love everybody?' he asked. 'Why do you need it to make creative music?'

The Beatles, deep into their acid-drenched *Sgt. Pepper's* phase, may have argued the point. Regardless, 'World' reached the UK Top 10 in December, just as 'Massachusetts' started its climb up the charts on the other side of the Atlantic, where it reached the US Top 10 and sold several million copies.

The Bee Gees were an unstoppable force. By the end of their first year away from Australia, they'd scored three UK hits, were making huge inroads in America, and had much of Europe under their spell. They had four Top 10s in Australia during the year, too. They'd filled London's Saville Theatre in late November—the same place where they'd first met with a hungover Stiggy—backed by a 30-piece orchestra, a rarity for anyone in pop; even the Fab Four hadn't played live with horns and strings. After a final appearance for 1967 on *Top of the Pops*—Robin cheekily offered a pound to anyone who could explain the meaning of the Beatles' 'I Am the Walrus'— Barry, Robin and Stiggy flew out for what they hoped would be a low-key Christmas in Oz.

It didn't quite work out the way they'd planned. Stigwood had tipped off the media and the manic response from their fans and the press was too much for the brothers, who scarpered back to the relatively safety of London after a few quick interviews, leaving Stiggy alone to continue talking a big game. 'Their current success is only the beginning,' Stigwood crowed. 'Without doubt they can repeat the Beatles' story again. Not in the same way,' he corrected, 'but just as big.'

Moments before departing, Barry hinted at a future on the big screen. He told a reporter from the *Sydney Morning Herald* that there was talk of a feature film in the works, a comedy-drama about the Boer War—shades of John Lennon's recent appearance in the Dick Lester-directed *How I Won the War*. 'It will be made in colour,' advised Barry, 'and in the cast will be the Goon Man himself, Spike Milligan.'

OK, the film was never made, but right then it seemed that anything was possible for the Gibbs. The Bee Gees were, to use the Beatles' own words, the 'toppermost of the poppermost'.

Barry and Robin didn't quite begin 1968 in the way they'd hoped. Their return flight from Australia stopped in Turkey, a last-minute break before getting back into the hurly-burly of London and, hopefully, another golden year. But fans and reporters were waiting at the gate at Istanbul; somehow they'd learned that a pair of Bee Gees was onboard. A dazed Robin and Barry, who took sedatives to endure the lengthy journey from Sydney, contacted Stigwood immediately—it was all a bit much. Couldn't they just have a holiday?

The brothers did manage a short break, in an Istanbul hospital, recovering from exhaustion. They finally reached London in the first week of January. Up next was the release of another album, the filming of a TV special, and more talk about a feature film. (Stiggy hinted at filming in Africa, of all places.) Every day, their schedule was jammed with commitments. They recorded, performed, travelled, partied, charmed the press—and then did it all over again. Sleep was a luxury. Work was everything. Well, almost everything: the brothers took a liking to collecting upscale motors, so much so that one day Barry looked out into the street where he lived and noticed that every car—be it a Roller, a Bentley, even a Lamborghini—was his. Mo was no slouch, either, buying a Rolls Royce Silver Cloud convertible and an Aston Martin DB6, among other prestige cars.

There was no shortage of great album releases in the early months of 1968: Aretha Franklin's *Lady Soul*, the self-titled Fleetwood Mac LP, *The Notorious Byrd Brothers*. The Beatles, fresh from meditating (and remonstrating) with the Maharishi in India, were writing what would become known as 'the White Album'; the Stones were living hard and working out songs for their upcoming *Beggars Banquet*. The Bee Gees' *Horizontal*, which hit stores on 30 January, was as good as any pop album released in another red-letter year for music.

The emerging cutting-edge music press, however, were no great advocates of the Gibbs. Writing about *Horizontal* and other early releases, *Rolling Stone* casually dismissed the Bee Gees as 'nothing if not professional … [prizing] gesture over authenticity, they made Sixties jukebox love songs … conveying genuine passion about as accurately as Hollywood kisses capture the mess and tangle of real love.' *Horizontal* rated a miserly one-and-a-half stars.

What *Rolling Stone* said was true, to a point, but the writer conveniently overlooked a simple truth: the Gibbs wrote pocket symphonies that lodged themselves in your memory. Sometimes a simple, melodic song was good enough; music didn't always have to change the world. The Gibbs were entertainers, not game changers.

And there was plenty to digest on *Horizontal*, as, in the words of a more favourable critic, the band drifted 'from the Beatles to the baroque'. And, again, there was at least one song with an intriguing inspiration. They may have often been damned for avoiding the personal narratives that characterised the work of Lennon and McCartney and Bob Dylan, but the Bee Gees did find ideas in unique places. In the case of the hymn-like 'Really and Sincerely', a train crash.

On 5 November 1967, Robin and his girlfriend Molly Hullis

were travelling on a London-bound train that derailed at high speed at Hither Green, Lewisham, South London. Four coaches tipped onto their side, showering sparks, twisted metal, splintered wood—and bodies—in all directions. Forty-nine passengers were killed and more than 100 were injured. It was the worst rail disaster in England in 10 years. When the train crashed, Barry and Maurice were waiting for Robin at a press conference; Mo, through the strange intuitive understanding that exists between many twins, sensed immediately that something was up. Although Robin and Molly escaped relatively unhurt, a shaken (and slightly stirred) Robin was treated afterwards at Lewisham Hospital. He insisted that this close brush with death made him rethink a few aspects of his life. '[It] made me realise just how pointless it is to get too hung up on trifling little matters.' There was no real evidence, though, that he did lighten up: Robin would remain the most tightly wound of the Gibbs.

The crash inspired him to write the song 'Really and Sincerely', a sad memorial to those who didn't walk away from the Hither Green crash site. Much of the song was written on a piano accordion he'd recently bought in Paris, which gave 'Really' an intriguing Euro flavour. Another lesser-known Bee Gees gem.

Also on *Horizontal* was Barry's 'Lemons Never Forget', a close cousin of the Beatles' 'Strawberry Fields', with its ominous, minor key soundscape. The Beatles connection ran deep with this song—Barry admitted it was a sly dig at Apple, the Beatles' company, which was going through some major upheavals in the wake of Brian Epstein's death and Stigwood's departure. Writing in the liner notes of the album when it was re-issued, Barry came clean. 'It was all over the industry that Apple was in disarray and the Beatles were breaking up,' he admitted. 'It was a bit of a send-up.'

Another song that didn't make the album, 'Sinking Ships', was an even less veiled dig at NEMS, Stiggy's former employers. Perhaps the Gibbs were responding to an off-the-cuff comment from Beatles' producer George Martin, who'd referred to them as 'junior rivals' of the Fabs. Junior rivals? That hurt.

Then there was 'Harry Braff', the Gibbs' light-hearted ode to an imaginary Formula One driver, written, interestingly, not long after Aussie Jack Brabham won his third Formula One championship. The brothers had been on an all-nighter with some industry types when the song came to them. On their way home in the early hours of the morning, still way under the influence, they decided to drop in on Stiggy and give him a preview. Stigwood loved the song but wasn't mad about the wake-up call. It was a fun throwaway, a chirpy strum that Barry admitted 'probably didn't mean a thing to anybody'. That wasn't quite true; Noel Gallagher of '90s Britpop leaders Oasis became a big 'Harry Braff' fan.

Elsewhere on *Horizontal*, 'World' and 'Massachusetts' reminded listeners that the Gibbs were a hit-making machine. And the album itself, while no *Sgt. Pepper's*, showed a few more sides to the Bee Gees.

All the while, the gaze of Stigwood and the brothers turned more and more to America. Breaking England was great, a huge achievement, but it was universally acknowledged that you weren't really a star until you'd conquered America—even the Beatles needed Ed Sullivan's approval on their way to superstardom. So the Bee Gees returned to North America in late January '68, miming 'And the Sun Will Shine' and 'Words' on the high-rating *Smothers Brothers Comedy Hour*, building their profile further, step by determined step. And it wasn't just the Gibbs who were becoming household names Stateside; when an LA radio station gave out the private phone number of Bee

Gee Vince Melouney, his phone rang off the hook. 'No more calls,' Melouney pleaded with the operator. He needed his rest.

Even at the time of their first UK success, Mo had hinted at trouble in paradise, as cracks started to show, egos grew and bad habits developed among the brothers. During one interview, Barry came off like the angry old man of pop, as he listed the many things they rejected: 'We're against sound effects, we're against Flower Power, we're against LSD,' he snapped. His pride, however, was in good shape, as he boasted that 'there are a hundred things we've done that have not yet been done by pop groups'.

By early 1968, *Horizontal* was a hit, peaking at No.12 in the US charts and in the UK Top 20. It also charted high throughout Europe and in Australia. Not bad for a band considered by many to be a 'singles-only' act.

The bandwagon, meanwhile, rolled on, as whatever sibling tension existed was cast aside, at least for the moment. In Germany, during another record convention, they were presented with a gold statue for sales of 'Massachusetts'; the statue was more than two metres tall. Back in the UK they received a gold disc for the same hit. 'Words' started to scale the US charts in late January, hitting No.15. Stigwood kept the Australian press in the loop, letting it be known that the Bee Gees' upcoming debut US tour would earn them US$1 million. 'It's the biggest deal of its kind in showbusiness,' he advised in typically-understated Stiggy fashion.

There were a number of firsts, too, during the early months of 1968. The Bee Gees made their debut live appearance in the US, a one-off at Anaheim's Convention Center in California on 27 January.

Interest was high in the Gibbs; the audience included members of the Mamas and the Papas, the Monkees, Buffalo Springfield, the Turtles and the Smothers Brothers. The Bee Gees played twice, at 6 p.m. and 9.30 p.m., with a setlist that included the hits ('Mining Disaster', 'Massachusetts', 'To Love Somebody') and the more interesting album tracks 'Every Christian Lion Hearted Man Will Show You' and 'World'. They picked up a handsome US$15,000 for the double-header, although Stigwood had to pay the 30-piece orchestra. The show went over well—so well, in fact, that the orchestra applauded the band when they came on stage for their second show. 'That doesn't happen at home,' mused Barry afterwards.

Their first full US tour would begin at the Hollywood Bowl in the northern summer, late July, taking in 25 cities. This was the tour Stiggy had been boasting would gross a million dollars.

Before that, the Bee Gees launched their first 'proper' UK tour on 27 March at the Royal Albert Hall. This was no regular rock'n'roll show; this time the Bee Gees were backed by a 60-piece orchestra, and their 50-minute set began with a symphonic overture—'Hooked on Bee Gees', as it were. Aside from the hits, they debuted a song in the works, 'I Have Decided to Join the Airforce', Barry earnestly dedicating it to the Royal Air Force, currently celebrating its 50th anniversary. The RAF band even joined them on stage. All in all, it was a big public splash, an event one journalist described as 'a victory hurrah for good pop music'.

Just prior to this London extravaganza, the Gibbs followed in the Cuban-heeled footsteps of the Beatles, making their debut on the enormously-influential *Ed Sullivan Show*. The super-square Sullivan may have been a throwback to the vaudeville era, but his weekly show drew an audience of around 13 million viewers, huge ratings.

The Bee Gees shared the bill with Lucille Ball, George Hamilton and the Dubliners—the entertainment version of the mixed grill.

It was a confusing appearance for the lads. Introducing them, Sullivan seemed to mistake Barry Gibb for a soloist, not the best of starts. As they performed 'Words', which was fast-tracking its way to the US Top 20, Robin sat uncomfortably at the piano, a forced smile straining every muscle in his face. Mo, who managed to lock himself in the toilet during rehearsals, chose a vomit-green suit for the occasion, not an outfit for the squeamish. Barry, admittedly, was golden, a burgundy scarf slung around his neck, his teeth a gleaming white, not a hair out of place, his eyes burning a hole in the camera. The Bee Gees were accompanied by a string and brass section, the players standing stiffly stage right. Edgy it wasn't.

Not everyone was clicking for the Gibbs. Their new single, 'Jumbo', was proving a hard sell back in the UK. And it wasn't their finest three minutes, feeling like a half-hearted attempt to fuse the guitar grit of the Kinks to the usual psychedelia. It was a strange, uncomfortable stab at diversity, and soon after its 22 March release, 'Jumbo' faded into Bee Gees obscurity.

'Jumbo' wasn't the only problem for the Bee Gees. Stigwood, who was now knee-deep in pre-production for the upcoming musical *Hair*, as his empire continued expanding, was starting to wonder whether there was simply too much Bee Gees product out there. 'Jumbo' was their eighth single release in just under a year, and they were already hard at work on their third album since docking at Southampton. There was a proposed film, *Lord Kitchener's Little Drummer Boys*—clearly another case of 'what's good for the Beatles is good for the Gibbs'—and their own planned TV special, *Cucumber Castle*. As if that wasn't enough, they were also slated to team with

Frankie Howerd on the comic's TV 'spectacular', *Frankie Howerd Meets the Bee Gees*. When combined with their endless media, radio and concert appearances, the workload—and the exposure—was staggering, putting a whole new spin on the term ubiquitous. The Beatles were masters at leaving the public craving more; the Bee Gees were doing the opposite.

None of this seemed to hamper their ability to write killer songs. Their next single was so good it erased such problems as over-exposure in one pop heartbeat.

'I've Gotta Get a Message to You' was a song with such a curious backstory that it made both 'New York Mining Disaster 1941' and 'Massachusetts' seem positively prosaic. In what could be generously described as an unlikely scenario, pampered pop star Robin imagined himself to be a prisoner on death row, with only a few hours before his fateful date with 'Old Sparky'. He tries to write a note to his wife, a farewell to the woman he loves. As lyrical scenarios go, it'd be hard to imagine something quite so dramatic. And no one did pathos better than the Bee Gees.

Robin delved deeper into the song's genesis in the liner notes for the *Ideas* album. 'It was like acting, you see—we said let's pretend that somebody, his life is on the line, somebody's going to the chair. What would be going through their mind? Let's not make it doom and gloom but sort of an appeal to the person he loves. Because right now that's all he cares about.' Another, far less tantalising explanation had Robin and Molly fighting and the song was his apology, but the electric chair angle was way more satisfying. They even threw in a rare lyrical joke, Robin advising the executioner he was 'in no hurry' to make their appointment.

Stiggy dragged himself away from *Hair* rehearsals to check in with the brothers in the studio, as the song came together. 'You should go back and re-record the choruses,' he said, as they listened to a playback.

'Why?' Barry asked. Stigwood was a huge fan of the brothers' three-part harmonies—and he felt that was something the song's chorus lacked. The ever-dutiful brothers did what Stigwood suggested, and 'I've Gotta Get a Message to You' was ready to go. As it reached the UK Top 10 in August 1968, and the US Top 10 the month after, they were once again keeping stellar company: the Beatles' 'Hey Jude', Diana Ross & the Supremes' 'Love Child', Jimi Hendrix's take on Dylan's 'All Along the Watchtower' and Joe Cocker's bluesy spin on the Beatles' 'With a Little Help From My Friends' were all in the Top 10, as was Mo's partner, Lulu, with 'I'm a Tiger'. It was the best of times.

But their debut US tour brought the Gibbs crashing to earth. In late July, with the band citing Robin's nervous exhaustion, dates in Phoenix, LA, San Francisco and San Diego were cancelled. The truth was that concert tickets weren't selling and the Stigwood Organisation was bleeding money. ('There was no nervous exhaustion,' Robin's partner Molly later confessed.) Ironically, one of the next concerts cancelled was in Rhode Island: 'Massachusetts' wouldn't be heard in Massachusetts, at least not in 1968. One of the few commitments the Bee Gees did meet was at the Ohio State Fair in Columbus, where they played four times in two days, sharing an unlikely bill with Roger 'King of the Road' Miller and comic George Kirby, playing to 100,000 people. Hugh Gibb shot some silent 8mm footage of the event, which would prove to be historic, in its own way—aside from an 10 August concert in New York, the Bee Gees wouldn't play in America again until 1971.

As more dates were cancelled, the group, Robin included, disappeared into Atlantic Studios in New York on 13 August—hardly the act of an exhausted pop star—where they worked on various new songs. By late August, Stigwood performed a mercy killing and canned the rest of the US jaunt; so much for their million-dollar payday. A token one-hour radio spot on LA's KRLA, with Barry and Robin providing weather reports and telling jokes, was an empty epitaph to the tour that never really was.

There were new signs of sibling tension in a strange TV spot for the *Dating Game* program, shot at the tail end of their US visit. Mo and Robin, along with five-time Olympic gold medal-winning swimmer Don Schollander, were the 'eligible bachelors'. (Lulu and Molly, clearly, didn't count when it came to Bee Gees business.) On the other side of the partition, screened from the three men, was a textbook Californian girl, a golden blonde named Debbie. She threw out 'zany' questions—'What do you like about the dark?', 'What would you do if you came home and found me talking to a banana?'—while the Gibbs and Schollander tried to play along. It made for cringeworthy TV. At one point, Mo's very English accent was so lost on Debbie that she asked the host for a translation.

'What would you do,' Debbie asked, 'if you came around to collect me and my father stepped in?'

'Smash his face in,' Mo replied, without a moment's hesitation.

'Well, as a gentleman,' Robin interjected, 'one cannot be violent in a case such as this ... So I'd see a solicitor first—and then hit him.'

By the time Mo was asked to name the softest thing he could imagine, he seemed genuinely agitated. The self-confessed peacemaker, who'd intervene when Barry and Robin clashed, exhibited a rare flash of temper. You could almost hear Maurice thinking, 'Do I really have to do this? What is the point?'

After what felt like hours, Mo sternly replied, 'Butter.' Bizarrely, stony-faced Mo won the date, although Debbie shrieked, 'I wanted them all!'

If uncomfortable TV spots like this weren't enough, Barry had begun hinting at an acting career. He'd had enough of the life of a pop star, he told the UK press—it was too debauched, too sordid, and he wanted out. Barry cited numerous film offers from his recent trip to the US, although Stigwood quickly hosed down the story. Clearly, the failure of the US tour was hitting hard. It would be many years before the Bee Gees became a profitable touring act, and it would only come after a major creative makeover.

*Idea*, the Bee Gees' third album in a hurry, hit stores in September 1968. It was another express delivery mix of hits ('I've Gotta Get a Message to You'), half-conceived ideas (the forgettable 'Down to Earth'), whimsy such as 'Kitty Can' and the usual melodramatic Robin showcases—including the 10-tissue weepie 'I Started a Joke' and the oh-so-sombre 'In the Summer of His Years'. Try as they might to suppress it, the growing tension within the group as they struggled with myriad issues—leadership, creative control, egos and boozing, just for starters—was bubbling to the surface. Robin suspected that Stigwood was pushing Barry more to the forefront. Jealousies simmered. The band of brothers, once so united, became divided.

The Gibbs had lived in each other's pockets all their lives, the last decade or more in a very public way—and *Idea* expressed the emerging divisions. The album felt like various solo efforts lumped together under the Bee Gees moniker. Only four of the album's 12 songs were brotherly co-writes; Robin had four solo credits, Barry three. Vince Melouney, who contributed the rootsy, rocky 'Such a Shame', was also feeling the pinch—he felt more and more like an outsider, unable to develop as a songwriter within the Bee Gees' creative straitjacket.

Spending money provided a handy distraction to the tumult. Barry had taken to collecting weapons; he once frightened off a prowler in his London home by waving an unlicensed revolver, which led to a few questions from the local constabulary and a £25 fine. (The judge famously told Barry that besides possessing two pistols, 'The only thing I can see Mr Gibb has done wrong is wear a white suit to court.') Mo kept chugging his Lennon-approved scotch and Cokes. 'I would have drunk cyanide,' he admitted, 'I was so in awe of the man.'

Mo also developed an unfortunate habit of driving his luxury cars into poles and fences and walls. The high life was getting the better of the once-grounded, once-practically-minded Gibbs of Redcliffe. Robin bought a splendid English manor house and collected musical instruments.

Yet rather than advising the lads to take some time away from each other, Stigwood continued to think big. It was the era of the two-album extravaganza, typified by the Beatles' 'White Album', Dylan's *Blonde on Blonde* and Cream's *Wheels of Fire*—the Who's epic masterpiece *Tommy*, too, was in the works. And Stigwood's connection with the Who ran deep—he was tight with their managers Kit Lambert and Chris Stamp, and worked as the band's booking agent. Stiggy could see the potential, both commercially and in credibility, of a big, bold musical statement. And the Who had only one key in-house songwriter, Pete Townshend; the Gibbs had three. How hard could it be? 'Boys,' Stigwood told the Gibbs in his avuncular way, 'you need to make a rock opera.'

Unfortunately, the album ended up killing the band.

While the record with the working titles of *Masterpeace* and *The American Opera* was still taking shape—they'd eventually settle on

*Odessa*—and around the same time that rivals the Beatles entered London's Twickenham Studios to shoot promo films for 'Hey Jude' and 'Revolution', the Gibbs, Melouney and Petersen were in Belgium, attempting to create their own unique mix of sound and vision. The occasion was a TV special named *Idea*, after their latest LP, which aired in September 1968. Other guests were Julie Driscoll, Brian Auger & Trinity and Jill Lindfors.

The opening set piece was 'Massachusetts', presented in a pop art/Dada style, flares and boots and scarves everywhere you looked, Barry sporting a jacket that could have been pinched from the Beatles' dressing room. The clip for the song 'Idea' was another pop art extravaganza, the band perched on a massive cut-out pistol, index fingers raised in some sort of abstract, late '60s statement, Andy Warhol-goes-to-the Continent.

Robin then took a solo turn for his 'I Started a Joke'. The others were in the shoot, but acted merely as props for Robin's aching melodrama. Yet again, pop art was the prevailing style. Vince Melouney was then given a solo spot, for the Kinks-ish 'La De Da', the band shot in a *Celebrity Squares*-like configuration, an oversized game of noughts and crosses.

This typified much of the *Idea* TV special—a lot of it seemed forced, the band doing their best middle-of-the-road impersonation of the counter-culture. Still, it had its moments. The thin-hipped, mutton-chopped Barry was in his pomp for 'When the Swallows Fly', prowling the set while staring meaningfully into the camera. He wasn't Otis Redding, but when pushed, Barry had some serious presence.

At other times, such as with the video for 'Indian Gin and Whisky Dry', it all came across as stilted, out of touch. The band's images were superimposed in glasses—they couldn't be any more literal if they tried—and the song culminated with a hearty toast from all, straight to camera, using real drinks, probably much to Mo's delight. This, and other moments during *Idea*, felt like a song in search of a visual concept. The Beatles' bumbling *Magical Mystery Tour*, rated a failure by most critics, was cutting-edge cinema by comparison. The clip for 'Harry Braff' was a clumsy attempt at music-hall whimsy.

The cameos of Julie Driscoll, a sort of Annie Lennox of the '60s, seemed far more natural than anything offered by the Gibbs. Euro songstress Jill Lindfors, with her funereal-grey make-up and cutting-edge wardrobe, delivered a version of 'Words' that was almost as earnest as anything the Gibbs could muster. Who cared if she was singing in German?

The brothers returned for 'I Gotta Get a Message to You', their latest hit. Barry stepped forward for the second verse decked out in his lucky bolero jacket, matched with dangerously puffy sleeves. Next up was 'Swan Song'; and this time Barry wore a garish violet ensemble, ruffles, the works, sporting wickedly-pointy flares and white boots. Despite his eye-popping gear, the elder Gibb somehow kept it together, once again staring into the dark heart of the camera as he delivered another sweeping popscape.

The big closer, such as it was, came in the form of 'I Have Decided to Join the Air Force', yet another overload of pop art, the guys swamped by posters of luscious thick red lips and placards with the lone word 'Yeah' etched upon them. Andy Warhol would have loved it. For all their efforts at spontaneity, the Bee Gees were no Beatles, as good as some of the songs were. At its worst, the TV production *Idea* was as convincing as a high school musical. As for the album on which the special was based, regardless of its patchwork nature, it was a hit on the Continent, charting well in West Germany and France; it also reached No.4 in the UK and made the US Top 20, selling more than a million copies in all.

More great numbers, especially for a band on the verge of a breakdown.

Even years after its creation, Robin admitted it was 'hard to speak about *Odessa* in any coherent way'. The Gibbs set out to create something that Stigwood could reproduce on the stage, as would happen with the Who's *Tommy*. But to write a cohesive, thematically connected series of songs was a tough challenge for any band, let along three siblings who were avoiding each other as much as humanly possible.

And the storyline of *Odessa* provided the Gibbs with a major creative challenge. '[It's] about a man on an iceberg after a shipwreck,' Barry explained, 'and his wife has run away with a vicar. It's very weird.' Deaf, dumb and blind Tommy had nothing on the vicar-cuckolded narrator of *Odessa*, who looked on as his fictional vessel, *Veronica*, sank beneath the waves. Not your typical pop fodder; more like *Titanic* with three-part harmonies.

As Barry explained, they were trying their best once more to please their manager. 'Because of *Tommy* and Robert's connection to these type of things, he wanted us to do a rock opera and we wanted to put it on stage. [But] instead of writing a rock opera, we just came up with a mish-mash, a bunch of songs that we thought we were going somewhere with. But I think we were extremely weary ... we could no longer deal with each other. The three of us drifted apart—in fact, I'd say the four of us drifted apart, including Robert.'

Barry, meanwhile, stuck by his line that he was leaving the band to become an actor, although he stressed that he'd meet all their existing commitments—another album, the proposed film, TV special and the rest of it, which would keep the Bee Gees busy until at least 1970. 'The group scene is not an everlasting thing,' Barry told British music mag *Disc*, 'you can only go so far.'

In the spirit of the Beatles' 'Hey Jude' or Richard Harris's 1968 classic, 'MacArthur Park', *Odessa*'s title track was an epic, at seven and a bit minutes, by far the longest song the Gibbs had committed to tape. The Gibbs even discussed splitting it over two sides of a seven inch 45, but then ditched the idea to release 'Odessa' as a single because they didn't want to be accused of copying the Beatles. Stigwood was a big fan of Robin's song, calling him in the middle of the night to express his feelings (and perhaps repay at least one Gibb for their habit of after-hours drop-ins). 'It's the greatest pop classic I've ever heard,' Stiggy told Robin.

As *Odessa* sessions consumed much of the final quarter of 1968, it was pretty clear that tensions between the brothers had reached a new low. While trying to complete one of *Odessa*'s more ambitious tracks, 'Lamplight', in late October, the usually-mellow Mo slowly came undone. By take seven, the band inched closer to a complete performance, but the ending was a mess. Take eight was even worse—somehow a platter of vegetables fell onto the piano at which Maurice was seated. 'This is the last time I'm doing it,' Mo announced, sweeping away the salad, as they prepared for take nine.

'So make sure you know the end,' Barry told him.

'I knew it after you started doing it,' replied Mo, 'but you've changed it 'round again for the second time.'

And so the squabble continued. Finally, by take nine, the

song was done, but the prickly exchanges in the studio typified the troubles in Gibbland. To complicate matters, Stigwood was preoccupied with staging *Hair;* for the first time since taking on the Bee Gees, it seemed he wasn't completely committed to the group. (*Hair* opened on London's West End on 27 September and ran for five years.) Stigwood's attitude didn't help, either, especially when he departed for another American trip and casually instructed Barry, 'Take charge of the boys.'

'He doesn't quite realise what a strain it can be,' a drained Barry told writer David Hughes, citing making the album and their myriad other obligations. 'Have you ever tried keeping your own brothers in order?'

Come early December, and Barry found himself alone in the studio. Robin and Maurice were long gone, nowhere to be found. There'd been few instances during the four months of recording when the brothers were in the studio at the same time. Ironically, Barry was putting the finishing touches to the problematical 'Lamplight', working with engineer Mike Wade on the final mix.

Looking around him, Barry took in the lonely scene. 'What's the point of this?' he asked Wade. And Barry meant every word.

The non-Gibb members of the band were voicing their own concerns. During a break from recording, as the band played a show in Hamburg, Vince Melouney came clean with a reporter. 'I have never really felt 100 per cent a Bee Gee,' he told the *New Music Express* (*NME*). 'Because the talent that I have doesn't come up to the standard of the Gibb brothers' talent.'

Melouney also grumbled about his treatment by Hugh Gibb; he felt Hugh treated him 'like an outsider'. It was quite the admission. On 11 November, Stigwood announced that Melouney was out, referring to 'a musical disagreement' between the guitarist and the Gibbs. In a 2006 interview, Melouney cited his problems with Hugh as the main reason for leaving the band; he also called himself 'too young, too naïve' to deal with the wild ride that was the Bee Gees. Colin Petersen hung in, but his time as a Bee Gee was also running short.

Bizarrely, none of this escalating drama slowed them down. In between sessions for *Odessa*, they criss-crossed Europe throughout November—even Robin's marriage to Molly Hullis on 4 December was a hit-and-run affair. They tied the knot at London's Caxton Hall registry office; their honeymoon would have to wait until *Odessa* was finished. Robin Gibb was still a few weeks shy of his 19th birthday. Curiously, Robin's 'I Started a Joke' began its climb to a US peak of No.6 within days of their wedding, but for reasons never fully explained, Stigwood decided against releasing the ballad in the UK. This could only have further supported Robin's suspicion that Stiggy was grooming Barry as bandleader.

A few days after Christmas 1968, while Barry was flying back to Sydney for some R&R, Mo appeared on Lulu's TV show, *Happening for Lulu*. After they performed Donovan's 'What a Beautiful Creature You Are', pop's It couple made an announcement: 'We're getting married.' They were due to become Mr and Mrs Gibb-Lawrie not long before Lulu sang for England at Eurovision in late March.

It seemed that the world would never stop spinning for the Gibb brothers, what with marriages, departures, escapes and the ever-mounting pressure of creating their big new musical statement. In a playful moment, with a TV camera whirring, Barry posed as a reporter, firing a question at Robin. 'What's all this about the band breaking up?' he asked.

Robin replied that there was as much chance of that happening as there was of him becoming 'the premier of Russia'.

It was a curious exchange: exactly why was Barry asking the question in the first place?

Given the huge expectations, with *Odessa* being talked up as the Gibbs' response to such era-defining records as *Sgt. Pepper's* and the Moody Blues' sprawling *Days of Future Passed*, it came as no great surprise that on its mid-February release, the record didn't quite meet expectations. While not shy of great chamber pop moments—the twangy 'Marley Purt Drive', with Barry on lead vocal, or the richly melodic 'Edison' and 'Melody Fair'—there was no obvious sense of unity. Like their previous albums, *Odessa* was a grab bag of songs, some great, some not so. If anything, it was the sound of a band breaking up.

*Rolling Stone* mag confronted the obvious and declared that *Odessa* was 'the *Sgt. Pepper's* copy all Sixties headliners felt driven to attempt'. However, they accepted that as knock-offs went, 'the Bee Gees' wasn't bad; faulting it for pretentiousness makes absolutely no sense'.

Pop culture's rear-vision mirror has treated *Odessa* well; the record is now considered an overlooked classic of the late 1960s. Even hipper-than-thou *Pitchfork M$^e$dia* rates *Odessa* very highly, stating: '*Odessa* is a feast that's hard to fault for ambition [although it's] too rich and occasionally too stodgy to take in one sitting.' The album rated a spot in cult guide *1001 Albums You Must Hear Before You Die*, while the Allmusic Guide also sang its praises. 'The myriad sounds and textures made *Odessa* the most complex and challenging album in the group's history, and if one accepts the notion of the Bee Gees as successors to the Beatles, then *Odessa* was arguably their *Sgt. Pepper's* album.'

With the title track now binned as a possible single, Barry's 'First of May' was given the green light. And this decision may well have been what transformed the good ship Gibb, which was already listing badly, into another *Titanic*. Robin was convinced his 'Lamplight' should have been the lead single, and didn't hold back in advising the media how he felt, letting fly when he spoke with a *Melody Maker* reporter.

Robin threatened to remove all his songs from the album 'if Mr Stigwood doesn't want to see eye to eye … I think "Lamplight" would be number one for weeks,' Robin added, predicting that 'First of May' '*might* make number 10'. (It did reach a UK peak of No.10, in March, but faded quickly thereafter. In the US it barely pierced the Top 40.) Robin even changed his phone number to put distance between himself and the others. RSO responded by telling the media Robin couldn't leave the band because his contract had a further three years to run. It was a very public donnybrook, with Barry, Mo and Stigwood on one side of the divide, Robin the other, and the press their only steady form of communication.

If the Bee Gees were to split, as seemed very possible, it wasn't any regular break-up. This was a close-knit family unit that now seemed totally unable to get along. A split wouldn't just terminate the band, it would break up the family. Barry and Mo retreated into the studio, perhaps the only safe place they knew, where they worked on even more new music, still recording as the Bee Gees.

Barry insisted that the Bee Gees would go on with or without Robin. Stigwood added that every row the brothers have 'always blow[s] over' and saw no reason to think otherwise with this latest contretemps. He was wrong. Robin Gibb was as good as gone.

In the midst of this sibling uprising, Mo and Lulu were due to be married on 18 February at Gerrard's Cross. There was no chance of a low-key ceremony—this was, after all, the nuptials of two of pop's biggest stars. Admittedly, most of the thousand-plus onlookers who descended on St James Parish Church were Lulu fans; she was pop's It Girl, the working-class lass who'd made it to the top.

'There was pandemonium,' the ever-so-condescending British Pathe newsreel voiceover proclaimed, as their camera tried to capture the chaos, the pushing and shoving, as fans and press struggled to catch a glimpse of the golden couple. 'Even the older ones in the crowd have a touch of pop fever.'

Maurice, wearing a smart white suit, waited a nervous 20 minutes before Lulu arrived in a green Roller. As she stepped out, dressed in a long, mink-trimmed white coat with *de rigeur* fur hood, the crowd surged forward. The police, who seemed massively outnumbered, formed a human chain, as Lulu pleaded with them to move back. 'Please let me in, please let me in,' she cried.

Barry had told Mo straight that he thought he shouldn't get married—only days before, a newspaper headline screamed: 'Maurice is too young to wed says big brother Barry'—but relented and showed up. Robin had buried the hatchet with his brother for the day and was Mo's best man. After the 30-minute service, presided over by Reverend Gordon Harrison, the newlyweds were forced to wait a further 15 minutes before a path could be cleared just so they could reach their getaway car.

'It was like a battlefield for the press men,' blithered the Pathe narrator, before concluding with this contender for the most patronising statement of the year, as Lulu and Mo's car drove off. 'The Bee Gees hadn't lost a man ... they'd gained a real honey.'

But just like his brothers, Mo's first stab at marital bliss proved anything but blissful. Many years down the line, Lulu admitted it was a bad move. She was as green as Mo; in fact when they wed she was still a virgin. 'The drinking was part of [the problem],' she confessed, 'but we shouldn't have got married in the first place. We should have just had a romance. I totally loved and adored him but ... in love with him? I was probably in love with love.'

It would take a few years before they split, but it seemed as though Barry might have been right all along: getting married wasn't the right thing for Mo. If anyone understood problem relationships it was Barry, who was currently heading into his own break-up, prior to marrying Linda Gray.

Robin seemed happy to be his brother's best man, but remained discontent with life as a Bee Gee. Barry and Mo now recorded without him; when the group filmed the BBC special, *The Talk of the Town: The Bee Gees in London*, sister Lesley stood in for Robin, singing with her brothers. That was a first—there was even talk of her own management deal with Stigwood, and a permanent role in the touring band. After *Talk of the Town* aired, Lesley spoke with Robin, who watched the show on TV and admitted to feeling 'very choked up about it'.

'Why don't you just come back then?' she asked him, which seemed perfectly reasonable. Robin didn't reply.

The split widened; if nothing else, Robin was stubborn. To further confuse the issue, Barry told a reporter that *he* felt like an outsider. On 6 March, the old firm of Robin, Maurice, Barry and Colin Petersen appeared together on *Top of the Pops*, promoting 'First of May', but it was a brief reconciliation—in fact, it was the last time that the quartet performed as the Bee Gees.

Robin's wife Molly was next to leap into print, insisting that her husband wasn't getting enough credit for his contribution to the group. Robin, meanwhile, made it widely known he was not talking with Stigwood under any circumstances. It was very, very messy, but somehow things got messier. In mid-March, RSO issued a writ against Robin, claiming 'damages and injunctions', although Stigwood had no real intention of taking the matter to court. All he really wanted to do was stop Robin making statements about leaving the group.

Then on 22 March, a media report announced that Robin was flying solo and would open a management company of his own named Bow and Arrow. A disgruntled Barry parried by saying that he was no longer interested in the much-talked-about Bee Gees film, *Lord Kitchener's Little Drummer Boys*, due to begin filming in April. The movie was quickly recast without the Gibbs but was never made.

When Robin failed to show with his brothers on the final episode of *Happening for Lulu*, in late March, Barry and Mo sent out a 'get well' message on air to their errant sibling, who was allegedly suffering from 'nervous exhaustion'. But it was hardly convincing.

Matters became so murky that in April, when another Bee Gees BBC special was scheduled, the director Michael Hurll admitted he didn't know how many brothers he was going to work with. Another stab at touring America was also on the cards, including a high profile gig at Madison Square Garden in New York, and the show would go on, with or without Robin, according to Stigwood. Robin, *NME* reported, was recovering from a 'minor breakdown'.

Barry seemed torn between brokering some sort of amnesty with Robin, and standing his ground. While he insisted his brother would be welcome back in the band, Robin would have to make the first move. 'I won't speak to him again until he speaks to me,' Barry told yet another reporter from the *NME*, coming off more than a little petulant.

Father Hugh weighed in. '[Barry and Maurice] have got to show Robin they can do it without him.' Hugh felt that a statement of independence on their part would lure Robin back into the fold, but that's not how the drama played out.

Robin, instead, issued his own statement: a debut solo single named 'Saved By the Bell', which was released mid-year. The mournful 'Saved' was a direct descendant of 1968's 'I Started a Joke'; if Robin had plans to break new musical ground, there was no evidence here. On 11 May, Robin emerged from his self-imposed public exile when he presented an award to Cliff Richard at the *NME* Poll Winners event, staged at Wembley in front of 10,000 fans. Maurice was backstage with Lulu and caught up with Robin. It was the first time they'd spoken privately in months. 'It's great to see you,' Robin told him, 'and we'll always be brothers, no matter what. But I'm out of the band.'

Maurice, always the man in the middle, stuck between Barry and Robin's war of egos, could do no more than shrug and smile and wish his twin well.

In late June, a weird family scenario played itself out in the UK charts—the battle between Robin's 'Saved By the Bell' and the latest Bee Gees' release 'Don't Forget to Remember'. To complicate things, Mo had helped Robin in the studio with 'Saved', playing various instruments and adding harmonies. In the end, it was a close race: Robin's debut reached No.2 in the UK and was a chart-topper in Ireland, South Africa, Holland and New Zealand, but failed to chart in America. Barry and Mo's 'Remember' also hit No.2 in the UK, topped various other charts—and sneaked into the *Billboard* Hot 100, then stalled at No.73.

Barry continued stirring the pot when he invited a reporter to his home in London's Belgravia. His news was interesting: the remaining Bee Gees were planning to audition new singers, the job requiring someone with 'Robin's range, harmonies and ability to write', no small ask. Barry revealed that they'd made overtures to Stiggy client Jack Bruce, formerly of Cream, which had recently disbanded. As mismatches go, this was hard to top: Bruce was deep into heavy bloozepower, Cream being the type of band that believed eardrums should be assaulted, not soothed. Not surprisingly, Bruce demurred. The Gibbs' little brother Andy, just 10, was way too young for recruitment, although Hugh did mention Andy's possible future as a Bee Gee in yet another press chat.

Barry made it known that every hopeful was welcome; his door was always open. 'If a young guy wants to audition,' he said, 'he can come around to my place and strum along just with me in the room.' This seemed a very strange way for a superstar group to go about their business; it smelled strongly of desperation.

In yet another of his too-frank-for-his-own-good press talks, Barry admitted that he'd heard Robin's solo album, *Robin's Reign*, which was currently being recorded. Barry was asked, would the LP be a hit? 'As for it being a very commercial hit record,' he replied, 'Frankly, I just can't agree.'

The new look Bee Gees—Mo, Barry and Petersen—returned to the *Top of the Pops* in late May, performing 'Tomorrow, Tomorrow'. They were introduced by expat Aussie DJ Alan Freeman; years later, in his posthumous solo record, *50 St Catherine's Drive*, Robin would dedicate a song to Freeman, one of several BBC broadcasters who played their part in the Bee Gees' rise. (Freeman was posthumously linked to the Jimmy Savile sex scandal.)

Mo continued doing what he now did best: partying. Returning from dinner in London, he crashed his Roller, emerging from the wreckage with a broken nose and two black eyes. Barry happened to be in the house when Mo stumbled inside; he drove his brother straight to hospital.

It seemed as though life for the Gibbs in 1969 was one big soap opera: break-ups, breakdowns, lawsuits, car wrecks, public spats, the works. When would it all end?

If there had been a peacemaker in the Gibbs' respective camps, his advice would have been simple: the warring brothers should make themselves scarce, just for a while, sort matters out privately, and then consider the future. But somehow this just didn't occur to the Gibbs or Stigwood; the two parties stumbled on, acting as if their sibling split was the most natural thing in the world (although by late June 1969, Barry had conceded that replacing Robin was an impossible task).

Robin powered on, with details leaked of a planned series of high-profile shows titled *An Evening with Robin Gibb*, featuring an orchestra, big production, the works. *Robin's Reign* would emerge in late June. There was also talk of a book, maybe even some acting. The sky wasn't even the limit for Robin, or at least that's the impression he was giving.

Stiggy, meanwhile, sought out a business plan that would appease the recalcitrant Gibb. A five-year deal was struck, which enabled RSO to run Robin's new publishing company. And RSO's Chris Hutchins was appointed as Robin's new manager, making it pretty clear that Stiggy hadn't given up on bringing the boys back together. He wasn't ready to sacrifice his very own Beatles that easily.

Stigwood quietly set to work reuniting the brothers, but not before giving them the room to learn if they could survive on their own. Barry continued to talk up his prospects as an actor, claiming he and Maurice had 'star parts in a big movie' that would begin shooting in the near future. Barry was also crowned 'Best Dressed Pop Star' by Carnaby Street retailer John Stephen, which just went to show that Stiggy's advice when they arrived in London—'go and buy yourselves some decent clothes'—had paid off.

By mid-August, Mo and Barry finally found themselves in front of a camera, shooting what they called 'a Tudor period, *Laugh-In*-styled' comedy named *Cucumber Castle*. Early rumours hinted the stellar cast would include entertainer Sammy Davis Jr (who did shoot a scene that didn't make the final cut), actor Vincent Price and Lulu, but the key players ended up being Barry and Maurice and *Carry On* stalwart Frankie Howerd. He had some history with the Gibbs, having hosted the Bee Gees on his TV special in 1967—Howerd would re-appear with the Gibbs several years later in the awful *Sgt. Pepper's Lonely Hearts Club Band* movie.

Shot for £50,000 and, in part, on Stigwood's impressive spread in Middlesex, *Cucumber Castle* was a camp, kitschy comedy, in which Barry and Maurice hammed it up as 'the Leeches', sons of the king, a role overplayed to the hilt by Howerd. A pre-shoot motor accident, involving director Mike Mansfield, should have served as an omen: this was one car crash of a movie. (Mansfield was replaced by Hugh Gladwish.) Revered stage and screen actor Richard Harris appeared on screen long enough to mutter a line that could have easily served as the film's epitaph: 'What am I doing in this century?' Harris asked. 'Get me out of here.' Barry and Mo looked on, dressed as oversized ducks. Dignity? Who needed it. The film didn't air until Boxing Day 1970, a good year after it was shot.

As actors, the Gibbs sure made great pop singers; the only redeeming aspect was the inclusion of 'Don't Forget to Remember', a UK hit for the brothers in September, their last UK Top 20 for three long years. Producer Stigwood managed to shoehorn in a totally incongruous performance cameo from English 'supergroup' Blind Faith (featuring his star client Eric Clapton), which might have captured a great band coming to life, and worked as a tidy promo for Stiggy's next big act, but had nothing to do with the film's paper-thin storyline.

If *Cucumber Castle* was to have been Barry and Maurice's statement of independence, it only served to make it clearer that family friction was affecting their decision-making. The film should never have been made. In keeping with the theme, Barry and Maurice dressed as knights, in armour, feathers and the rest of it, for the soundtrack LP cover, but they looked lost in time and short of ideas. The stately 'Don't Forget to Remember' and the passable country and western pastiche 'Bury Me Down By the River' were the only standouts in yet another set of songs that felt like rushed cast-offs.

Interestingly, Lulu cut her own version of 'Bury Me' soon after, in 1970. Highly regarded American Arif Mardin arranged the Lulu version—and in a few years time he would play a major role in the second coming of the Bee Gees.

During the recording of the album that would accompany the *Cucumber Castle* TV show, in September 1969, Colin Petersen was fired from the band, which was now reduced to a party of two. His scenes were duly cut from the film, a ruthless send-off for a man who'd been a dutiful Bee Gee since their arrival in early '67. His dismissal was by letter, delivered by Stigwood's chauffeur. Petersen countered with a writ, against Barry, Mo and RSO, requesting they cease operating under the Bee Gees name until the matter was settled in court. The Gibbs responded by insisting the name was theirs and no one else's. Petersen's writ was thrown out of court in late September; a High Court judge ruled Petersen was a 'minor attraction' within the group, which must have hurt.

Afterwards, Barry revealed that Petersen felt the band wouldn't survive without Robin. Barry didn't link this to Petersen's sudden dismissal, but it wouldn't be hard to connect the dots. Loyalty was all for the Gibbs, especially in these troubled times. (Barry later wrote to Petersen, telling him that it was Stigwood who instigated his sacking, and that he regretted it. Barry told Petersen his departure was 'a loss to the Bee Gees sound'.)

Maurice, meanwhile, had a strange encounter during a break in filming *Cucumber Castle*. Diminutive Monkees singer Davy Jones, Lulu's former beau, met Mo in early August 1969 to discuss the possibility of covering some of Maurice's songs. It's not clear who brokered the meeting, given its awkward back story—Lulu took up with Mo only after being jilted by Davy—but both stars put on a brave face afterwards, although no recordings were ever attempted. They got on well, insisted one insider, because they 'both come from Manchester'. Lulu remained uncharacteristically silent.

Throughout the latter months of 1969, Robin had virtually no communication with his brothers and the rest of the family, although he seemed ready to unload whenever a reporter's microphone was near. (Robin's new plans included two musicals, one his personal twist on Dickens' *Christmas Carol*.) Hugh Gibb told a journalist that he hadn't spoken with Robin in three months. And Robin's latest change of management—he was now represented by Vic Lewis at NEMS, of all places—prompted a vague legal threat from Hugh, along with a writ from RSO. Robin, allegedly, responded to Hugh with hints of physical violence, implying his Dad might end up in a pair of 'concrete boots'. Robin was still only 19.

When Mo sat down for the latest in a seemingly never-ending series of interviews, this time with a reporter from *Disc*, he admitted to feeling no anger when Robin went solo. 'I simply understood the situation,' said perennial pacifier Maurice, who did admit that Robin never got along with Melouney and Petersen, sometimes criticising them on stage. Mo went on to say that the last time he was able to contact Robin was when his twin appeared on *Top of the Pops*, and he called the studio to wish him well.

It still took a few more months before the in-bloody-evitable happened and the brothers agreed to disband the Bee Gees, not too long after the Beatles called it quits, in an interesting co-incidence.

Yet these final few months of Bee Gees version 1 were as hectic as ever, despite the relentless sniping. There was an unavoidable sense that they were trying to squeeze in as many appearances, releases and recording sessions—Mo and Barry in one London studio, Robin in another—as humanly possible, just in case the chance never came their way again.

Barry and Mo's proposed American tour didn't happen; instead they said they were concentrating on shooting episodes for the planned *Cucumber Castle* TV series. They talked up the possibility of working with George Harrison and Eric Clapton on the next Bee Gees LP. But neither this nor the TV series eventuated; instead, a gap-filling best of the Bee Gees collection hit the stores in the first week of November, and rapidly climbed the charts.

In mid-November, Barry caught up with Australian journalist Ian 'Molly' Meldrum. 'Will the Gibbs ever get back together?' the *Go-Set* reporter asked.

Barry thought this through for a moment before replying. 'Just because we are apart now doesn't mean we are enemies,' he said, neatly avoiding the question. 'I never speak out against Robin, but Robin has a lot of fun speaking out against us.' Curiously, Barry had only recently stamped his foot and said that if Robin 'walks back into the group, I walk out'.

Two weeks later, a dejected, defeated Barry announced that he was leaving the Bee Gees. Barry said he felt 'fed up, miserable and completely disillusioned'. He was off to shoot a film with Vincent Price and work as a solo artist. Mo and Robin would be solo acts too. They'd all had enough.

act

fever

The British and American charts and airwaves were as rich as they'd ever been in the early months of 1970. There were hits from a revitalised Elvis Presley, the ubiquitous Motown—Diana Ross, Marvin Gaye and Stevie Wonder were all in the midst of a purple patch—along with Simon and Garfunkel's pop/gospel fusion 'Bridge Over Troubled Water' and Led Zeppelin's roaring 'Whole Lotta Love'. For the first time in a few years, the Bee Gees were silent. They'd racked up seven hits in the UK and almost as many Stateside since their 'Mining Disaster' breakthrough in early 1967, but now they were Missing In Action, torn apart by sibling rivalry, jealousy and rash public statements. Stigwood blamed 'a certain entourage' that surrounded each of the Gibbs, all giving advice when not requested. Mo blamed a lack of maturity, along with the usual complications that come with success: money, booze, lovers, lifestyle. Robin felt it was a classic case of the 'too much too soon' syndrome, although that conveniently neglected the decade they'd spent in Australia with little or no success. Barry blamed drink and drugs—Robin mixed speed with 'downers', Barry smoked, Mo drank—and the fact they were 'very high on ourselves'. Ego.

Whatever the cause of their split, they spent these early months of the new decade carefully avoiding each other. 'Blood's thicker than water,' said Barbara Gibb, when asked whether her boys would ever reunite, '[after all] they're brothers.' But before any reformation, each of the Gibbs had to heal. Mo boozed it up with Richard Burton and Ringo Starr. Robin plotted his solo career. Barry spent a lot of time in his flat in London, firing his BB gun at the chandelier and idly flipping through the pages of the *TV Guide*.

Barry was the first to make a post-Bee Gees move, heading into a London studio mid-February to work on a solo project that would rank among the Gibbs' more mysterious. Barry always had a thing for country and western; a lot of the band's Australian recordings came with an unmistakable twang, emulating such Oz stars of the day as Slim Dusty and Tex Morton. And this, Barry's 'lost' solo album, called *The Kid's No Good*, had a pretty strong whiff of tumbleweeds and the front porch. Admittedly, this was a golden era of country, with such stars as Charlie ('Behind Closed Doors') Rich, Charley Pride, Johnny Cash and Jeannie C. Riley (of 'Harper Valley PTA' renown) crossing over into the mainstream, but a Bee Gee gone country seemed odd.

Yet, said Barry proudly, 'I love country music and I probably allowed it a little more than I should have to influence me.' Arranger Bill Shepherd—'the only arranger I'll ever work with'— was back on board, along with backing vocalist P. P. Arnold and an unlisted cast of supporting players.

The recording did have its moments. 'Clyde O'Reilly' was a classic story-song with a moral, the type of tune that American Kenny Rogers would soon base his career upon. 'I'll Kiss Your Memory' was an archetypal tears-in-your-beer weepie. But the album wasn't strictly country. The opener 'Born' came with a soulful punch and ranked with the best songs currently coming off the Motown production line. Vocally, Barry seemed unbound, liberated. 'I was born to be free,' he sang, as the song rocked and rolled. ('Born' would be recorded by American-born, UK-based soul singer P. P. Arnold, with Barry producing, but was never released.) 'One Bad Thing', with its sweeping strings and hooky chorus, would have sat comfortably alongside the pick of the Bee Gees' late '60s hits. Like 'Born', 'One Bad Thing' was also covered, first by Barry's Aussie friend Ronnie Burns, then by the Freshmen, New Horizon and Wildwood.

Elsewhere, 'The Day Your Eyes Met Mine', a *Cucumber Castle*-era track, was the kind of tender ballad the Gibbs would master a few years later when creating songs like 'How Deep Is Your Love'. It, too, was covered, by American Lou Reizner, better known for his production work with Rod Stewart and David Bowie. The mellow 'Peace in My Mind' was reinterpreted (in German) by Katja Ebstein, while 'Mando Bay' was also given a Teutonic makeover, by Peter Maffay. The Texan rockabilly rebel Roy Head cut 'Clyde O'Reilly'. Clearly, Barry's songs weren't cast-offs, judging by the diversity and quality of their interpreters.

If nothing else, *The Kid's No Good* provided some solid returns for Barry's publishing coffers. The bootleg, all 70 minutes of it, generated some good press, too, one critic noting: 'One could think of [these songs] as the equivalent of lost solo tracks by the Beatles from the same era, except it's clear that *The Kid's No Good* ... was a finished work, thus making the bulk of these songs considerably more satisfying than, say, a bunch of unfinished John Lennon or Paul McCartney tracks off of *Let it Be*. There probably isn't a hit single here, at least for the American market, but it's all good listening.'

Even today the album remains a forgotten artefact—only the lyric 'the kid's no good' would end up on a Bee Gees record, 1973's 'Come

Home Johnny Bridie'. (Robin, too, would record a 'lost' solo album during this time, known as *Sing Slowly Sisters*. Mo did likewise with a record titled *The Loner*. All three records have been widely bootlegged.)

Barry, meanwhile, finally divorced Maureen and prepared to marry Linda Gray. They wed on 1 September, his 24th birthday, within a week of his divorce being finalised. At least Barry had his personal life in order.

As for the recalcitrant Robin, he powered on as if his brothers and this monster called the Bee Gees didn't exist. As Barry worked on *The Kid's No Good*, Robin prepared a third solo single, 'August October', another sampler of his upcoming *Robin's Reign* LP. He headed to New Zealand for a rare solo performance, backed by a local orchestra. He played only two Bee Gees' songs, 'I Started a Joke' and 'Massachusetts'; during the latter, Robin was targeted by a tomato-throwing member of the audience. He shrugged and kept singing.

Maurice, meanwhile, plugged away at his own solo record, a mix of novelties ('Take it Easy, Greasy') and songs such as 'The Loner' and 'Laughing Child' that would draw a clear, bold line under his role in the ongoing family drama. Yet by late January 1971, in a peculiar about-face, Mo was denying that the band, or at least he and big brother Barry, had actually split. 'Barry was bored and said the wrong things in the wrong way,' he told an *NME* reporter.

In the same breath, Mo talked about taking dancing lessons—Lulu was never home, apparently, and he needed something to do—and appearing in *Sing a Rude Song*, Stiggy's next planned musical, due to open in a few weeks time. He was even intending to shave off his beard. Mo also helped Beatle buddy Ringo with his own solo recording, a homely take on 'Bye Bye Blackbird'. The studio seemed the only safe haven for each Gibb brother.

It was becoming increasingly hard for anyone outside the family to get a handle on the real story about the brothers' relationship, especially when Mo told another reporter that the Bee Gees 'are alive and well and living in London', even while Barry and Robin continued to fly solo. The release, on 13 March, of a 'new' Bee Gees single—strictly a Barry and Maurice collab, 'IOIO'—further confused the issue. Barry and Maurice posed for the single's front cover, as hairy and toothy and upbeat as ever, but it was a flop, charting for all of one week at No.49, and promptly disappearing. The song's chirpy, upbeat disposition seemed in stark contrast to the current state of play within the Gibb family.

Stiggy was saying little, at least in public, being busy producing *Sing a Rude Song*, which opened in February at London's Greenwich Theatre. In it, Mo co-starred with *Carry On* star Barbara Windsor.

But all this activity seemed like a distraction from the big issue: did the 'real' Bee Gees have a future? *Did they even exist?*


Robin's full-length album debut, *Robin's Reign*, was released in February 1970 in the UK and March in North America. It was an album borne of anger and resentment, with a title that could have been lifted from some dodgy British sitcom, but it was also a surprisingly strong record. It also showed that if a Gibb adopted the Beatles' approach, and took the time to truly craft an album—Robin had worked on *Reign* for much of 1969—then they could pull off something truly ambitious. Of all the Gibb brothers' work during their split, *Robin's Reign* was the only album to be given a commercial release.

Mo, as always, didn't let business get in the way of family, and contributed to a couple of tracks, playing a variety of instruments. Robin found his own Bill Shepherd in arranger Kenny Clayton— and Clayton helped create a record of orchestral pop, albeit with odd weird twists such as 'Farmer Ferdinand Hudson', a quasi-psychedelic moodpiece, and 'Lord Bless All', which sounded like an ancient hymn.

The genesis of many of the songs was dead easy: Robin would play a melody on the organ, add a guitar and a drum machine track, then some voices, before handing it over to Clayton. But when the lush 'August October' and 'Saved By the Bell' blasted from the speakers listeners were reminded that 'understated' was not a word in Robin Gibb's vernacular. And while his lyrics tended to retreat to the safe ground of love won/love lost, the album's original title—*All My Own Work*—served notice that this was Robin's declaration of independence.

Robin's reputation as the stroppiest, most complicated Gibb was reinforced when he spoke about his album to the press. In one interview he compared himself with Bob Dylan; in another he calmly listed the seemingly endless projects he had lined up: a book, a screenplay, two scores, a musical version of Shakespeare's *Henry VIII*... (What, no moon landing?)

Yet talk inevitably returned to the Bee Gees saga: What happened, Robin? Will you ever get back together with Barry and Mo? 'Music to me is an adventure,' Robin told *The Guardian*, 'and I can do far more on my own. It was restricting writing for the Bee Gees but I enjoyed it until they began to judge what I was doing.'

He left it dangling there, but it's likely that Stigwood, rather than Mo or Barry, had been Robin's biggest critic, beginning with his rejection of Robin's 'First of May' during the *Odessa* period. Moving on was not something Robin did particularly well—and he could bear a grudge.

'As it was,' surmised the *Allmusic Guide*, in its mixed review of *Robin's Reign*, 'the album couldn't get far enough away the Bee Gees' own roots to count as more than a footnote—albeit an often beautiful and reasonably entertaining one—to their history.'

Tellingly, despite its merits, *Robin's Reign* didn't register in the UK, US or Australia. Its only chart placings were a paltry No.19 in West Germany and No.77 in Canada. When Maurice's debut solo single, April's 'Railroad', came and went without a murmur—and the recently released *Cucumber Castle* soundtrack album stalled at No. 57 in the UK—the writing was pretty much on any wall that the Gibbs or Stigwood cared to look at: as solo artists, the Gibbs made for a great group. The only path to success was for the trio to work again as the Bee Gees. But how to reunite them? A rumour that Barry was preparing to relocate to the US—which he swiftly denied—once again muddied waters that were already murkier than the Thames at low tide.

A curious middleman in the ongoing soapie was Steve Kipner, who grew close to the Gibbs during those long, late nights at the St Clair studio back in Sydney's Hurstville and relocated to the UK in the late 1960s. Kipner's band, known in Australia as the Kinetics but now rebranded Tin Tin, was signed to RSO, on the encouragement of his buddy Mo, and placed on a hefty weekly retainer of 15 quid. Kipner was in an interesting position to see the Bee Gees' drama unfold: he was a labelmate, a peer and a friend.

'I believe Robert was trying to keep the individual Bee Gees occupied. So Maurice became Tin Tin's producer and we were on RSO,' Kipner observed.

A self-titled Tin Tin album, with Maurice multi-tasking as producer and playing everything from harpsichord to bass and drums, didn't generate much interest, but a gently sentimental ditty named 'Toast and Marmalade for Tea', with Steve Kipner on lead vocal, recorded in 1970, became a hit in America, reaching No.1 in numerous east coast cities and peaking at No.20 on the *Billboard* Hot 100 during 1971. The Bee Gees hadn't charted highly in the US since 'I Started a Joke', so Mo must have derived some satisfaction from producing this out-of-nowhere hit. (Tin Tin dissolved in 1973 but Kipner moved on to a stellar songwriting career in the US, writing 'Physical' for Olivia Newton-John, and huge hits for Chicago and Christina Aguilera.)

As 1970 progressed, it seemed it was no longer a case of 'will the Bee Gees reform?', but *when*. If they continued delivering solo projects that crashed and burned, Stigwood would turn off the cash and their careers would be over. This would be a particularly bitter pill to swallow when the oldest member of the group, Barry, was just 24. The Beatles had recovered from their troubled period in the late '60s to produce the masterpiece *Abbey Road*; perhaps the Bee Gees could do likewise.

The ice started to melt around the middle of the year. There were hints in the musical trade papers. When asked about the likelihood of a reformation, a spokesman for Stigwood's company had an each-way bet. While denying an immediate reunion, he revealed: 'There is strong speculation that the Bee Gees trio will be reactivated this year.' 'Trio' being the key word—although use of the term *reactivated* made some wonder if Stiggy and RSO viewed the Bee Gees as a pop music machine rather than three troubled brothers.

The human factor, however, kicked in on 7 June, when Robin joined Mo in a London studio to work through four takes of a song called 'Conquer the World', Robin singing the lead. It would never be released, but clearly a change was in the summer breeze. The duo worked on another track, 'Distant Relationship', Robin's tribute to Molly's father George, who had died suddenly at 60. George spent the last few days of his life in Robin and Molly's London home. A little further down the line, the song would be transformed into a Bee Gees cut, 'Sincere Relation'.

Barry returned from a holiday on the Continent in June to read a press report that the three Gibbs were 'once again talking', with Robin leading the push for a reunion. This was quite something to swallow along with his toast and tea; after all, Barry's solo single 'I'll

Kiss Your Memory' was just about ready to roll. He also had a brief return to Australia planned later in the month to be a presenter at the *Go-Set* Pop Poll Awards. 'I'd like to see how ["Memory"] goes,' Barry said, 'before committing myself to anything else.'

However, Barry's wariness didn't stop Robin and Mo from continuing with their collaboration. On 21 June they were back in the studio, working once again as a twosome, on a track named 'Come to the Mission', the first part of an ambitious three-song suite. Though 'Mission' would remain in the vaults, the collaboration suggested that a full family get-together couldn't be far off. It seemed that Robin's temper—and runaway ego—had finally cooled. 'It's no fun if you're on your own,' Robin told a reporter.

But then, while in Australia, Barry threw up yet another road-block. He cited songwriting credits as a spoke in the wheel of their creative relationship; even their solo efforts were credited to all three brothers—'the same as when Paul McCartney writes a song, John Lennon automatically gets a credit,' he grumbled (although that wasn't strictly the case with Bee Gees credits). Yet in almost the same breath, Barry predicted a bright future for the Bee Gees, stating they could go on for 'another 20 years or more'. He'd had enough of working with artists outside the family, and his immediate goal was to write a hit, 'the sort of record the public wants to hear', which was something no Gibb had been able to achieve during their period of alienation.

A key turning point happened on 1 August, once again in a London studio. Mo and Robin worked on a track named 'I Can Laugh', which Robin had brought to the session, convinced it was perfect for the group. When the tape of their efforts was stored away, the title scrawled on the outside of the box told a story. It simply read: 'Bee Gees.'

Not everything attempted during these ongoing Robin/Maurice sessions was musical gold. During 1970, more Bee Gees songs were left on the studio floor than ever before, or after. It was the year of the outtake. A few tracks would be dusted off for their next album, *2 Years On*, but most were cast aside forever. Yet the simple process of singing and recording together again—even if it was only Mo and Robin at this stage—was a key part of the healing. What they struggled to say to each other in person seemed to be more easily expressed through music.

Stiggy didn't keep the public in the dark too long. On 24 August, on the eve of RSO being floated on the English stock exchange, *Daily Variety* printed what everyone had suspected for some time: the Bee Gees had officially reformed. Stigwood said it was necessary for the brothers to make peace before they could work together again, although the unspoken truth was that they also first needed to fail as solo acts.

'We want to apologise publicly to Robin,' Mo told *Melody Maker*, 'for the things that have been said.' He made it clear the band was now just the three of them, with a session drummer sitting in. The insular Gibbs were drawing even tighter than before.

As for the return of Robin, the English press speculated how much this would cost Stigwood when RSO did go public, as the recalcitrant Gibb needed to be bought out of his existing solo contract with NEMS. The figure bandied about was around £50,000. In the words of *Daily Variety*, Robin 'cost Stigwood some fancy coin'. But that would prove to be money well spent over the ensuing years. As for the float, RSO sold two million shares and placed a £3 million value on the company, increasing its worth, according to some estimations, by as much as £500,000. Any lingering doubts that RSO wasn't a musical powerhouse to rival NEMS were now dismissed.

September saw the brothers continue their search for not just the perfect song, but also the perfect studio. Their reunion was significant in itself, but they needed a comeback hit. They shifted base to London's Morgan Studios, where Beatles Paul McCartney and Ringo Starr had recorded, as had the Kinks.

Among the many new songs the brothers were recording for the unimaginatively titled *2 Years On* was 'Lonely Days', which was finished by October. 'Days' had started out as a spare instrumental, which Mo scratched out on a piano, but changed shape considerably when Barry and Robin joined him and started ad-libbing vocals, just like in the old days, before all the drama. 'It was new, fresh,' Mo said of the recording, 'the energy we had from our time apart all came out. It was a wonderful session.'

Maurice wasn't overstating the case. Another sketch that emerged from the same period was the aching 'How Can You Mend a Broken Heart', which would do some useful Bee Gees business a little further down the line. As Mo surmised, 'Not a bad day's work. Two [future] No.1s.'

'Lonely Days', which made it clear the Gibbs had been tuning into the Beatles' moving swansong *Abbey Road*—especially McCartney's 'Golden Slumbers'—started its rapid chart ascent, especially in America, during November. In fact, it set a new high for the brothers Stateside, peaking at No.3. Yet in the UK it didn't fare quite as well, only reaching 33. Still, 'Lonely Days' was ample proof that the Gibbs had lost none of their songwriting nous; their honey-dipped harmonies were in full working order. Split? What split?

In the jarringly stylised film clip for 'Lonely Days', the brothers were presented as sophisticated young men about town: Mo stepping into his Roller, Barry walking his oversized mutt Barnaby through the city streets, Robin contemplating his collection of gold records and pointy statuettes before taking the air at his country estate. Only as the song reached its soulful coda did the brothers actually appear together, joining hands and then climbing into their cars and driving together into the future. The symbolism was clunky but the message was clear enough: the family that drove fancy motors together, belonged together.

The *2 Years On* LP, which dropped in November 1970, didn't rival *Abbey Road*—it didn't match *Odessa*, for that matter—but it had its moments, even though it sold less than half a million copies worldwide. The title track, with its soaring strings and crashing percussion, summed up the brothers' troubles of the past couple of years, all Sturm und Drang. Barry's 'Portrait of Louise' was genuinely lovely and 'Lonely Days' was one of their best singles yet. There was little filler in an album of polished popcraft and tasteful arrangements.

Yet Robert Christgau, the self-appointed 'Dean of American Rock Critics', who wrote for New York's *Village Voice*, dismissed it in a few quick keystrokes, perhaps a little too harshly. 'This is a little better than the LPs the Gibb brothers came up with during their separation,' Christgau sniffed, '*Cucumber Castle*, which at least sold some, and the solo flop *Robin's Reign* ... Presumably they broke up because they sensed that the formula was getting stale. To try to re-create it yet again is to guarantee the transformation from good commercial group to bad one.'

As US sales of 'Lonely Nights' ticked into the low seven figures, the Gibbs began their first and long-overdue 'proper' tour of America with an 11 February 1971 show at the Palace Theatre in Albany. Bearded drummer Geoff Bridgeford, from their extended RSO family Tin Tin, joined the brothers on stage. There were also TV appearances booked, including *The Tonight Show* with Johnny Carson, where they'd cross paths with avuncular comic George Burns, an unlikely future Bee Gees collaborator.

Despite high praise from *Billboard*, which described their New York show at the Philharmonic Hall as 'impeccably perfect', the two-week run wasn't a great success. There was a bomb scare at the New York show—a hoaxer called the theatre, screaming that the Bee Gees were 'fascist pigs'—and less-than-full houses on the west coast. A band spokesman blamed a recent earthquake for the mediocre attendance. Stigwood shrugged and told the press that the tour was also an effort to get more American artists to cover Gibb songs; it wasn't all about ticket sales. And word did spread that middle-of-the-road crooner/TV star Andy Williams—who hosted the Bee Gees on his show on 6 March—was interested in recording 'How Can You Mend a Broken Heart' Wisely, the Gibbs would keep that one for themselves; it became their first US No.1 in July, beating James Taylor, Marvin Gaye and Carole King to the top spot.

Having promised a working return to Oz ever since they boarded the SS *Fairsky* back in early 1967, the Bee Gees' troupe finally reached Australia, also in July 1971, with dates booked in all the capital cities. They were touring again with drummer Bridgeford, as well as a 16-piece orchestra. Long-time arranger Bill Shepherd was their musical director.

Yet the tour almost didn't happen. Several local impresarios thought the Gibbs were a financial risk, that they wouldn't fill venues, until promoters Ron Blackmore, Paul Dainty and David Trew took up the option (and pocketed some useful change, as it transpired). When the roadshow rolled into Sydney on 11 July, the Gibbs were given the full homecoming hero treatment, even though they hadn't lived in Australia for almost five years. The ongoing tussle as to who exactly 'owned' the Gibbs, and where they called home, was now being played out in public.

Before their Sydney date, the Gibbs—including father Hugh and sister Lesley—were 'presented' to Sydney Lord Mayor Sir Laurence Emmet McDermott. Barry, for one, looked genuinely chuffed. 'We always played on the steps [of the Town Hall],' he beamed when a TV crew caught up with him, as he flashed back to their early days. 'And we said one day we're going to go up the stairs.'

A hastily arranged press conference took place where, almost immediately, talk turned to what was still recent news—their reformation. 'How did you get it back together?' asked one reporter.

'Brothers,' said Barry—as simple as that. 'You can't get away from it. You're together all your lives. And when we broke up, we were children ... We believe in what we're doing. It's not musical knowledge, it's not something we've been taught, we just grew up doing it. And if you're doing anything else ... I don't know what the word is. Whatever we're doing, we're doing naturally.'

Mo, decked out in a sharp, light-coloured double-breasted jacket, slipped easily into his customary role as band funny man. 'We were together for a month before our manager knew it,' he said, smiling slyly, ensuring that Stiggy wasn't nearby.

'We're brothers. We fight,' added Robin. 'No one in this room hasn't fought with their relatives. Ours was made public. So we all went our separate ways. I was the first, in March 1969. [But] why stay alone when you can be so much happier and better together?'

Robin appeared a little worse for wear at the press conference, hiding his late-night eyes with dark shades. He sidestepped a question about making another solo record—his first wasn't even released in Australia—insisting not altogether lucidly: 'We have an obligation to bring to our audience our sound.'

Much praise was heaped on Bill Shepherd, who'd worked on most of their bigger hits; according to the brothers, the arranger did his best work with the Bee Gees, even though he'd recently recorded with the Rolling Stones. 'When he works with Mick Jagger, he's terrible,' quipped Robin, briefly removing his shades.

Another recurring subject was drugs; somehow, despite their cleanskin image, the Gibbs' 'Every Christian Lion Hearted Man Will Show You' had been interpreted as a drug song, so much so that one punter had pulled Mo aside in a Paris street, gushing: 'Wow, man, that song—*what are you on?*'

Barry, of course, decided it best to shut down all this wayward talk. 'Our music has never been directed towards drugs, ever.' To drive home his point, the elder Gibb sipped a cup of tea as he spoke. 'When we started writing things like "New York Mining Disaster", no one was on drugs. We just arrived in England; we were green.' Green? The pot reference might have been unintentional, but the press scrum found it hard to suppress its mirth. Green, huh?

Mo moved the conversation towards a new track, 'The Greatest

Man in the World', calling it 'Barry's best song yet'. An impromptu run-through on acoustic guitar led to a jam of the Everly Brothers 'Bye Bye Love'—always the Everly Brothers, the siblings that got them started in music all those years ago.

To round off the gathering, a Festival Records exec stepped forward to present gold records to each Gibb for the chart-topping *Best of the Bee Gees*. Their recent studio albums weren't doing much business, but their best-of was selling just fine, having eclipsed 20,000 sales in Australia, reaching No.6 and remaining on the charts for more than a year.

Barry, as ever, appeared humbled. Robin, however, took exception. 'Excuse me,' he said cheekily, pointing to the gold plaque, 'but mine says The Hollies.'

The tour, which drew full houses in each capital, was a success, a far better money-spinner than their recent disappointing run of dates in America. Their 15-song setlist was a greatest hits package, including 'New York', 'Words', 'I've Gotta Get a Message to You', 'To Love somebody', 'Massachusetts' and 'I Started a Joke', with 'Spicks and Specks' dusted off as the encore. Mid-set, Mo took a solo vocal turn for 'Lay It On Me'.

Their on-stage patter may have been a bit clunky, the brothers seemed stuck fast between the music hall and the cool pop world of the late-'60s, but local audiences lapped it all up. 'They're gorgeous,' raved one fan when a film crew caught up with some admirers. 'They're very polished,' stated another. Female fans squealed throughout their concerts, especially when Barry took centrestage.

'The Bee Gees ... have packed every concert and brought every audience to their feet for a standing ovation!' declared local music rag *Go-Set*. 'In Sydney and Canberra the crowds leapt from their seats and yelled for more. Canberrites have rarely been known to show such overwhelming enthusiasm for a visiting act of any sort. In Sydney the applause was deafening almost ten minutes after the Bee Gees had left the theatre and were on their way to their hotel! In Melbourne an extra concert was arranged to cope with the huge demand for tickets and crowd reaction was spectacular.'

Statesman Barry insisted the band would be back sooner than later. 'We love Australia,' he told the gentlemen of the press. 'It's partly our home and England's partly our home.'

He remained true to his word; the Gibbs would return within a year for another run of Oz dates, this time in larger venues. The UK and America may have been a harder sell for the reunited Bee Gees, but they remained reliable seat-fillers in Australia. Maybe that's where their future lay.

Despite the feverish response in Oz, the Bee Gees were about to bottom out commercially. In 1972 they hit a career lowpoint. 'How Can You Mend a Broken Heart', a US hit in mid-1971, and 'Run to Me', which reached the Top 20 a year later, were their last chart hits in the States until their mid-decade resurrection. While spanning only a few calendar years, their dry spell was a lifetime in the pop world. 'There's nothing worse on earth than being in the pop wilderness,' Barry said in 2014, looking back. The Gibbs may have patched up their fraternal relationship, but somewhere along the way they'd fallen out of step with the marketplace.

So what was big in 1972, and why wasn't it the Bee Gees? The Rolling Stones had surfaced from exile in France with the gutsy, raunchy *Exile on Main Street*. David Bowie found the near-perfect fusion of glam elegance and rocky swagger with *Ziggy Stardust and the Spiders from Mars*. Lou Reed achieved something similar on the other side of the Atlantic with *Transformer*, produced by Bowie and catapulted into the charts on the back of the seductive and quietly sinister 'Walk on the Wild Side'. Folk rocker Neil Young got back to the country with *Harvest*, inspiring a bounty of imitators, starting with soft-rockers America; some fans even mistook their hit 'Horse With No Name' for a new Neil Young song.

Meanwhile the Gibbs were spinning their wheels creatively, still relying on the heavy orchestration and surging melodrama that had brought the magic in the 1960s (and still sometimes did bring shivers, such as with the gorgeous 'Walking Back to Waterloo', a standout of the brothers' under-rated late 1971 *Trafalgar* album). But times were changing; musical fashion was evolving. In comparison with Bowie's elegantly-wasted character Ziggy Stardust and reptilian New Yorker Reed, the Gibbs were wholesome and way out of step, their music and entire approach a throwback to different times. Even peers the Hollies, equally white-bread, had evolved, moving from the chirpy 'Carousel' and 'Carrie Anne' to the edgier 'Long Cool Woman (in a Black Dress)', a song that was more Creedence Clearwater than Merseyside. It was a big hit, too, a US No.2 in mid-1972.

Other breakout artists, such as singer-songwriters James Taylor and Carole King, were turning inwards, poking about in their own lives and feelings, but this was the type of reflection that the Gibbs always seemed wary of. They were more comfortable with lyrical abstraction, not self-examination and exposition. Taylor's 'Fire and Rain', with its themes of madness and loss, was definitely not a Bee Gees kind of song.

Maurice decided it was time to get out of London, relocating to the Isle of Man, where he and the others had grown up during the 1950s, before their move to Redcliffe. Hugh and Barbara now lived on the island with teenager Andy; they ran the local post office. Barry and his family (and Barnaby the dog) also relocated there. Robin remained on the mainland.

Mo's marriage to Lulu was headed for the divorce courts (it was made official in 1973) and he insisted that he had little money left, having blown much of his fortune on cars and the fast life. According to Mo, as 1972 rolled on, all he had to his name was a blue Roller 'and about eight grand in the bank', as hard as that was to believe, given the Bee Gees' success. Mo lived in a small townhouse, next door to the local chippie. 'It was real rough,' he recalled, 'it was bloody cold. Mind you, the fish and chip shop was good.'

The Bee Gees seemed as good as done by the early 1970s. Barry, for one, genuinely thought it was the end of the road, unless they could unearth some new musical direction—and fast. Mo passed the time as Andy's driver, collecting him from school in the Roller, until he was forced to sell the car, his savings now gone. Stigwood's time and energy were consumed elsewhere—Eric Clapton, one of his other star clients, had hit the jackpot with his new group Derek and the Dominoes; their superb *Layla and Other Assorted Love Songs* album was one of the best releases of the early 1970s, a big hit for the Robert Stigwood Organisation. Stiggy was also preoccupied with crack songwriting team Andrew Lloyd Webber and Tim Rice and the film version of the hit musical *Jesus Christ Superstar*—the movie would gross close to $11 million in 1973 and $25 million worldwide, proving that RSO was much more than the home of the Bee Gees. The big screen seemed to be the future. One unknown actor who auditioned for *JC Superstar* was a brooding New Jersey teenager named John Travolta.

'The record company didn't want to know us, our management lost interest,' Mo said of this nadir, astutely not mentioning Stigwood's name, even though he and his company wore both hats. 'All of a sudden we were left alone. We didn't have a career. I was drinking a lot more. If you don't drink and don't party,' he explained, 'there's nothing to do.'

Yet still the brothers kept writing and recording; they were nothing if not persistent, their work ethic beyond reproach. There was also a 30-city American tour with labelmates Tin Tin and an orchestra of college-aged kids, who backed the Gibbs on stage, everyone travelling in a Greyhound bus. But even that was a disaster, as they played to near-empty houses. In Nashville, the Gibbs and the guys from Tin Tin were given a crisp $100 bill to cover their day-to-day expenses. One of the troupe ordered a drink and not knowing one greenback from the other, left a $90-something tip on the bar. That costly stuff-up neatly summed up everything Bee Gees-related in the early 1970s.

Don Pietro was a popular American radio DJ of the era, and he managed to track down the Gibbs in late 1972 while they were holed up in the Record Plant studio in Hollywood working on yet another new album. Despite all the upbeat talk and laughs, the group was in a dire state: no hits, no direction, no clue. The smell of desperation was as thick as the LA smog.

Rising above Mo's Goon Show impressions, with Robin his giggling sidekick, Pietro threw a few softball questions their way. Did the band have 'lots of exciting things in the works for 1973?' he asked.

They did, Barry insisted. There was a world tour, starting in May, covering North and South America, Asia, Europe and Australia. There was also the new record they were recording—or, as it turned out, attempting to record—with the help of drummer Jim Keltner and guitarist Alan Kendall. It had only been months since the release, and subsequent demise, of their most recent album, *Life in a Tin Can*, also recorded in the Record Plant during September 1972, a record that *Rolling Stone* had savaged, and would sell a dismal 175,000 copies worldwide.

'We're cutting our second album in advance,' Barry pointed out, 'because we have a lot of good material, we want to get it down.'

Great, said Pietro, but what was with the album's working title, *A Kick in the Head Is Worth Eight in the Pants*—what the hell did that mean? Was it some kind of cryptic message? Between nervous giggles, Mo admitted that he didn't know the answer and passed the question along to Barry. He didn't have much of a clue, either. 'Would you rather have a kick in the head or a kick in the pants?' was the best response Barry could muster.

Clearly, Pietro had no answer because he moved onto a discussion of film work. Mo mentioned one movie project that had been shelved, although, he said, there might be something happening after the world tour. But as with almost everything Bee Gees-related in the early 1970s, nothing was especially clear, all was vague. And if little came of either project, Mo added with a shrug, 'We'll be back in the Record Plant making *another* album.'

Moving to safer ground, Pietro asked about their old hit 'I Started a Joke' and its meaning. Barry and Mo immediately looked at Robin, as if to say, 'Hey, it's his song, best ask him.' Robin recalled how he was on a Viscount plane and the roar of the engines reminded him of a Strauss composition, 'and the tune came to me'. After a nervous pause, Barry added, 'With a lot of our songs, you need to make your own personal meaning, read into them what you want.'

Barry had crooned how 'I held a party and nobody came,' on 'I Held a Party', from the lukewarm *To Whom It May Concern* LP, which crashed and burned in 1972. Now it seemed that his forlorn lyric was coming true. Just one single was lifted from the *Kick in the Head* sessions: June 1973's 'Wouldn't I Be Someone', and it failed to chart anywhere bar Australia, where it barely scraped into the Top 50. Stigwood was savvy enough to recognise a dead album when he had one on his doorstep, and found time in his busy schedule for a sitdown with the Gibbs. 'It's not worthy of you,' Stigwood said, referring to *A Kick in the Head*. 'It's not commercial enough.'

The brothers reluctantly agreed; Barry later referred to *A Kick in the Head* as 'an awful album'. Stiggy pulled the pin and the record was never released, even though a handful of the finished tracks would see daylight over the next few years. *Life in a Tin Can* was a dud, *To Whom It May Concern* a flop, but *A Kick in the Head* was a disaster. Could the Gibbs sink any lower?

While his siblings were LOST in America, sifting through the ashes of their flagging career, 16-year-old Andy Gibb was taking his own musical baby steps back on the Isle of Man. An easy-on-the-eyes, golden-haired kid, Andy called his first band Melody Fayre, the name borrowed from the Bee Gees song 'Melody Fair'. Clearly, Andy had no issues letting the world know about his family connection; he even let mother Barbara manage his band's affairs. She also helped choose the band's name. Not only did Andy resemble big brother Barry, but he admired him enormously. Barry would joke that his parents had given birth to two sets of twins, only he and Andy were born 12 years apart.

Andy, despite the age difference, thought of himself as a Bee Gees 'understudy', ready and willing to join the troubled group whenever the call came. One night, Barbara noticed that Andy was crying; he told her that he felt lonely, with his brothers away on yet another tour. She suggested that instead of waiting for a call that might never come, Andy should find some local musos, buy some good equipment, and get his own group started, which was how Melody Fayre—whose other members were drummer John Stringer, bassist Jerry Callaghan and guitarist John Alderson—was born. Hugh helped out, too, finding the fledgling band work in local pubs and hotels.

Their early sets included covers of the Bee Gees' 'Down the Road' and 'Every Second, Every Minute'. And Melody Fayre's first demos, which were recorded in a studio on the Isle of Man, included versions of the Gibbs' 'Wouldn't I Be Someone' and 'The Most Beautiful Girl'. The band also covered songs from Neil Diamond and Paul Anka; it seemed they liked the view from the middle of the road.

Just prior to their public debut on 4 June 1974, at a local hospital fundraiser, Barry returned and helped Andy and his group with their setlist, adding 'I've Gotta Get a Message to You', a challenge for any singer, let alone a neophyte like Andy. Still, the crowd of around 400 seemed happy enough, even if the shy Andy lacked much in the way of on-stage swagger. Despite their faults, Melody Fayre was on its way.

A few days later, when the band gathered at the Gibb house for rehearsals, the other members were stunned when they were greeted by Barry Gibb, fully-fledged pop star (though currently in decline), wielding a new-fangled video camera. Maurice also dropped in to check on Andy's progress. This and future nights were spent watching *Cucumber Castle* or Hugh's home movies, which dated all the way back to Redcliffe.

Melody Fayre spent much of that northern summer strumming and singing for guests at the Peveril Hotel on Loch Promenade. Rather than promote the band, the clumsily worded ads for these shows made it abundantly clear who was the main attraction: 'Appearing Nightly,' the flyer read, 'The Youngest Brother of the famous BEE GEES, ANDY GIBB and his music: The Show for the Young at Heart.' Mo and Barry sometimes looked on from the audience as Andy and the band played many of their songs. Sometimes Hugh would sit in on drums, making it every bit the family affair.

By the end of the year, two things were clear: Andy Gibb had a future in music, and that future didn't reside on the Isle of Man. There were only so many times he and the band could fill the Peveril Hotel. Hugh and Barry understood this, and discussed it with Andy. 'Go to Australia,' Barry advised him. 'Try and get a start there like we did.' Sister Lesley still lived in Oz with her family, so he'd have a solid base. There was also talk of getting his music, when it was ready, into the hands of Stigwood, to secure a deal with RSO.

Melody Fayre's flight touched down just a few days before the Bee Gees began their next Australian tour in October 1974. And it was a relief for the Bee Gees to be back in Australia; during their recent tour of the UK they were relegated to playing such venues as the Batley Variety Club to a few hundred disinterested patrons and their dogs.

The Australian orchestra, perched a little precariously above the main stage, would burst into an overture of 'New York Mining Disaster' just as a spotlight hit Barry, leading the band, as always. In Melbourne, at that very moment, the seated and hitherto sedate audience burst into screams—for a second the brothers must have flashed back to the heady days of the late-'60s, when they ruled the pop world. And Barry did look pretty damned good, in snug red pants and a printed shirt, his face framed with a beard, his teeth pearly white, his outfit adorned with just a hint of bling. He was golden, sexy. The twins were more than presentable, too, Robin in high-waisted white flares and a red shirt; Mo's dark ensemble topped off by an ever-so-slightly psychedelic jacket.

They opened most sets with 'In My Own Time', Robin taking the lead. The song had a gently funky undercurrent, but he was no mover, Robin. Rather than dance, he'd shoot an occasional smile in Mo's direction, or cup his ear with his hand, a signature Robin move, losing himself in the song. He was also trying valiantly to hear himself sing above the screams; on good nights it was fierce enough to strip paint from the walls.

Despite the undercurrent of pop hysteria, the Gibbs seemed hell-bent on reminding the home audience that they were family-friendly entertainers: After each song, the brothers would take a theatrical bow. Everything was slick and professional, from the stately venues, to the orchestras, well-rehearsed moves and dramatic use of spotlights. This was grown-up pop; it was almost impossible to imagine that within a few years they'd be at the vanguard of a disco-pop revolution. Occasionally Barry would burst into a smile, but for the most part he was all focus and determination, scrubbing away at an electric guitar. Their harmonies, meanwhile, were as pristine as ever.

Their sets offered up an odd selection of songs, perhaps in keeping with the group's uncertain place in the pop landscape. Older tunes ('I Can't See Nobody' and 'World') were mixed in with oddities ('Alexander's Ragtime Band', played as a goofy three-parter, just like when they started out) and new songs such as 'Down the Road', which was about as groove-heavy as the Gibbs had ever been. During the latter, Barry encouraged the audience to clap along, his arms raised to the heavens.

Little was said between songs, until Mo briefly took centrestage. 'This is my turn to do a solo,' he smiled, breaking into a country song. He was more at home, though, hamming it up on piano during the intro to 'Run to Me'—where Barry took full flight—and when introducing his brothers.

**ABOVE** A 1963 promotional shot of Barry, Maurice and Robin. **RIGHT** Recording 'How on Earth' at Liverpool Cathedral in 1967. **BELOW** The group's first album, *The Bee Gee's Sing and Play 14 Barry Gibb Songs* (1963), and first international release, *Bee Gees' 1st* (1965).

OPPOSITE PAGE A rare shot of the group with sister Lesley out front (replacing Robin) for a 1969 BBC TV recording. ABOVE 1971's *Trafalgar* LP. RIGHT Robin and accordion at his English estate, 1970. BELOW Maurice, Robin and Barry meet the press at Sydney Airport in 1971—their first trip 'home' in several years; in the early 70s, their careers adrift, the Gibbs returned to the Isle of Man, where they had spent some of their childhood.

ABOVE Golden boy Andy Gibb. RIGHT Maurice, Barry and Robin on the set of *Top of the Pops*, where Mo met his first wife, British pop star Lulu. BELOW Andy joins his brothers for the all-conquering 'Spirits Having Flown' tour in 1979.

ABOVE Barry, Robin, Maurice and Andy Gibb at the 1977 Billboard Music Awards. BELOW Maurice in 1979, a time when his drinking threatened to end not only the group but his life. RIGHT the group's multi-million-selling soundtrack to John Badham's *Saturday Night Fever*.

ABOVE 1979's *Spirits Having Flown* album marked the end of the group's superstar era. BELOW the *E.S.P.* LP from 1987; Barry at Shepperton film studios, London, in April 1989, recording a video for *One*, the first Bee Gees album released after Andy's death.

LEFT Maurice, Robin and Barry back together again for the 'One for All' tour, 1989. BELOW The Gibb brothers with father Hugh and mother Barbara, backstage at Wembley Arena, London, June 1989; the 1998 live album *One Night Only*, recorded the previous year at the MGM Grand in Las Vegas.

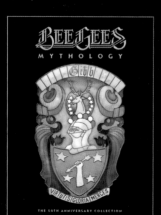

**ABOVE** The four Gibb brothers at home in Miami, Florida, surrounded by friends and family, including manager Robert Stigwood. **LEFT** The career-spanning *Mythology* boxed set, released in 2010. Its four discs are split equally between the four Gibbs.

Mo told the Melbourne crowd that Barry was 'England's answer to Ernie Sigley'. Mo then apologised to local TV star Sigley, in case he was looking on. Robin, naturally, was 'England's answer to [Sigley's sidekick] Denise Drysdale ... my other half.'

Comic spot now over, it all came together during 'To Love Somebody', Barry's vocal tour de force, where the brothers and the orchestra brought the works, kitchen sink included. 'Massachusetts' was the big finale.

These sold-out Australian shows were indeed a long way from Batley in the chilly north of England, but that gritty English industrial centre would have its place in Gibb history. While playing a club there in April 1974, the recently divorced Mo had met a blonde waitress, Yvonne Spenceley. 'I'm gonna marry her,' Mo told a friend. Within months they'd moved in together.

Barry and Linda, meanwhile, now had a son, Stephen, who was born in 1973. He was the first of their five children. Spencer, the first of two children for Robin and Molly, was born in 1972.

While it seemed that the brothers were gradually rebuilding their personal lives, their career remained a mess. Yet by the time of their 1974 Australian tour, they had already connected with the person who would be their saviour.


Arif Mardin was a smooth, sophisticated Turkish-born music man, a close friend and colleague of the equally smooth and sophisticated (and Turkish) Nesuhi Ertegun, who co-founded Atlantic Records with his brother Ahmet. In his multiple roles of producer-arranger-composer, Berklee College of Music graduate Mardin had been the guiding force behind hit records by Aretha Franklin, Bette Midler,

Carly Simon and Diana Ross. (Later he'd work with Hall & Oates, Phil Collins, Culture Club, Jewel and Norah Jones.)

Mardin seemed an unlikely collaborator for the moribund Bee Gees—his specialty was 'blue eyed soul'—but, as Barry Gibb freely admitted, the Bee Gees needed to change style and direction; they had to stop trying to be the Beatles. And Atlantic, where Mardin had worked from 1963, was making some of the most exciting music of the era. In 1973 alone, Atlantic delivered new releases from Bette Midler, Tom Waits, Roberta Flack, Stephen Stills, the Eagles and the Byrds.

On the recommendation of fellow Atlantic producer Jerry Wexler and Ahmet Ertegun, Stigwood had brokered a meeting between the Gibbs and Mardin in late 1973. Mardin, who was on staff at Atlantic, was able to work with the Bee Gees because Atlantic was RSO's American partner. It was agreed that the sessions for the *Mr Natural* album, their first collaboration with Mardin, would take place in the Atlantic Studios in New York and two London studios, between mid-November 1973 and late-January 1974.

During those sessions, Mardin unearthed a new and fresh sound from the Gibbs. The dated acoustic leanings of recent records such as the unfortunate *Kick in the Head* and *Life in a Tin Can* were shelved in favour of something warmer, more R&B-oriented. There were even shades of church during 'Give a Hand, Take a Hand', a song that dated back to the *Cucumber Castle* era (and which was later covered by gospel greats the Staple Singers). A direct line could be drawn from the liquid keyboards and soaring synths of such songs as 'Throw a Penny' to future smash hits 'More Than a Woman' and 'Night Fever'. Most crucially, during 'Dogs'—a song that was more substantial than the title suggested—there were traces of Barry's falsetto, the sound that would soon become the Bee Gees' platinum-plated trademark.

For once, the Gibbs were slightly ahead of the musical curve: the danceable nature of *Mr Natural*'s better tracks emerged in a year that was dominated by big ballads (Barbra Streisand's 'The Way We Were'), hard rock (Grand Funk Railroad's 'Locomotion') and the country pop of John Denver. Disco was for the moment still a gay-club phenomenon.

The flipside of the Bee Gees' evolution was this: with the introduction of more 'outside' musicians in the studio, including electric guitarist Alan Kendall, keyboardist Geoff Westley and drummer Dennis Bryon, there was little for Maurice to do creatively. Barry sang lead on six of the album's eleven tracks; Mo only contributed to the writing of four songs: 'Give a Hand, Take a Hand', 'Voices', 'Can't Let You Go' and the hypnotic closer 'Had a Lot of Love Last Night'.

Perhaps this explained why Mo dismissed *Mr Natural* as a 'total disaster', before quickly adding that it was 'like a rehearsal' for the career resurrection that was just around the corner. Nor, when it was released in mid-1974, were critics overly enamoured with *Mr Natural. Rolling Stone*'s Ken Barnes applied such terms as 'monumental turkey' and 'slushy' to individual songs on the album. Barnes did however concede that the title track was a 'natural hit that wasn't' and that 'Lot of Love' was 'quite pretty'. He was also sufficiently prescient to note that the album had a 'vigour missing from recent records'. Yet most other music publications didn't even bother reviewing the LP.

'Mr Natural' the single did some business—it hit the Australian Top 10, the Bee Gees' first real success since 'Run to Me' two years earlier—but the album barely touched the *Billboard* 200, despite a great guest spot on the high profile *Mike Douglas Show*, where the brothers performed 'Mr Natural' pretty much live, their voices chiming together beautifully. Still, *Mr Natural* was a good, sometimes great record, which established their working relationship with the estimable Mardin, and pointed the way for the Gibbs' musical future.

Soon after the record was completed, Mardin pulled the Gibbs aside. They were despondent at the lukewarm response to the album; three singles had been released and each one flopped. Their confidence dented even further, they were expecting the worse. 'That was a good start,' Mardin said, in his heavily-accented English. 'Let's do another album.'

Barry, Maurice and Robin exchanged hopeful smiles. They hadn't expected this type of ongoing support, especially from such a successful music-maker. The Bee Gees needed a true believer, and they'd found one in Arif Mardin.

Andy Gibb and the guys from Melody Fayre had been part of the Bee Gees' entourage during their 1974 Australian tour. It was quite the heady introduction to life in Australia, viewed through the darkened windows of their personal limo and from the cocoon of five star hotels.

Col Joye and his brother Kevin Jacobsen, who'd played significant roles in the early development of the Bee Gees, also took an interest in the youngest Gibb. Andy and the group had written a few songs of their own, and plans were set in place to record them for Joye's ATA label, which he'd established in the mid-1960s to release his own records. ATA had since become the label of choice for the 'Bandstand family', such peers of Joye as Judy Stone, Little Patti and Sandy Scott, all regulars on Channel 9's hit show—as the Bee Gees had been in the early 1960s. Joye had recently returned to the charts with the smash 'Heaven Is My Woman's Love', while the label had also scored with releases from singer-songwriter Kevin Johnson.

Andy's first recording for ATA was cut in September 1974, a song named 'To a Girl', with Mo adding backing vocals. Despite a cameo on the TV show hosted by the same Ernie Sigley the Bee Gees had joked about on stage, Andy's single was never officially released. Soon after, Andy cut another six tracks for Joye and ATA, including

'Flowing Rivers', which a little further down the line would become the title of his debut LP.

The local media quickly gravitated to Andy—the Gibbs, after all, were Australian music royalty. One newspaper reporter likened him to Neil Diamond and Perry Como, which made it hard to tell exactly whether they approved of his music. Andy became a regular on TV; even without an official release, it seemed as though his pretty face was everywhere.

Barbara, meanwhile, kept Melody Fayre on a tight leash, rejecting their request for a weekly retainer, insisting that paying gigs were in the works. 'Just wait,' she told them. 'Just wait.' Yet apart from hours in the studio working on new music for ATA, the bulk of Andy and the band's early days in Oz were spent lazing at the beach. Stringer and Alderson flipped burgers at a fast-food outlet. By the time Andy returned to the studio in mid-1975, his backing band had returned to the Isle of Man. So Andy teamed up with a crack outfit of session musos, many culled from Sydney jazz-rock combo Crossfire, and, in a very Gibb-like manner, got on with his solo career.

The mid-1970s must have been a strange time for Hugh and Barbara Gibb—while their youngest son was building a career in far-flung Australia, his brothers were slowly rebuilding theirs in Miami, a city that would eventually become a home-away-from-home for the Gibb family. (The brothers each owned houses there by 1976.) Eric Clapton, one of Stiggy's A-list clients, had rebuilt his career in Miami after a lengthy bout with heroin addiction; the resulting record, *461 Ocean Boulevard*, was perhaps the best Clapton had ever released.

The title of Clapton's LP was a nod to the house in which he stayed during the recording sessions, which took place in nearby Criteria Studios. Clapton loved everything about Miami: the house, the studio, the vibes, the warmth. 'You must record there,' he told the Gibbs.

With nothing left to lose, they readily agreed, and settled into Criteria during the early months of 1975. It was a sunny respite from the northern winter; the weather reminded them of their early days in Redcliffe. Producer Arif Mardin was again down for the ride, this time with an even more notable selection of session players, the most prominent being keyboard whiz Blue Weaver, a Brit who'd built his career in the bands Strawbs (where he replaced Rick Wakeman) and Mott the Hoople. Weaver would become a key member of team Bee Gees over the crazy next few years.

Recording sessions for the *Main Course* album began in Criteria on 6 January and continued until 21 February. The new music made during this creative burst would be a revelation for the becalmed Bee Gees—and would also help kickstart a musical revolution.

During the first sessions, the Gibbs recorded three fairly straightforward Bee Gees' tracks: 'Was It All in Vain?', 'Country Lanes' and 'Wind of Change', only the latter hinting at anything especially danceable. Again, they seemed to be treading water, fearful of experimentation. Stiggy felt it was necessary to have another chat with them. 'Are you sure this is how you want to sound?' he asked them. 'Why not try something new, something with rhythm?'

What was new in 1975 was disco, until recently strictly a product of the gay scene and underground dance clubs. Funky, supercharged cuts such as Gloria Gaynor's 'Never Can Say Goodbye' and 'Get Dancin'' from Disco Tex and the Sex-O-Lettes were burning up the American hit parade and dancefloors, muscling aside the guitar bands and sensitive singer-strummers who'd dominated in recent years. Rock was out, dance was in, and here were the Bee Gees in Miami, a hotbed for much of this new music, a city that soaked up Caribbean and Latin influences like a sponge. The city was hot, *the city was funky.*

Miami's very own Henry Stone, who ran TK Records, even boasted about having invented disco with George McCrae's massive 1974 smash, 'Rock Your Baby'. Club promoters in Chicago and New York might have argued Stone's claim, but there was no disputing the fact that McCrae's subtle, sexy hit was a breakthrough for disco and put Miami on the musical map. Locals KC and the Sunshine Band—whose members Harry Wayne 'KC' Casey and Wayne Finch wrote 'Rock Your Baby', when not working in the TK warehouse— were also poised to raid the charts and the airwaves, via songs like 'Get Down Tonight' and 'That's the Way (I Like It)', monster hits in 1975. Both were TK releases, as was Foxy's No.1 soul hit 'Get Off'. Anita Ward's 'Ring My Bell' was released by Juana, another of Stone's labels.

Mega-club 1235 was Miami's answer to New York's Studio 54, the place to be seen—if indeed you *could* see through the club's high-tech lighting, or hear yourself think over its eardrum-bursting sound system. Miami's chic-est hung out there, coke spoons on proud display around their neck, dripping bling, their tans positively glowing. Surely, some of this high-octane energy could rub off on the Gibbs, if only they'd open their minds—and ears—to their new environment.

The turning point came on 30 January, as the brothers drove from 461 Ocean Boulevard to the studio, their car crossing the Julia

Tuttle Causeway that connected Biscayne Bay to Miami. 'Can you hear that?' someone asked. A strange rhythm, a distinctive *ch-ch-ch-ch* sound, the noise of the car's tyres on the causeway surface, fed through the bridge's reinforced steel frame, wafted in the air. A song was co-written in a flash by the three, en route—it was originally called 'Drive Talkin'' but then changed to 'Jive Talkin''. The scratchy guitar rhythm that opens the track was Barry's attempt to re-create the sound their car made as it crossed the causeway.

While recording, Mardin asked them if they knew what the term 'jive talkin'' referred to. The Gibbs had overheard the phrase but weren't quite sure of its meaning.

They thought it was a term for dancing, you know, *jiving*. 'Something like that, right?' they asked.

Mardin laughed. 'No, no,' he said, 'it's a black term for bull-shitting.'

A quick rework of the lyrics captured their exchange; the song now opened with an admission: 'Jive talkin'/so misunderstood.'

'Arif was brilliant, full of ideas,' said Maurice. 'He knew all the feels and the grooves and was so experienced.'

'I think the main lesson we learned from Arif was that the music had to be vibrant,' said Barry.

And vibrant was just the word to describe 'Jive Talkin'', which was swathed in the swirling keyboards of Blue Weaver and built upon an irresistibly-funky undercurrent, anchored by Maurice's bouncy bassline and trailblazing use of an ARP synthesizer, a so-called 'synth bass', which Stevie Wonder also used to great effect in 'Living For the City', 'Superstition' and elsewhere. In a snappy three-and-a-bit minutes, 'Jive Talkin'' perfectly captured the disco movement. It was funky, it was alive, it was sly and sexy—and it was a far cry from 'I

Started a Joke'. The brothers Gibb were now essentially white artists trying their hand at black music. And with the exception of the even-more-unlikely Average White Band, a gang of Scots who'd gone very large in early 1975 with 'Pick Up the Pieces', the fair-skinned Bee Gees pretty much had the market to themselves. The group who wanted to be the new Beatles was poised to become peers of the Jackson 5, Silver Convention and the O'Jays.

Another key song from the *Main Course* sessions was 'Nights on Broadway'. As they worked on the track, Mardin had an idea for a vocal ad-lib for the 'outro' of the song. 'I need someone to scream,' he asked the Gibbs. 'Can one of you do that?'

Barry had improvised a falsetto once or twice beforehand in the studio, and offered to give it a shot, although he feared he would just sound like a Bee Gee screaming out of tune. He stepped into the vocal booth, his hands covering his headphones, his eyes closed, while the instrumental track was cued. During the outro, Barry let loose the kind of high-pitched wail that could shatter crystal. When he returned to the control room, everyone—Mardin, his engineer Karl Richardson, Mo, Robin and all the musicians—were stunned. It was perfect. 'Now,' Mardin asked Barry, 'can you do the same—but this time with lyrics?'

Barry was up for the challenge, and the results, which made the final version of 'Nights on Broadway', presented a whole new approach for Barry and the other Gibbs. They'd truly stepped into the unknown.

'I could sing a whole song in falsetto!' Barry exclaimed. It was a massive turning point for the Bee Gees. From now on, Barry wrote almost exclusively with his falsetto in mind. He quickly tried the same approach on 'Fanny (Be Tender With My Love)', a gorgeous song about the housekeeper at 461 Ocean Boulevard. It worked brilliantly.

Funnily enough, in between these tracks they recorded 'Come On Over', later a hit for Olivia Newton-John, but right now a square peg of a song, lacking the juice of 'Nights on Broadway' and 'Jive Talkin''. It sat oddly out of place on the finished album, especially considering that *Main Course* opened with the funky triple threat of 'Nights on Broadway', 'Jive 'Talkin'' and 'Wind of Change', songs that defined the new approach of the group.

So Barry had stumbled upon something sensational in the studio, but where did that leave perennial middleman and peacemaker Mo? Just like his brothers, his confidence had taken a fair beating over the past couple of years. If anyone needed a boost it was Maurice, who tended to drown his sorrows in buckets of booze. Enter, once again, band saviour Arif Mardin. While recording 'Wind of Change', Mo made a cursory run through his bass part; to him it felt like the definitive take one, which he could improve upon. Mardin thought otherwise. 'That stays,' he told Mo, who looked a little shocked.

'You don't want to change this?' Maurice asked. 'Are you sure?'

Mardin shook his head. It stayed. This was just the affirmation Mo needed. Confidence restored, he grinned all the way back to 461 Ocean Boulevard and played beautifully through the *Main Course* sessions.

RSO delivered 'Jive Talkin'' to radio stations at the end of May in a plain white cover, with no credits—just like 1974's *Mr Natural* album, which had featured the image of a lonely barfly on the album cover and not a Gibb in sight. It was only when a DJ placed the record on a turntable that they learned 'Jive Talkin'' was a Bee Gees song—the one place their name appeared was on the inner sleeve.

This time it proved to be a smart marketing move on the part of RSO: radio's response was purely about the song, not the fact it was the work of the trio who once warbled 'I Started a Joke'. And given that the Bee Gees' market value was still pretty low in 1975, not having cracked the US Top 10 since 'Broken Heart' four years back, it felt like a fresh start for the band. No preconceptions, no baggage, just this remarkably fresh and dynamic song.

Mo summed it up perfectly when he talked about the reaction to the record. 'Everyone went, "Who, the Bee Gees? *The Broken Heart Bee Gees?*" Are you kidding? The same group? Whoa!'

The commercial response was euphoric, as 'Jive Talkin'' swiftly began to scale the business end of the US charts. By July 1975 it was a gold record—Van McCoy's disco smash 'The Hustle' was No.1—and come 9 August 'Jive Talkin'' hit the top of the *Cashbox* Top 100, a feat it would repeat on the *Billboard* and *Record World* charts. It also peaked at No.5 in the UK.

It was an amazing year all-round for disco; when 'Jive Talkin'' reached No.1, 'The Hustle' was still clinging to the Top 10, while such breakout hits as KC's 'Get Down Tonight' and Earth, Wind & Fire's 'That's the Way of the World' were also charting highly. LaBelle and the Ohio Players had already scored No.1 mainstream hits, while even David Bowie brought a little Studio 54 bump and grind to his latest hit, 'Fame'. And if Bowie, the Thin White Duke himself, was doing disco, surely it was part of the zeitgeist. No less than five dance songs featured in the top 10 of *Cashbox*'s year-end Top 100 singles for 1975. America was getting loose, getting laid, dancing up a storm. Discos were opening on what seemed like every other street corner. Designers were also taking note, as heels grew higher, collars wider and flares billowed like the sails of a ship. And that was just the men's fashion.

Upon release in August 1975, the *Main Course* album was received just as enthusiastically as its lead single. What the Gibbs and Mardin had touched on during *Mr Natural*, they now embraced in one huge satin-shirted bear hug—or at least for the most part, it should be noted. There was still the odd clunker, such as the mawkish 'Country Lanes' or the twangy 'Come On Over', which just went to show that the Gibbs could be their own worst editors. Those songs didn't belong on *Main Course*, which was also the first Bee Gees record to feature the distinctive band logo, designed by US artist Drew Struzan. Missteps aside, the bulk of the album was exuberant and highly danceable, yet not disposable. All three brothers sang like birds, their high, sweet voices perfect for this new direction. Mardin and his crew had brought off the most amazing musical makeover.

'*Main Course* marked a huge change in the Bee Gees' sound,' noted one reviewer. 'The writing was simpler ... it was made up of catchy dance tunes in which the beat and the texture of the voices took precedence over the words.'

Even arch Gibbs critic Robert Christgau conceded that they'd made a heck of a comeback record; he bestowed a B+ rating on *Main Course*. 'At first I was put off by the commercial desperation that induced these chronic fatuosos to turn out their brightest album in many years,' sniffed the *Village Voice* scribe. 'But commercial success validated it: "Nights on Broadway" and "Jive Talkin'" turned out to be the kind of fluff that sticks.'

The shift of Barry Gibb's falsetto to front and centre was also regarded as a smart tactical move on the part of the band and Mardin, although the producer with the Midas touch downplayed his part in this. 'Basically, I just said, "Can you take it up an octave, please?" ' Mardin modestly told *Billboard* magazine.

In his review of the album, *Rolling Stone*'s Stephen Holden felt that the group had succeeded in rebranding their sound. 'My guess,' Holden said, 'is that it should succeed.'

He was right, of course. What was probably the most commercial and trailblazing album of the Bee Gees' lengthy career reached a chart high of No.14, selling more than 500,000 copies in America alone, and producing genuine hits in 'Jive Talkin' ', 'Fanny' and 'Nights on Broadway', another US Top 10 in September 1975.

But the Bee Gees' remarkable rebirth had only just begun.

Stuck in West Ryde in suburban Sydney, living with Barbara, Andy must have felt mixed emotions as his brothers underwent their commercial resurrection. While he was undoubtedly proud, where did this leave him? And why was he still in Australia—hadn't he served his apprenticeship? What about America and Stigwood?

Post Melody Fayre, Andy had connected with a new band named Zenta, and continued playing the Sydney circuit of shopping centres and clubs—hardly the high life. Things looked on the improve when they opened for international acts the Bay City Rollers and Sweet in 1975, but little came of these high-profile supports.

Andy's recording career, such as it was, consisted of one single issued from the sessions with the guys from Crossfire. 'Words and Music' was released by ATA in August 1975 and hit a chart 'high' of 78 in the Oz charts soon after. The album, which was scheduled for release sometime in 1976, never appeared. Andy did, however, score a spot on ABC TV's high-rating weekly pop show, *Countdown*. Irrepressible host Ian 'Molly' Meldrum introduced Andy with a story about first meeting him in the company of his brothers in the UK a few years earlier, when Andy was just a kid. 'Now he's 17, he's good-looking and he's a very good songwriter, like his brothers,' Meldrum declared, while a gaggle of teenaged girls anxiously awaited the appearance of the youngest Gibb. 'He's written a song called "Words and Music" and I think it's going to be a monster hit.'

Andy stepped out to croon the soggy ballad, looking just about perfect in a silvery jacket and maroon shirt, open to the waist, every inch Barry Gibb Jr. The *Countdown* teenybopper audience swooned at his high notes. But 'Words and Music' wasn't the song to launch his career. If his brothers had recorded it, they would have been accused of retreating into the past: it was maudlin, and stuck in the middle of the road. Andy, too, needed to juice up his music, loosen up, get down.

And again very much in the family tradition, Andy found security in a female partner, a suburban Aussie girl named Kim Reeder. Kim's father was a bricklayer, her mother worked in a factory. Andy quickly became a surrogate member of the Reeder family; their solid working-class roots were in stark contrast to the gypsy life of the Gibbs. Within months of meeting her, he'd proposed marriage.

Just a few weeks before their planned wedding, Andy received a call from Barry, who was in Alaska, of all places. Barry had big news: if Andy was ready to come to America, he and RSO might just be able to help him out. Barry had been in Stiggy's ear about his younger brother, and had played him some of Andy's demo recordings. Andy represented something that Stiggy understood better than most: a pop star in the making. 'Here's the deal,' Barry told his younger brother. 'I want to produce your records and Robert [Stigwood] wants to manage you. Plus he wants to sign you up for his label.'

As career perfect storms went, Andy couldn't have asked for anything more: he'd just nabbed a high-profile record producer, manager and label in one hit. Andy immediately agreed to the proposal, though in the back of his mind he also knew that he was buying into a complicated situation—was it his own talent being recognised, or was he hitching a ride on his brothers' shiny coat-tails? Would he be regarded as something other than a Gibb clone? And something concerned Barry, too; he felt Andy was too young to marry. He'd made that mistake himself, as had Mo. But on that Andy held firm; after all, he'd already given Kim the money for her wedding dress, drawn from his Christmas club account.

On 11 July 1976, less than a year after they first met, Andy and Kim were married at Sydney's Wayside Chapel. Andy was 18. The newlyweds honeymooned at Stigwood's salubrious digs in the Bahamas. In between doing the things newlyweds do, Andy sat down and signed his recording and management contract with Stigwood and RSO. As for Andy's Sydney band Zenta, they only learned of Andy's departure when a call came in on the afternoon of their next gig, telling them that Andy was gone. *He'd left the country.* Andy was as driven to succeed as his siblings.

While the unstoppable rise of disco had done wonders for the Bee Gees' rebirth, Andy also had timing on his side. When he shifted base to the USA in the northern summer of '76, teen idols were back in favour. Pin-ups David Cassidy (both with and without the Partridge Family), Bobby Sherman, expat Aussie Rick Springfield and squeaky-clean Mormon Donny Osmond had weakened the knees of young girls via such songs as Osmond's 'Puppy Love' and Springfield's wholesome 'Speak To the Sky'. Their sugary-sweep pop confections were tailor-made for kids too young for the after-hours freakiness of disco.

On the surface, Andy Gibb blended in perfectly; he appeared to be straight off the teen-idol production line, with his glowing good looks, heartbreaking smile and soaring voice. Now all he needed was the right song to launch his career.

His brothers, meanwhile, got some bad news around Christmas 1975. Until now, RSO had done all its business in America with Atlantic, hence the magical relationship with Arif Mardin. But business came first and Stigwood decided on a shift to Polygram in America, which already handled RSO products for much of the world outside America. This spelled the end of the Bee Gees' time with Mardin, the man who'd breathed life back into their corpse. And their next record was crucial: they needed to find a way to capitalise on the success of *Main Course* and their shift in musical direction. This was something they'd hoped to do with Mardin.

Mardin continued to believe in the group. 'You can do it alone,' he assured them in early 1976, when they got together. 'You'll be fine.'

It was eventually agreed that Barry would man the producer's chair, alongside Mardin stalwart engineer Karl Richardson, and 'musical adviser' Albhy Galuten, who'd been involved with the *Main Course* sessions. Richardson and Galuten passed as Criteria's 'house hippies', with their long, lank hair and beards, but they felt groove deep down in their bones.

Initially, however, the Gibbs did try working with an outside producer, the very successful Richard Perry, in LA. Perry's CV included Carly Simon, Barbra Streisand and Art Garfunkel; the *Village Voice* declared that in the 1970s, 'the rungs on the ladder of success seem so much closer when Perry [was] your guide'. Despite this, the Gibbs opted to go it alone after a few days' trial with Perry, when he rejected their song 'You Should Be Dancing'. With Barry now in charge, the sessions continued until the middle of the year.

It was a smart move: the first two songs the Bee Gees recorded post-Perry would soon become breakout hits—'You Should Be Dancing' and 'Love So Right', both featuring Barry's skyscraping falsetto. The Bee Gees, flush with confidence, unleashed two disco powerhouses in quick succession. The Gibbs couldn't understand why Perry rejected 'You Should Be Dancing' and for good reason. It was a hit.

Just as remarkably, the next three songs they laid down—'Subway', 'You Stepped Into My Life' and 'Love Me'—ended up as either B-sides of their own singles or, in the case of 'Love Me', a smash hit for another RSO artist and *Jesus Christ Superstar* alumni, Yvonne Elliman. Not a bad way to begin a new album, all things considered. Clearly, there was no space for filler on the record that would be called *Children of the World*. Of the 10 tracks that made the final album, Barry sang lead on seven, and shared vocals with Robin on the rest; Mo joined in during 'Lovers'. There was no doubt now as to who was the leader of the band.

Maurice, meanwhile, struggled to keep a lid on his boozing. During a brief return to the Isle of Man, where his parents still resided, his blue Roller parked outside the local pub was a familiar site. When he volunteered as a marshall at a race day on the island, his dedicated section of the track was the scene of major chaos. Another time he was arrested while driving on the footpath, decked out in an American cop's uniform—Mo had become an avid collector of police regalia during the 1970s. He was fined £80 and suspended from driving for two years. It was a relief for everyone, especially Yvonne, you must imagine, to get him back to Miami for the album launch.

*Main Course* may have raised a few eyebrows on release and taken some time to connect with the group's new audience, but there was no such problem with *Children of the World*, which hit stores like a hurricane in September 1976. By this time 'You Should Be Dancing' was already No.1 in America—across the pop, dance, disco *and* R&B charts—and was charting highly throughout Europe and Australia. (There was a whisper that Stiggy wouldn't release the album until 'You Should Be Dancing' reached No.1; his wait was short.)

Dance music, thanks to the likes of Wild 'Play That Funky Music' Cherry, KC and the Sunshine Band, and Earth, Wind & Fire, was now so ubiquitous that it had inspired its first send-up, Rick Dees and His Cast of Idiots' 'Disco Duck', a huge hit around the time of the new album's release. Nothing says zeitgeist more than a parody. The Bee Gees would cop their own, too, when Brits the Hee Bee Gee Bees—stagenames Garry, Norris and Dobbin Cribb— warbled 'Meaningless Songs in Very High Voices'. Everything, from their heliumated vocals to their starch-laden scarves and windswept manes, was right on the money.

*Rolling Stone* now had no problems singing the brothers' praises (also, ideally, in very high voices). ' "You Should Be Dancing",' noted Joe McEwen, 'rocks KC's "Shake Your Booty" right off the turntable (or dance floor) in head-to-head competition. It's an impossibly propulsive track, whose only rival in the genre is KC's "Get Down Tonight".'

In blessing the record with a not-always-easy-to-achieve B rating, Robert Christgau seemed keen to damn *Children of the World* with faint praise: 'Their closed-system commitment to a robot aura renders embarrassing questions about whether they mean what they're singing irrelevant, which is good,' he wrote a tad unclearly. 'Too often, though, their pleasure in artifice doesn't wholly irradiate the rather patchy material. Best hook: Blue Weaver's organ part on "Subway".'

Others, such as Bruce Elder, writing for the *AllMusic Guide*, had no such issues. 'The result still sounds a lot like Mardin's production from the previous album,' he noted, 'and the group [is] in very good form—stretching out not only on disco numbers ... but also delivering beautiful soul ballads such as "You Stepped Into My Life" and "Love So Right" ... The album is also somewhat experimental in its way, making more use of synthesizers in a pop music setting than had ever been heard on a mainstream, commercial long-player before.'

The Bee Gees seemingly couldn't miss; when 'Dancing' finally started to slip out of the charts in November 1976, 'Love So Right' passed it heading in the opposite direction, all the way to No.3. 'Love' even fared well on the Black Singles chart (these being pre-PC times), reaching No.27, not a bad achievement for a pale-faced trio from the wrong side of the world. The *Children of the World* album was also a hit, hitting a chart high of No. 8 and selling more than a million copies in America alone.

By the end of the 1976, there was no doubt about it: the Bee Gees were back on top. Mo summed it up neatly when he spoke with an interviewer. 'We were so knocked out that we had an audience again.'

As if rebuilding his own group's career wasn't enough, Barry, during 1976, also set to work with brother Andy on his debut LP. In true Gibb style, Barry pulled in those currently close to him—including Albhy Galuten and Karl Richardson—to work on what would be the *Flowing Rivers* album. Barry, his songwriting mojo once again functional, co-wrote the record's two key songs, 'I Just Want to Be Your Everything' and '(Love Is) Thicker Than Water'.

Not everything about this slick, mainstream pop record went by the book. The Eagles were next door to Andy and Barry in Criteria during October 1976, recording *Hotel California*, their bittersweet valentine to LA's fast life. Eagles' guitarist Joe Walsh, a man alleged to carry chainsaws in his luggage just in case a hotel room needed redecorating, stepped in to play guitar on 'Everything' and 'Thicker Than Water', both destined to be hit singles. The Gibbs had friends in the oddest places.

Freddie Mercury, the shamelessly camp frontman of English group Queen, who were riding high via their epic glam ballad, 'Bohemian Rhapsody', also played a curious role in Andy's rise. It must have made for an interesting scene when they met briefly in Munich, Germany. Andy spoke with Mercury, complaining that he, quite literally, had trouble finding his own voice. Mercury's advice, to simply sing like his brothers, made perfect sense. 'Just get out there,' he told Andy, insisting that he reach for the highest possible notes. 'It's your family's trademark.'

It all came together for Andy when he returned to Criteria; he wrote every song on the album apart from Barry's two singles. Galuten also helped write a couple of tracks, 'Dance To the Light of the Morning' and 'Too Many Looks in Your Eyes'. And life changed dramatically for Andy when 'I Just Want to Be Your Everything' was released in mid-1977. Virtually overnight, on the strength of his visual appeal and this one smartly constructed pop song—and the immense market value of the Gibb name—Andy stepped out from the shadow of his brothers and became a solo star. Yet he never denied the role that Barry, in particular, played in his climb to the top. When asked about his sudden success—by July 1977, 'Everything' was No. 3 in the US, pipped only by Barry Manilow and fellow teen idol Shaun Cassidy— Andy willingly paid his dues. 'I believe I owe it chiefly to my brother Barry, who produces my records. He's always steered my career.'

This would be both a blessing and a curse for Andy, who, in his more insecure moments, couldn't be sure if it was his talent, or his brothers' reputation, that helped his rapid rise, despite his skills as a singer, guitarist and composer. 'I don't intend to lean on them my whole life,' Andy stated, as 'Everything' clung to the top of the charts.

Andy hit what Barry later called his 'first fame' in August, when the song reached No.1. It stayed in the charts for a heady six months— only to be replaced by his brothers' barnstorming 'How Deep Is Your Love'. The Gibbs, and RSO, were on the crest of a remarkable run.

Yet Andy's personal life was a mess. He gravitated to LA, where he developed a taste for the high life, partying, snorting, bingeing. Then Kim told Andy that she was pregnant with their first child;

she also told him that he needed to straighten up. When he failed to take her strongly worded hint, she moved back to Australia to have the baby—daughter Peta was born on 25 January 1978—while Andy stayed behind in America. Their relationship was fast coming undone. Soon enough, Andy was linked to Olympic figure skater Tai Bailonia (who would describe him as 'such a sweet person; almost too sweet for the world he was in'), while actress Susan George was another confidante. American singer and actress Marie Osmond would become a close friend.

Despite his off-stage drama, Andy rang in the new year with a bang when '(Love is) Thicker Than Water' became his second No.1 in February. Andy's Munich advisor Freddie Mercury was nipping at his heels with Queen's latest hit, the anthemic 'We Are the Champions'. When Andy stepped out to promote the song on such programs as the *Wolfman Jack Show* it was hard to drag your eyes away from him; he looked almost flawless, angelic, a mirror image of his big brother. Like it or not, Andy was the Barry Gibb clone that, in his darkest hours, he'd feared becoming.

When he arrived to play a concert at a venue in Dallas, Texas, with mother Barbara by his side, Andy was appalled by the site that greeted him. The marquee read: 'Andy Gibb—Younger Brother of the Bee Gees.' 'Have that thing taken down!' he roared at an assistant.

But it was all part of life as a junior Gibb. Andy quickly became a regular face on American chat shows and tonight shows, but the line of questions invariably turned to his elder siblings: 'What's it like having such famous brothers?' 'How hard is it to be a solo Gibb?' 'Is there any sibling rivalry?'

Andy may have been the fastest-rising star in America, but he was still a Gibb brother, for better or worse.

In its 7 June 1976 edition, *New York* magazine published a brilliantly-evocative investigative piece, 'Tribal Rites of the New Saturday Night', written by Nik Cohn, an expat Englishman adrift in America. At the story's centre was 18-year-old Vincent, 'the best dancer in Bay Ridge', an Italian-American-Catholic kid from Brooklyn who only really came to life when he pulled on one of his dozen or more floral shirts, tucked into his distressingly-tight flares and hit the dance floor of a local club named 2001 Odyssey. Nothing mattered to Vincent more.

In a journalistic flourish, Cohn had captured the essence of disco mid-'70s style, with suburban dreamer Vincent his mouthpiece. This wasn't the upscale highlife of Miami's 1235, or Manhattan's Studio 54, where Andy Warhol gossiped with Bianca Jagger and Truman Capote, while sexual debauchery took place in the downstairs dungeon and Bolivia's finest was inhaled by the spoon-load. For Brooklyn kids like Vincent, 2001 Odyssey was the ultimate escape, more like a clubhouse, somewhere to hang out on Saturday, be the centre of attention, dance the Hustle, the Bus Stop or the Odyssey Walk and live the type of life that was unattainable for the rest of the week. 'Once inside,' Cohn wrote, '[they] were unreachable. Nothing could molest them. They were no longer the oppressed, wretched teen menials who must take orders, toe the line. Here they took command, they reigned.'

In an interesting twist, Cohn was a confidante of Pete Townshend of the Who, a band that worked closely with Robert Stigwood. Even more interestingly, Cohn would later denounce his 'Tribal Rites' story, saying that much of it was based on a mod he knew back in England. Authenticity be damned, however; the article became the basis of the plot and characters of a film tentatively named *Saturday Night*, to be produced by Stigwood, who had quickly snapped up the rights to Cohn's story. The success of *Jesus Christ Superstar* had given Stiggy a taste for the big screen. His mind flashed back to the kid who'd auditioned for *JC Superstar*, John somebody. He might just be right for the *Saturday Night* male lead.

Stigwood, director John Badham and screenwriter Norman Wexler set to work on the film, casting Travolta in the lead role, renamed Tony Manero. Travolta was by now well-known for his ongoing role as Vinnie Barbarino in TV's *Welcome Back, Kotter*. TV actress Karen Lynn Gorney was cast as Stephanie Mangano, Tony's dance floor partner. Broadway actress Donna Pescow signed on as Annette, Tony's ex. Initially considered 'too pretty' for the role, Pescow chowed down and added 40 pounds (18 kilograms) to her slim frame, and rediscovered her Brooklyn accent. Travolta's mother and sister were given minor roles in the film. Rusty-voiced Fran Drescher, later of *The Nanny* fame, had a small part.

The movie had a low budget, just $3.5 million, modest even by mid-1970s standards. Director Badham took advantage of local Brooklyn sites, filming in the Bay Ridge, Sunset Park and Bensonhurst neighbourhoods. He also shot at the local White Castle burger joint and Phillips Dance Studio. Tony Manero pulled shifts at Six Brothers Hardware and Paints on Brooklyn's Fifth Avenue and hung out with his crew at Lenny's Pizza on 86th Street. It was as authentically Brooklyn as the Verrazano-Narrows Bridge, which also played its part in the film.

The film was deep in production when Stiggy put in a call to his star clients, who were holed up in a chilly French recording studio. He had a proposition for the lads.


In the wake of the success of *Children of the World*, the Gibbs had hit the road, squeezing every drop out of their golden run of hits. They'd also been toasted very publicly by their Svengali Stigwood: while on tour in New York he had them open RSO's new 'international headquarters' on 57th Street, as much a boutique, à la the Beatles' Apple, as a place of business. It was a big occasion, as was the garden party Stiggy hosted for the brothers in New York, which set him back a cheeky $15,000. James Taylor, Carly Simon and Andy Warhol were all prominent faces in the crowd. Clearly, the Bee Gees were once again Stiggy's star clients.

The group recorded many of their 1976 shows and decided to package a live album, a first for the brothers. It was to be called *Here at Last ... Bee Gees Live*, and was taken mainly from a pre-Christmas 1976 show at the Forum in LA, the final date of the tour. While mixing the record and working out some new tunes in French studio Le Chateau, where Elton John had recorded his *Honky Chateau* album, Stiggy dropped in to give them an update on his disco movie. At first, the idea of some guy who worked in a paint store and danced by night didn't impress the Gibbs.

'Nice one, Rob,' Mo said to Stigwood, perhaps still smarting from the *Cucumber Castle* debacle. 'Good luck with that.'

Yet Stigwood persevered, telling them the film truly had hit potential. 'Boys,' Stigwood asked, sounding more and more like Alfred Hitchcock as he moved into his comfortable middle age, 'Do you have any new songs?'

'Funnily enough,' Barry told him, 'we do.'

*Saturday Night* was about to be transformed from a gritty B-grade melodrama to a bona-fide pop culture sensation.

Stiggy couldn't have dreamed of a better selection of new songs. 'Stayin' Alive', 'More Than a Woman' and 'How Deep Is Your Love', each a potential hit, were among the songs the brothers were piecing together. It was a magic time for the Gibbs, who were now assuming full control over their commercial direction, with Barry very much at the helm. If disco was hot—and pretty soon it would get even hotter—then they'd write smash hit disco songs until the world told them to stop.

Duly impressed by the songs he had heard, Stiggy thought he'd press his luck. 'Do you have anything that might work as a title track?'

'What about something called "Night Fever"?' Barry suggested. 'That sounds like a good title.'

'Oh no, that'll never do,' Stiggy replied. 'It sounds too pornographic.'

Regardless, the film once known as *Saturday Night* soon had a new title: *Saturday Night Fever*. It also had a solid-gold soundtrack-in-waiting.

What's most intriguing about the Gibbs' contribution to the movie is that they didn't read the script, nor did they really know the storyline apart from Stiggy's brief rundown. 'Saturday night fever' could have been the name of a third world disease, for all they knew. They were simply writing catchy, commercial disco/pop tunes—and Stiggy had a home for them. They had no idea how their songs would be used on the soundtrack. In fact, while the movie was being shot, because the Bee Gees' songs were not ready, John Travolta was gyrating to Boz Scaggs' 'Lowdown' and the music of Stevie Wonder.

The Gibbs only saw the finished film when it was screened in a cinema—and then they thought the music was too soft; they could hear the slap of the dancers' feet on the dance floor. Stiggy agreed and the music's volume was increased. The Bee Gees were effectively songwriters for hire, working in post-production. Yet the tracks they delivered for the movie—the lush ballad 'How Deep Is Your Love', the pulsating 'Night Fever' (originally called 'Saturday Night'), the romantic 'More Than a Woman'—became integral components of the storyline and the massively-successful soundtrack. (There were eight Bee Gees tracks on the film soundtrack, with Tavares covering 'More Than a Woman' and Yvonne Elliman cutting the Gibbs' 'If I Can't Have You'.)

The placement of the Bee Gees' songs set in train a device that would drive such future films as *Grease* and *Flashdance*: pop music as narrative. Why bother with dialogue when a hit song could cut straight to the emotional heart of a scene? The trio almost did Hollywood scriptwriters out of a job. *Rolling Stone* agreed. 'The Bee Gees' "Stayin' Alive",' the magazine noted, 'not only provides the disco pulse of this blockbuster ... it also communicates the spirit of the film: corny, but somehow deeply resonant.'

It was the Bee Gees' film as much as it was John Travolta's. *Fever* opened with the rhythmic throb of 'Stayin' Alive', and the song set

Tony Manero and his story in motion. Paint can in hand—which seemingly swung like a pendulum to the pulse of the Bee Gees on the soundtrack—Manero hit the Brooklyn streets over the credits, still dressed in his Saturday night finery of flares, satin shirt, boots and a sharp, tailored jacket. He ogled girls, swung by Lenny's Pizza for a slice and generally strutted his stuff, all the while with 'Stayin' Alive' pumping out of the speakers. Travolta was constantly in motion, his hips seemingly in a world of their own.

The scene then shifted to Tony stripped to his jocks, Narcissus personified, gazing in the mirror, psyching himself up for a big night out, scanning his wardrobe for that perfect outfit. We then flashed to the dance floor of Odyssey, this time with 'You Should Be Dancing' blaring, Manero busting moves all over the place—so much so that the other dancers stepped aside to let him do his thing. It was a brilliant five-and-a-bit-minute opener, the perfect juxtaposition of sound and vision.

The positioning of the soft and silky 'How Deep Is Your Love' was just as effective in what was, frankly, a fairly routine script. 'How Deep' provided the note-perfect backdrop to a heavy-hearted scene involving Manero, half-asleep on the subway, his face bloody and battered, dealing with the dark side of Saturday night. Elsewhere, when Tony and his Odyssey crew broke into formation to the strains of 'Night Fever', intercut with images of the man in his bedroom getting his coiffure just right—'watch the hair; you know, I work on my hair a long time,' he told his family over dinner—Travolta seemed, as one critic noted, 'Like a peacock on amphetamines; he struts like crazy.' Yet without the Gibbs' music, these scenes wouldn't have had anywhere near the impact.

By the time of the soundtrack's release on 15 November, 1977, a brace of Bee Gees singles were well on their way to the top of the American charts: 'How Deep Is Your Love' (No.1 in December), 'Stayin' Alive' in February '78 (with Andy's '(Love is) Thicker Than Water' at No.2) and 'Night Fever' in March. Yvonne Elliman's cover of 'If I Can't Have You' reached the top of the charts in May 1978; Andy's 'Shadow Dancing' was another No.1 for composer Barry in June. It was a dream run that even exceeded the Beatles' tsunami of hits in the 1960s.

Things just got plain silly in March 1978 when America's top four singles—'Night Fever', 'Stayin' Alive', Andy's 'Thicker Than Water' and 'Emotion', covered by Aussie Samantha Song—were all written and/or performed by the Gibbs. That was something even the Beatles hadn't managed: complete chart domination. That week, the brothers hit the Big Apple, and were greeted by a Times Square billboard that screamed: 'BEE GEES HAVE THE #1 SINGLE AND #1 ALBUM IN BILLBOARD, CASHBOX AND RECORD WORLD. CONGRATULATIONS! 5 HITS IN THE TOP 10!'

'It was like being in the eye of a storm,' observed Barry, who in between all the madness was busy writing a song named 'Grease' for Stiggy's next big-screen smash, to be sung by Frankie Valli of the Four Seasons. Once the *Fever* hit, said Mo, 'the world just went crazy'.

Back in Miami, the Gibbs were named honorary citizens of Florida. They refused to answer the phone, which just kept ringing. People—fans, crazies, the lot—tried to scale the fence that surrounded their Miami compound, hoping for a glimpse of the biggest stars in the business. Cars cruised slowly past, blaring 'Stayin' Alive' at 120 decibels. The always insular brothers grew a little bit closer, more shut off from the outside world; it was the only way they knew how to deal with the craziness that *Fever* had set in motion.

'We couldn't breathe,' recalled Barry.

When cornered by a writer, Robin admitted that they'd become spokesmen for Generation Disco. Their new music captured 'the imagination of millions of people. It goes beyond being a hit album,' figured Barry, his Florida tan now a glowing brown 'We're the group that disco was built around.'

Five Bee Gees *Saturday Night Fever* songs were lifted as singles in Australia, which gave them a stranglehold on the local charts for the best part of a year, and their virtual chart monopoly was replicated across the globe. 'How Deep Is Your Love' clung to the Australian charts for 31 weeks; 'Stayin' Alive' charted for six months straight; 'Too Much Heaven', a 1978 single that would be included on the Bee Gees' *Spirits Having Flown* album, hogged the Top 40 for 22 weeks.

In a *Billboard* retrospective of the decade, the Gibbs had five songs—'Stayin' Alive', 'Night Fever', 'How Deep is Your Love' plus Andy's 'Shadow Dancing' and 'I Just Want to Be Your Everything'— in the Top 10 of the Top 100 Songs of the Seventies. And to think that in the first few years of the decade they couldn't get a gig, let alone a hit record.

Robin Gibb tried to sum up the *Fever* era for a reporter. 'The record business was pretty angry,' he laughed, 'because they couldn't get [other] records on the playlist.' Robin was right: by and large, when the mainstream's focus wasn't on the Bee Gees, or others covering their songs, it shifted to the younger member of the family, as Andy Gibb badges, T-shirts, bubble gum, even jigsaw puzzles, flooded the teen market.

'We weren't on the charts,' Mo added, 'we *were* the charts.'

Naturally, as the hit singles piled up, sales of the *Saturday Night Fever* double album soundtrack skyrocketed. The album also included tracks from Tavares, Kool and the Gang, and KC and the Sunshine Band, all big disco-era names. When the movie hit cinemas just before Christmas 1977, the soundtrack album was already selling between 175,000 and 200,000 copies a *day*; almost a million albums had been sold even before the film opened, purely on the strength of the Bee Gees' songs. The album was No.1 in America, Australia, Canada, Holland, France, Japan, Norway, Sweden, the UK and Italy, and would remain the highest-selling album for the year in all these countries.

*Saturday Night Fever* would eventually shift more than 40 million copies worldwide, become the highest-selling soundtrack ever and is in the top ten bestselling albums of all time. It resided at the top of the *Billboard* album chart for 24 weeks, and stayed in the charts for more than two years. It topped the UK charts for 18 weeks. The Gibbs scooped the Grammy pool; their wins included Album and Producer of the Year—due recognition for Galuten and Richardson, as well as Barry—and Best Pop Vocal for 'How Deep Is Your Love'. The album remained so popular it won the Bee Gees Grammys in 1978 *and* 1979. ('They ain't heavy,' Andy mugged as he stood at the Grammy podium alongside Donna Summer, 'they're my brothers.')

At its peak in late 1977 and early 1978, the *Saturday Night Fever* soundtrack tripled the sales of its nearest rival, Billy Joel's *The Stranger*. It was the ultimate crossover success, straddling formats from R&B to pop; both 'black' and 'white' radio stations flogged it mercilessly. And all this from an act who insisted that dance music 'didn't enter their minds' as they were writing and recording these songs.

As cheesy as disco now looks in pop culture's rearview mirror, *Saturday Night Fever* was a platinum-plated phenomenon, powered by the brothers' music. The Bee Gees stuttered 'you shhhhhould be dancing' and it seemed that the western world took them up on the suggestion. Wherever you looked, flares billowed and body shirts were worn open to the waist, revealing more gold than Fort Knox. Cleavage and heels ruled, hair was primped and permed. Discos popped up on every street corner, from New York to Newcastle, London to Lisbon.

The album and film, of course, were unashamedly mainstream entertainments; they weren't made for critics. Still, the reviews of the film and the album were typically more generous than anything the Gibbs had received during their recent commercial rebirth. Even hard-bitten *New York Times* critic Janet Maslin singled out

186

the brothers' contribution to the film. 'Among the movie's most influential principals—although they never appear on-screen—are the Bee Gees, who provided the most important parts of its score,' Maslin wrote. 'It could be argued that the Bee Gees ... now [have] this kind of music down to a science, and that originality is not exactly a key ingredient in the disco mystique. In any case, at its best, the music moves with a real spring in its step, and the movie does too.'

*Village Voice* critic Robert Christgau was his usual snippy self, once again damning the Gibbs with the faintest of praise, despite awarding the soundtrack album a B+ rating. 'So you've seen the movie—pretty good movie, right?—and decided that this is the disco album you're going to try ... Well, I can't blame you. The Bee Gees side [of the album] is pop music at a new peak of irresistible silliness, with the former Beatle clones singing like mechanical mice with an unnatural sense of rhythm ... [But] there's one more problem. While you're deciding to buy this record, so is everyone you know. You're gonna get really sick of it. Maybe you should Surprise Your Friends [sic] and seek out Casablanca's *Get Down and Boogie* instead.'

In a more balanced review, *Rolling Stone* observed, 'Few sound-tracks have defined a genre; this one did, and more. Released ... just as disco reached its populist brilliance/commercial bogus-ness tipping point, it matched proven club hits (the Trammps' "Disco Inferno", Kool and the Gang's "Open Sesame") with a clutch of Bee Gees songs intended for their own forthcoming album. From "Stayin' Alive" and "More Than a Woman" to KC and the Sunshine Band's "Boogie Shoes", the peaks on this double album can still turn any wedding dance floor into a seething caldron of joy and embarrassment.'

In a future poll, *Rolling Stone* would rank *Saturday Night Fever* the fifth best soundtrack of all time, noting: 'It's okay to think that disco sucks, but there's something different, and dare we say special, about the Bee Gees-and-beyond soundtrack to John Badham's love letter to leisure suits ... perhaps it's about catching the zeitgeist at just the right moment.'

Exactly.

In London, the Beatles' producer George Martin listened to most of the *Saturday Night Fever* songs and simply couldn't equate the music with that of the group that once went hit-for-hit with his protégés. 'I thought [the songs] were written by someone else,' he quietly chuckled, 'they were so good.' Martin found the music irresistible, admitting 'even old men like me would get on the [dance] floor.' Martin and the Gibbs would soon work together.

Back in the US, Michael Jackson, the star member of another family band, lost himself in the deep grooves and silky harmonies of 'More Than a Woman', et al. *Saturday Night Fever* and the Bee Gees would have a huge impact on his album *Thriller*, an influence he'd readily admit when his album exploded in 1982. Over time, Jackson would draw close to the Gibbs, especially Barry. Sometimes he'd hide out at Barry's house in Miami.

Stigwood's RSO reaped some useful returns from the soundtrack; by 1978 it was grossing in the neighbourhood of $100 million annually. In 1977 alone, the Bee Gees netted somewhere between $12 and $15 million on the strength of *Saturday Night Fever* LP. They'd come a long way from $100 travel allowances and criss-crossing America in cramped Greyhound buses. Now they could afford to buy Cucumber bloody Castle.

In May 1978, brother Andy hit a high only matched of late by his all-conquering siblings. Andy's latest single, 'Shadow Dancing', became his third successive US No.1, topping the charts for seven weeks, beating off such quality challengers as his brothers' 'Night Fever', Gerry Rafferty's 'Baker Street' and the Rolling Stones' 'Miss You', the Stones' own stab at disco. With that, Andy became the first solo artist in American chart history to reach No.1 with his first three singles. He celebrated by purchasing a 58-foot cruiser named the *Shadow Dancer*—and hired a full-time bodyguard to keep the over-eager fans at bay. He kept a .357 Magnum and two semi-automatic machine guns on board to scare off Caribbean pirates. Sadly, 'Shadow Dancing' was his last chart-topper.

Again, the fingerprints of big brother Barry were all over 'Shadow Dancing', which all four brothers co-wrote quickly one night in LA. Barry co-produced the track with studio partners-in-hit-making Galuten and Richardson. He even wrote the song's orchestral arrangement. Andy's ever-present dilemma intensified: was he succeeding on his own merits, or riding in his brother's slipstream? Was Andy nothing but a 'puppet on a string', as he sighed in 'I Just Want to be Your Everything'?

Andy also had to confront the short lifespan of a teen idol. 'Three to five years and you're out,' he told a reporter. His future plans included searching out more 'meaningful' music, songs with an appeal beyond his core female audience. 'They're the ones [that] keep you going,' Andy said.

The youngest Gibb's private life, meanwhile, was a shambles. Back in Australia, his estranged wife Kim had given birth to baby Peta on 25 January 1978 after a tough 40-hour labour. Andy was nowhere to be seen, despite his promise that he'd be present at the birth. Only a fortnight earlier, Kim had opened a Sydney newspaper to learn that she and her superstar husband were about to get divorced. This was news to Kim. But the rumour was true; the divorce papers arrived within days. She suffered a near-breakdown, her post-childbirth weight dropping to a pencil-thin 45 kilos. Her ex, meanwhile, was partying hard back in the States, coming 'close to being in love'—his words—with eight-years-older British actress Susan George. And he was about to consumed by a blizzard of cocaine.

Still, Andy's popularity was such that he was tapped—*sans* brothers—to guest star on the hour-long *Olivia!* NBC TV special, with Swedish invaders ABBA, which aired in the US on 15 May 1978. It was a banner year for expat Aussies: the feather-haired, moist-lipped Newton-John was all over the charts and the big screen, thanks to her star turn in *Grease*, a film that was busy turning its modest $6 million budget into a hefty $100 million box office windfall. Newton-John's 'You're the One That I Want', complete with its ever-so-racey video clip, was in a friendly fight with Andy for the No.1 position in the charts. Her 'Hopelessly Devoted to You', also from *Grease*, would soon join the battle.

The *Olivia!* special defined Andy's place in the mainstream. During the musical centrepiece, Andy, 'Livvy' and ABBA sang a super-medley, starting with Olivia's 'If You Love Me Let Me Know' before segueing into the Swedes' 'Fernando'. Andy, looking like a million dollars, his hair shining, shirt open to the navel, sporting tight red pants and a slick white waistcoat, stepped forward to join forces with ABBA's Frida and Agnetha on 'I Just Want to Be Your Everything'. It was then back to Olivia for 'Have You Never Been Mellow' and 'Please Mr Please', before the microphone returned to Andy for 'Love is Thicker Than Water' and 'Shadow Dancing'. The studio audience's biggest screams came during Andy's solo turns. This 15-minute production number, a solid-gold medley of chartbusters, ended with the ensemble reprising 'If You Love Me Let Me Know'. The stars then joined arms and sang their hearts out on the closing number, 'Thank You for the Music'.

*Olivia!* personified wholesome mainstream entertainment. Thirty million Americans tuned in, most of whom would have been shocked had they known of Andy's off-stage thing for white powder and the high life.

Andy followed his *Olivia!* gig with a guest spot on the even more family-friendly and high-rating *Bob Hope's All-Star Christmas Special*. The scripted exchange between the droll, ski-nosed comic and the singer was painfully awkward. Hope smugly introed Andy as 'the hottest-selling export from Australia since lobster tails'—and it headed downhill from there.

'I can't believe I'm standing here on the same stage as Bob Hope,' Andy gushed.

'Well it is I,' Hope smirked. 'You know, the nose, the soulful eyes, the chin. I'd know me anywhere.'

Andy did his best to exclaim excitedly how only a few weeks ago he'd worked with ageing wisecracker George Burns. First George Burns, now Bob Hope—who'd have thought? What were the chances? He'd come a long way from suburban Ryde, in a heartbeat, or so it seemed.

'George who?' Hope grinned, pretending not to know his longtime co-star.

'Burns,' Andy replied hopefully.

'Oh yes,' Hope snapped. 'Elderly fellow. Small. Bony. Dry wit. Cigar smoker.'

'Oscar winner,' Andy shot back.

'Never heard of him,' continued Hope, who didn't have an Oscar on his mantelpiece. A few seconds of silence passed.

Talk turned, of course, to Andy's famous name. After all, what was a conversation with Andy Gibb without a mention of his siblings? 'I can't take all the credit [for my success],' Andy offered humbly, 'because I come from a big musical family.'

Hope asked Andy how it felt to be an overnight sensation. 'When I first came to America,' Hope reminisced, 'it took me a long time before I made it.'

'You had problems I didn't have,' was Andy's response. 'First off, you were fighting the Indians.'

With that lousy joke and yet another smirk from Hope, Andy repaired to the snowflake-adorned set to serenade the crowd with 'Shadow Dancing', a light sheen on sweat on his smooth brow, his every pelvic thrust bringing shrieks from the audience. It may have been American entertainment at its most cornball, but the Hope special captured Andy Gibb at his pop peak. He was a superstar.

Stardom can be fleeting. After the mind-blowing success of *Saturday Night Fever*, the Gibbs disastrously chose to appear in a Robert Stigwood film adaptation of the Beatles' album *Sgt. Pepper's Lonely Hearts Club Band*, which sneaked into cinemas in late July 1978 and then sneaked right out again. What was supposedly a study of corruption in the crazy world of entertainment—set to a soundtrack of reconstructed Beatles songs—only proved that singers can't carry bad movies on the strength of their voices and good looks.

On paper, at least, the *Sgt. Pepper's* project seemed like a grand plan. As Barry would admit, 'If somebody had said to you, "I want to make a movie of *Sgt. Pepper's*, and I want you to play a member of the band," you'd say, "Fantastic." ' Barry, Mo and Robin agreed to the movie, in a heartbeat.

The Gibbs had always genuflected at the altar of the Beatles, having recorded *Abbey Road*'s 'Sun King', 'She Came in Through the Bathroom Window' and 'Golden Slumbers' / 'Carry That Weight' for the odd (and fatally flawed) 1976 doco-slash-musical *All This and World War II*. Rod Stewart, Bryan Ferry, the Four Seasons and Elton John (alongside John Lennon, posing as Dr Winston O'Boogie) all contributed songs to the doco, but it sunk like a stone, barely lasting two weeks in cinemas. A stunned reviewer asked whether its PG rating stood for 'positively ghastly'. This was pre-*Fever*, of course; who knows what business the film may have done if it was released after *Saturday Night Fever*.

As for *Sgt. Pepper's*, well, it was the Fabs' finest 40-odd minutes—why wouldn't the Gibbs want to be involved in a movie based upon the album? Stigwood, having already produced a live Broadway show titled *Sgt. Pepper's Lonely Hearts Club Band on the Road*, had secured the rights to 29 Beatles songs. What could go wrong?

Stigwood had negotiated with Dee Anthony, a bulldog-like New Yorker manager, for Anthony's client the flaxen-haired Brit Peter Frampton to star in the film alongside Stiggy's 'lads'. On the strength of the multi-million selling *Frampton Comes Alive!*, Frampton was currently the brightest solo star on the planet. Frampton and the Bee Gees sing the Beatles: surely, believed Stigwood, it was box office gold.

The press releases started flowing. 'I am happy and proud to be associated with Dee Anthony,' crowed Stigwood. 'Peter Frampton's presence brings the ultimate in true stardom to *Sgt. Pepper's*.'

'We are deeply privileged and honoured to be associated with Robert Stigwood,' returned Anthony.

In a remarkable coup, Stiggy even persuaded Beatles producer George Martin to work on the new versions of these wonderful songs. Martin had procrastinated, knowing the Beatles wouldn't have approved, but when his wife reminded him that if he didn't take the music producing job on the film, someone else would—potentially ruining some of his finest work—Martin signed on. Stigwood guaranteed Martin full creative control over the soundtrack.

'It's going to be a fantastic film,' Barry gushed. He flashed back to hearing the LP in Stiggy's office on its day of release in 1967. 'No one could believe the album. It was a milestone in recording.'

The Bee Gees were (mis)cast as the Henderson Brothers, members of the reformed Sgt. Pepper's Lonely Hearts Club Band, whose main role in what passed as a plot was to play the featured songs. Frampton was to portray Billy Shears, the grandson of Sgt. Pepper. In supporting roles, Stiggy cast Billy Preston (who had played sessions with the Beatles) as a gold-lame wearing black messiah, risen from the dead, along with comic Steve Martin, veteran actor Donald Pleasence, *Carry On* star Frankie Howerd, who'd worked with Barry and Mo on *Cucumber Castle*, and acts-of-the-moment Aerosmith, Alice Cooper and Earth, Wind & Fire. George Burns had the only speaking part, playing Mr Kite, the narrator, but the job of trying to tie together a narrative described as the 'ultimate fantasy' proved too tough an ask even for the seasoned Burns.

There were the usual behind-the-scenes dramas: KISS rejected the role taken by Aerosmith, fearing it would damage their reputation. Then the guys from Aerosmith refused to be killed by Peter Frampton in their fight scene, not keen to be snuffed by such a lightweight. Their deaths were re-staged as an accident. Aerosmith were especially incensed when they learned that each of the Gibbs and Frampton were being paid something like a million dollars for the film, while they were being paid significantly less. Alice Cooper had to arrange day leave from rehab to film his scenes as the Sun King.

Stiggy was in his element when it came to the film's big finish, shot early in January 1978. For the all-star reprise of the title track, he cracked open his Rolodex, inviting 400 A-listers, B-listers and anyone else willing to attend a day-long, all-expenses-paid Hollywood party in exchange for a little mimed singing and a bit of swaying in time to the music. Anyone who agreed was given carte blanche access to a limo and hotel suite. That one day of filming alone cost Stigwood something like $500,000.

Just before the grand opening of *Pepper's* in LA on 18 July 1978, Frampton was seriously injured in a car crash. He was in a New York hospital when the film was screened. The Manhattan premier was staged at the grand Radio City Music Hall, on what was declared Sgt Pepper Day, 21 July. It turned out to be a black-letter day for the Gibbs, Frampton, Stigwood and pretty much anyone else closely involved with this train-wreck of a movie. Maybe Frampton's accident was a warning.

As awful as the *Sgt. Pepper's* movie clearly was, the Gibbs, as always, dutifully talked it up when asked, toothy smiles plastered across their faces. One of their promo ports of call was the *Merv Griffin Show* couch, this time with a grinning Stiggy in tow, straight off the plane from Bermuda. He was introduced cheekily as 'Andy'. Rather than pick apart the movie, talk quickly turned to Stiggy and the lifestyles of the very rich and famous-by-association. Barry referred to his manager as Scrooge McDuck reincarnated. 'He's got a huge money bin, you know,' laughed Barry. 'And he's got a worry room that he walks around.'

'I deny all this,' chuckled Stiggy, sounding even more Hitchcockian than ever. 'I live in Bermuda. I'm an American taxpayer. And I have a medium-sized white house.'

As the interview progressed, it became clear that no one wanted to discuss the movie they were supposedly promoting. They compared recollections of their first meeting with Stigwood soon after arriving in London—it was agreed that Stiggy did have the mother of all hangovers, although the presence of his two male minders was disputed—and discussed whether Stiggy had a great ear for a hit or

TRAGEDY

was tone deaf. Stiggy opted for the latter, but did confess to being 'one of the most fortunate people in the world; my work is my hobby'.

Also on Griffin's couch was *Pepper's* co-star Frankie Howerd, who talked about the contrasts between the Beatles—with whom he'd also worked—and the Bee Gees. While the former were 'irreverent, outrageous, anti-establishment', the Gibbs, to Howerd, were pros, 'very eager to be helped; they weren't at all cocky'. Yet again, the Gibbs were seen as 'good lads', unwilling to upset the status quo. Conformists. To reinforce the stereotype, Mo mugged for the audience, Robin said little, Barry directed the traffic, like the polite older brother he was.

The interview ambled along and still no talk of *Sgt. Pepper's*; even some footage aired from the film, showing Peter Frampton, the Gibbs and George Burns during the 'For the Benefit of Mr Kite' production number, failed to prompt any sort of diligent plugging. Instead, chat moved to the future, a new album that the brothers were currently recording, a record that Stiggy assured everyone watching 'was going to surprise the world'. He singled out 'Too Much Heaven' as 'one of the most beautiful songs the Bee Gees have ever written.' (He was referring to the *Spirits Having Flown* album, released in February 1979, that would sell 16 million copies.)

Brother Andy was still riding high in the charts, Griffin noted— what chance Barry working with the 'other' Gibb brother? 'Andy is doing so well on his own that I think we should just leave him alone.'

'What are you doing with your millions of dollars?' the host enquired.

'What are you doing with *yours*?' Barry retorted, as the audience laughed and clapped.

Stiggy steered the chat to the *Saturday Night Fever* soundtrack,

197

which, he reminded everyone, was currently zeroing in on sales of 18 million. So, he demanded, why no Academy Award nomination? He was referring to 'Stayin' Alive' not being nominated in the 1978 Best Original Song category. 'There's never been a more perfect marriage of movie and music,' Stigwood insisted. 'I think by popular consensus the Bee Gees won the Academy Award.'

Once the applause settled down, Stiggy rounded out the interview with talk of 'another feature' starring the Gibbs, post *Sgt. Pepper's*. At last he was talking up the reason he and the Gibbs were on the Griffin show, *Sgt. Pepper's*, the dud that would end the Bee Gees' movie career.

American critic Leonard Maltin summed up the disaster succinctly. The picture, he wrote, 'ranges from tolerable to embarrassing and just doesn't work.' It was true—little of the film was watchable, with the exception of Steve Martin's manic turn, hamming up 'Maxwell's Silver Hammer', and Stiggy's over-the-top finale, with cameos from Barry Humphries (as Dame Edna Everage), Peter Allen, Carol Channing, John Mayall, Curtis Mayfield, Helen Reddy, Connie Stevens, Frankie Valli, Tina Turner, Donovan, Seals & Croft, Leif Garrett and a glowing Stigwood himself.

*Pepper's* returned barely half of its $18 million budget during its short cinematic run in the summer of 1978. It derailed the Bee Gees' seemingly unstoppable momentum and also unleashed hell on the career of self-destructive star Peter Frampton, who struggled to bottle the magic of *Frampton Comes Alive!* and swiftly fell off the radar. *Sgt. Pepper's* director Michael Schultz wasn't spared; critic Paul Nelson quipped that Schultz would 'need direction to merely find the set, let alone the camera'. As for the Gibbs' acting, as Leonard Maltin noted, 'if you can't say something nice ...'

*Sgt. Pepper's* was a creative and commercial disaster, but still the masses snapped up virtually every ticket for the Bee Gees' 1979 North American tour, the brothers' last hurrah in their amazing decade of rebirth. The 'Spirits Having Flown' tour itself would be a sight-and-sound spectacular, all retina-wrecking lights and explosions and pyros and relentless grooves. The Gibbs had been involved in pre-production with personal manager Dick Ashby and lighting designer Delton Bass, but they were still shocked when they arrived at the venue for the opening night, Fort Worth's Tarrant County Convention Center, where they'd sold all 14,000 tickets weeks in advance. 'I've never seen as many speakers as that,' Barry exclaimed to interviewer David Frost and his crew, his mouth slightly open at the sight, taking it all in.

'The lights look … incredible,' said an equally shellshocked Mo.

'Now,' Barry joked, aware that a TV camera was watching over him, 'all we need now is a band … and a manager … and a hit.'

The three Gibbs spoke about their hardscrabble past, when they had driven to gigs in Britain in a battered green van, earning bugger all. Times had changed and all in the course of a few fast years.

Nowadays, five semi-trailers accompanied the Gibbs from city to city, lugging their computer-operated set, with lighting capable of 40,000 different patterns. When the show reached overdrive, the stage would light up like a dance floor; it was enough to make the usually static Robin wiggle his hips ever so gently. The brothers and band—which included Blue Weaver, guitarist Alan Kendall and drummer Dennis Bryon, key contributors to the Bee Gees' disco/groove makeover, as well as Galuten and Richardson on the sound desk—would fly to each gig in a leased 55-seater Boeing 720, the jet's livery changed to display the Bee Gees' black, red and gold logo. The plane's $1 million price tag was a minor inconvenience; after every gig the brothers, sometimes with Andy along for the ride, would fly home to Miami. Who needed hotels?

'You need a family, no matter what happens,' Barry told Frost, who travelled with the band making a documentary for NBC.

It was interesting that the Gibbs, who were currently making music purely for the hips—and whatever else came afterwards between consenting adults—saw themselves as homebodies, solid-state citizens. Hedonism was a big part of the disco movement, and their new music was blissful, exuberant, full of life, but the Bee Gees insisted they'd rather stay home and play with their kids.

But right now the Gibbs were keen to play and meet their audience, the people, according to Barry, 'to whom our records mean a lot'. It was a completely different experience making a record, he told Frost, while holed up in Miami, and then getting on stage and seeing how audiences responded. Nothing could replicate that feeling. They enjoyed getting back in touch with their people; they'd had enough of the emotional disconnect of the recording studio. And how many red carpets could you walk, after all?

The sheer logistics of the 41-date tour, by far the largest the Bee Gees had ever undertaken, were pretty damned spectacular.

Beginning in Fort Worth on 28 June 1979 and wrapping up three and a half months later with a 'hometown' show at the Miami Stadium, the brothers played to some 800,000-plus people, pulling in $10 million-plus at the box office alone, huge numbers for 1979. Tour merchandising would have doubled, perhaps even tripled that figure. Scalpers shopped tickets for $700 apiece at some shows; in LA, on the night of the show, Bee Gees merchandise sold at the rate of $3000 *per minute*. The Gibbs and Stiggy laughed all the way to the bank, forgetting, at least temporarily, the nightmare of *Sgt. Pepper's*.

The stats really were eye-popping; the Bee Gees were pulling the type of crowds reserved for big sporting events or Papal visits. They filled New York's hallowed Madison Square Garden each gig of their three-night stand—a run during which, Barry admitted, they rarely slept, running on some heavy adrenaline. 'I can't figure out how we did it,' Barry said in 2014. 'Youth, I guess.'

In Cleveland they drew a crowd of 35,000, in Chicago slightly more than 36,000, Cincinnati 33,000-plus. Rarely did ticket sales fall below the 90 per cent mark; in most cases the houses were full. More than 29,000 filled the Spectrum in Philadelphia, 36,270 packed the Silverdome in Pontiac, 26,000 squeezed into Providence's Civic Center. Lines stretched seemingly for kilometres outside each venue, evidence that the Bee Gees were far and away the hottest concert ticket of 1979, even as disco breathed its last gasp.

Never the kind to tinker with a successful look, let alone a formula, Barry, Mo and Robin took the stage each night decked out in identical white satin pants and white spangled jackets, a fair sprinkling of Vegas now in their wardrobe, shirts open to reveal ample chest hair and a smattering of bling. Andy would don the same outfit when he joined them most nights for 'You Should Be Dancing'. It was the closest, as one writer noted, to Andy ever becoming a Bee Gee. The screams that continued through much of the show grew just that much more shrill when Andy joined the others.

At one point during his nightly cameo, Andy turned to Maurice off-mic and shouted above the din, 'Can you believe this craziness? Can you believe it?'

'No,' Mo responded, shaking his balding head. 'It's incredible, isn't it?'

Sidestage, personal manager and long-time *aide-de-camp* Dick Ashby stuck cigarette filters in his ears to alleviate the crowd noise. Cops at Shea Stadium did likewise.

The Bee Gees had always wanted to be the Beatles, and now with this tour they were experiencing the closest thing America had seen to Beatlemania: Bee Gees Fever.

Each show, 'Nights on Broadway', the song that represented a huge creative turning point for the Gibbs, Barry's first serious stab at his now trademark falsetto, was the big production number, mirrored disco balls and the Bee Gees logo descending as if from the heavens. But they hadn't forgotten their past: Robin would step forward for 'How Can You Mend a Broken Heart', Barry would take centrestage during 'Words', while 'Massachusetts' and 'I Started a Joke' were also high on the setlist. But while those blasts from the past may have been beautifully crafted and emotionally rich, the huge crowds had come to boogie.

A frenetic 'Jive Talkin'' closed each show and then they'd return for a one-song encore, 'You Should Be Dancing', an explosion of live horns and blazing lights, the Gibbs and backing vocalists the Sweet Inspirations in full voice, the entire crowd out of their seats and shaking it like there was no tomorrow. This big climax ended with a lengthy jam and a massive rumble of percussion. By that time the Gibbs, sweaty and satiated, were entombed in their limo, heading for the airport and another night flight to Miami.

There was no shortage of special guests, both on and off stage. On 30 June in Houston, a bearded John Travolta, taking a break from shooting his next film, *Urban Cowboy*, joined the four Gibbs for 'You Should Be Dancing', reproducing some of his fancy footwork from *Saturday Night Fever*. Billy Joel, Al Pacino, Diana Ross and KISS, who were about to undergo their own disco makeover with 'I Was Made for Loving You', were among the faithful at the Garden in Manhattan. Among the 60,000 crowd at LA's Dodger Stadium were Rod Stewart, Olivia Newton-John, Karen Carpenter, Jack Nicholson and, significantly, Barbra Streisand.

Just before their 24 September spectacular in Washington, DC, the trio was invited to the White House by President Jimmy Carter, who acknowledged their work for UNICEF. (The Bee Gees had headlined a NBC TV show for the charity back in January, with Andy also appearing. Over time, royalties from their performance of 'Too Much Heaven' generated some $7 million for UNICEF.)

After the tour, Barry said he really felt the stress and strain that came with maintaining such a high-profile, big-budget roadshow, but at least on a public level it was a love-in from coast to coast. Drug-free, too, according to an FBI agent assigned to security on the tour, although Mo maintained his ritual of a scotch and Coke for breakfast, occasionally two, which probably explained his sometimes woozy on-stage presence.

David Frost's NBC TV special screened at the end of the tour. It was a by-the-numbers doco, executive produced by Stigwood and Frost, that captured the Gibbs in various guises: at play at Barry's waterfront spread in Miami's Millionaires Row, with their respective families—Mo's son Adam was born in 1977, Robin's children Spencer and Melissa also featured, as did Barry's ever-expanding brood— and planning the tour with Delton Bass, Ashby, Stiggy and others. There were unlikely cameos from country greats Willie Nelson and Glen Campbell, jamming Everly Brothers songs with the Gibbs and pulling off a pretty effective 'To Love Somebody', proof that Barry's finest few minutes was a song for all musical moods. A tanned Hugh and Barbara were also given air time, reminiscing about the day they came home to Keppel Road and discovered their boys singing like birds in their bedroom. Hugh threw in an aside that his boys had never held down a regular job, that 'music was their life'. Stiggy put in a cameo.

The most revealing few moments were shot in Miami, as they worked with Galuten and Richardson on the song 'Tragedy'. The track sounded great, everyone agreed, but it needed something more. What about an explosion just before the chorus, to give it even more muscle, asked Barry? A quick conference was held, and again everyone agreed. But short of nipping out to buy some TNT, how could they re-create an explosion?

Barry had an idea. He stepped into the vocal booth while everyone else looked on. Galuten and Richardson cued the track, Barry psyched himself up, and at the chosen moment cupped his hands in front of the microphone and mimicked the sound of an exploding bomb. It sounded more wet fart than orgasmic blast, but the idea was solid.

When Barry returned to the control room, and the track was played back, Richardson said, 'Not bad... but it sounds awful.'

'More saliva,' Robin suggested. 'Loosen your shirt,' added Mo.

When the laughs died down, Barry returned to the vocal booth—and nailed it. Big smiles were exchanged; it was yet another successful day in hitsville, Miami Beach. The song reached No.1 in America in March 1979.

In the main, the NBC special was a live Bee Gees showcase, capturing all the pizzazz and flash of *Spirits Having Flown*, the brothers looking slightly stunned by the sheer scope of the production and the size of the crowds they pulled each night. They'd come a long way from Redcliffe Speedway.

Disco, just like punk and so many other cultural phenomenons, proved a fad. Even in the midst of the 'Spirits Having Flown' tour, there were rumblings of disco-discontent. Just as the Bee Gees headed to Seattle on 13 July, the Chicago White Sox hosted a baseball double-header against the Detroit Tigers. Popular local DJ Steve Dahl used the game to host what he called 'Disco Demolition Night', a sort of surrogate anti-Bee Gees rally. Fans were encouraged to bring along their unwanted disco vinyl and exchange it for a discounted ticket. Instead of having their albums collected by staffers, fans hurled them like frisbees onto the baseball diamond, making a huge mess. Dahl duly blew up the pile of records during a break in the game. The crowd left en masse after the 'demolition' and the chaos led to the cancellation of the second match.

The charts were reflecting that disco was on the wane. Whereas in 1978 and 1979 the Hot 100 was clogged with product from the Bee Gees, brother Andy, Chic, Earth, Wind & Fire and Donna Summer, the emergence of bands such as the Knack, Styx and Foreigner marked the re-emergence of rock as a force in the mainstream. By early 1980, disco breakouts such as KC and the Sunshine Band were only connecting with their big ballads rather than more danceable, upbeat fare. 'Please Don't Go' was KC's last charting hit in the USA, the end of an era.

Disco's uniform of body shirts and slim-hipped flares was being rendered obsolete by the skinny ties and black jeans of new wave. Guitars were wiping out synths and falsettos and mirror balls. Scowls were in, hedonism out. Speed yes, coke no. Discos started to shut their doors, replaced by sweaty live venues. Goodbye KC and the Sunshine Band, hello XTC and the Cars.

Time was being called on disco superstars the Bee Gees, too. Their 'Love You Inside Out' had hit the US Top 20 in May 1979, but they wouldn't bother the business end of the charts for another decade.

After a crazy five years at the vanguard of a musical phenomenon, the Gibb brothers were about to become shadowy figures on the pop landscape. It was time to slow down.

act

tragedy

The 1970s had been all about rediscovery and creative rebirth for the Bee Gees, who had scaled unimagined pop heights. As Mo said during the 'Spirits Having Flown' tour, 'Even getting bomb threats was great! If you weren't important,' he explained, 'they wouldn't bomb you.' He was making a strange kind of sense: the Gibbs couldn't get arrested at the start of the decade—OK, Mo did once, for drink driving, on the Isle of Man—yet by the end of the 1970s they were as ubiquitous as the Beatles had been in the 1960s.

But as a new decade dawned, the world was tiring of the Gibbs. 'America needs a rest from the Bee Gees,' noted Timothy White, editor of *Billboard*. Disco was done. *Sgt. Pepper's* was an embarrassment. The Gibbs needed to drop out of the spotlight, take stock. And Maurice, Robin and Andy, especially Andy, had personal demons that needed urgent attention. The brothers were about to change course again.

It was Mo who warned Andy about the seductive dangers of the high life. He was, after all, speaking from experience, drawing on the lowpoint in the late 1960s when the band first split and he retreated to the Isle of Man, owning little more than a blue Roller and some spare change, his first marriage on the skids. And perhaps Mo was also thinking of more recent times, the wild nights on the *Spirits* tour, when he'd be carried back to his room, as good as comatose after yet another lively after-party.

'This is a nice house, Andy,' Mo told him one day when they caught up. 'And that's a nice Porsche outside. But you're not going to keep all this, you know.'

Andy gave the impression he didn't understand. 'What do you mean?'

'You keep doing what you're doing,' Mo said, clearly referring to his younger brother's addiction issues, 'and this stuff'll vanish. Your career, everything.'

Andy said nothing; he just nodded his head. He did understand what Mo was trying to tell him. But it was hard to tell, judging by soon-to-unfold events, whether the message actually sunk in.

In early 1980, Andy's estranged ex, Kim, brought their daughter Peta, now almost two, to the States. It was the first time she'd met her father. Any dream Kim may have nurtured of a bond forming between father and daughter, however, faded quicker than a cheap perm. Peta's only memory of the time was Andy buying her a can of Coke. That was it. They'd talk on the phone from time to time, but there was no further physical contact between them.

Andy's problems extended into the studio. He was recording a new album, appropriately titled *After Dark*, once again working with Albhy Galuten. But Andy was unreliable, unpredictable: he missed sessions, and when he did bother coming into the studio to sing, it was clear that his toxic lifestyle was damaging his voice. Barry, always Andy's protector, was forced to step in and cut some vocals on his behalf.

Released in February 1980, the first musical offering from a Gibb in the new decade, *After Dark* flopped, despite a stellar cast, including numerous contributions from Barry and vocals from the ever-supportive Olivia Newton-John. The album hit a US peak of No.21 before sliding quickly out of the charts, despite some reasonable reviews, even from the typically Gibb-resistant *Rolling Stone*. '*After Dark* may have scant appeal to rock fans, but on its own pop terms, it's a production triumph,' noted critic Stephen Holden. 'There's no cheap filler. As ice-cream parlour music for Romeo and Juliet, it's first-class.' 'Desire', the lead single, was a remake of a track from his brothers' *Spirits Having Flown* album, but it failed to gain any airplay. 'I Can't Help It', a duet with Newton-John, fared a little better, reaching the US Top 20 in late March. But that was pretty much it.

Label boss and manager Stiggy tried to help by shielding Andy from all his money so he didn't blow the lot on drugs. It didn't help. Andy was less than impressed and reacted badly. 'You become the enemy,' admitted a heartbroken Stiggy, who chose to keep his distance from Andy. A *Greatest Hits* collection would surface later in the year, ending Andy's deal with Stigwood; he was dropped from the RSO roster after four years with the label. His records had stopped selling and he'd become too big a liability. It was an astonishingly rapid fall from grace.

Despite *After Dark*'s failure, Andy remained a favourite on the family-friendly circuit, being tapped once again by Bob Hope for the *All-Star Comedy Party*, his latest United Service Organisation special for US servicemen and women, which aired on 28 May. Introduced by Hope as 'the hottest-selling import to hit our shores since Toyota', Gibb still looked great, his blond mane swept back, floral shirt open to the navel, a gold medallion draped around his neck. Before he had a chance to speak, Hope laid on another hefty serving of hype, this time describing Andy as 'the most exciting thing to hit the teenage market since the printed T-shirt'.

Host and star began their scripted chat discussing their shared English roots—Hope had been born in London, emigrating to America with his family when he was five—and Andy's Aussie upbringing. Andy asked Hope about a trip he took to Australia. 'The people of Australia are so nice,' Hope said, his trademark smirk in place, 'especially for a non-English speaking country.'

'What do you mean, Bob?' asked Andy, cocking an eyebrow. 'Australians speak the King's English.'

'They do?' continued Hope, twirling his golf club. 'Whenever I hailed a taxi, no matter what I told the cabbie, he always took me to the airport.'

Banter done, Andy headed centrestage to mime 'After Dark', mingling with the uniformed audience. In hindsight, it presented a bizarre scenario: a 22-year-old in the midst of a dangerous downward spiral hamming it up with the maestro of the mainstream. Somehow Andy pulled it off.

Brother Robin, meanwhile, had dramas of his own. In what he'd later euphemistically refer to as a 'messy period', Robin and Molly were breaking up. She'd filed for divorce in May 1980. While he maintained a base in Florida, she still lived in their house in Weybridge, with their two young children. Theirs was no ordinary split. In the words of a *Daily Mail* reporter, their divorce was 'one of the bloodiest and dirtiest in the inglorious annals of showbusiness break-ups ... a tale of jealousy, deceit, money and dark sexual mores of a star known globally for his high-trousered, high-voiced, wholesome Bee Gees' image.'

FBI files, which were not released until 2012, soon after Robin's death, revealed that the situation leading up to the split between Molly and Robin—who still had a taste for speed, upholding his role as the 'Pilly' Gibb—had reached such a nadir that he had claimed, in a telegram to Molly's UK solicitors Haymon & Walters, that he'd hired a hitman. 'I have taken out a contract,' Robin wrote. 'It is now a question of time.'

Robin was convinced, for no tangible reason as it turned out, that Molly and an unnamed male acquaintance were trying to extort £5 million from him. He even entered her Weybridge home while Molly was in New York, searching for 'evidence'. As it was still technically their marital home, when Molly learned of Robin's search, she couldn't have him arrested. Robin subsequently handed along some documents he thought meaningful—he called it 'bombshell evidence'—to the FBI and British police. But they contained nothing that hinted at any kind of planned 'fleecing'. It seemed to be little more than paranoia.

It would have seemed almost comical if it wasn't for the impact on their two children, Spencer and Melissa, aged six and four. When the Gibbs' custody battle was fought out in the courts, Robin was banned from seeing the children. This ban would stay in place for another six years, which Robin admitted left him 'on the verge of madness'. (In September 1983, he was arrested and sentenced to 14 days' imprisonment for breaking a court order and speaking to the press about his marriage to Molly, although he was freed on appeal within hours.)

The Gibbs had just lived through the most amazing decade of their career, but clearly that didn't guarantee them domestic bliss.

Andy's next move shifted him ever so slightly away from the life of a teen idol, something he'd been trying to do almost since he first burst onto the charts. *Solid Gold* was an American syndicated music TV show that first aired on 13 September 1980, a slicker, smoother version of Australia's *Countdown* or UK perennial *Top of the Pops*. The show's one unique quality was the *Solid Gold* Dancers, painfully thin dancers in leotards and headbands, who'd bust suggestive moves to the sound of the hit records of the week. 'Costumed like a Las Vegas version of punk fashion,' Jon Pareles wrote in the *New York Times*, 'their routines typically have a minimal connection with the songs that back them up.' Lester Wilson, choreographer for *Saturday Night Fever*, was one of three *Solid Gold* choreographers. The show rated highly, especially during its first three seasons.

Vocal star Dionne Warwick was *Solid Gold's* first host, initially accompanied by comic Marty Cohen. Then Andy was recruited as co-host, joining Warwick for the first time on 27 September 1980, having sung several times in earlier episodes of the program. On his first night as host, Andy welcomed renowned singer-songwriter Paul Simon, who performed 'One Trick Pony', as well as Rocky ('Tired of Toeing the Line') Burnette, before joining Warwick to croon 'I Just Want to Be Your Everything'. As always, he looked golden—solid golden, perhaps—and seemed at ease in front of the cameras and the hefty TV audience.

Not too long into his stint on *Solid Gold*, Andy appeared on an episode of *The John Davidson Show*. The star-friendly Davidson was probably best known as one of the hosts of TV's *That's Incredible!*; he also sometimes sat in for Johnny Carson on *The Tonight Show*. The date, 6 January 1981, would always be significant for the youngest Gibb.

In what seemed like a throwaway comment, Davidson asked Andy about his 'dream women'. Andy, who'd been linked to such stars as Susan George and the thoroughly-wholesome Marie Osmond, mentioned Bo Derek, whose star was shining very brightly due to the hit film '*10*'. Andy also namechecked Victoria Principal, one of the stars of super soap *Dallas*, a show currently four years into its decade-plus run. Little did Andy know, but Principal was elsewhere in the studio, and Davidson whisked her out to the set. Andy looked gobsmacked; this wasn't a set-up—a dream was playing out before his starry eyes. Principal sat down and the chemistry between them was immediate and tangible; you could just about cut it with a knife.

'So,' a smiling Davidson asked, referring to Andy's 'thing' for the beautiful Principal, who, like Susan George, was eight years older than Andy, 'when did you first realise this was the reason you watched *Dallas*?'

'From the very first time I saw her,' Andy replied in a heartbeat. Though still in shock, his eyes darted towards the actress. In fact, he couldn't take them off her. 'Never missed an episode,' Andy said. 'I really don't care who shot JR.' The audience erupted into laughter.

Andy and Principal quickly became an item. Between their very public love affair and his ongoing gig with *Solid Gold*, Andy Gibb seemed, at least to his adoring public, to have his world in order. For the moment, Andy and Principal were Hollywood's hottest couple.

The appearance of superstar Barbra Streisand at the Bee Gees' show at Dodger Stadium in 1979 was no random occurrence. 'Babs' was striving to return to the pop charts, a move kickstarted by her recent hit duet with Neil Diamond on the schmaltzy 'You Don't Bring Me Flowers'. She was in search of the perfect producer-cum-collaborator and right now there was no better man for the job than Barry Gibb, the most successful producer-songwriter-performer of the 1970s.

In fact, it was Diamond whom Barry called as soon as he was asked about working with Streisand. 'What's Barbra like to work with?' Barry asked. He'd heard the whispers—that Streisand was a diva, that she threw tantrums and made life in the studio unbearable.

'She's fantastic,' Diamond replied, much to Barry's relief. 'You should go for it.'

Barry, with Robin on board, did just that. They needed a new sensation, something that didn't carry the Bee Gees moniker, and the Streisand project was perfect. The two Gibbs began writing a song a day at Barry's home, in an upstairs room.Quickly they had seven demos ready, with vocals by Barry which they despatched to Streisand HQ.

Soon after, Barry's phone rang. It was the lady herself. 'I love them,' she said. 'Let's get started.' To which she added this reassuring coda: 'When we're in the studio, feel free to criticise me.'

With that, and Diamond's reassurance, Barry held no fears of studio drama. Along with touchstones Albhy Galuten and Karl

Richardson, he started the sessions in Miami during February 1980 and then in March shifted to the west coast, Streisand's base.

Barry had studied Streisand closely; he understood her range, her abilities as a vocalist, and crafted the songs accordingly. He knew she wanted a contemporary sounding record, and likened the experience to 'writing a screenplay for her, to make her do something different'.

Barry's role in *Guilty*, as the album would be called, was much more than gun-for-hire; it was a true collaboration. As a songwriter, he contributed to each of the album's nine songs, five of those in tandem with Robin. Barry also co-produced the record with Galuten and Richardson and sang on various tracks. He even posed in a clinch with Streisand for the album cover, both resplendent in virginal white.

*Guilty* was released in September 1980, just as Andy was settling into his role at *Solid Gold*. 'Woman in Love', a Barry and Robin collaboration, was the lead single, and it nailed what they'd all set out to achieve: to bring diva Streisand, better known for her takes on standards and show tunes, smack dab into the mainstream. The song had a sultry, sensual ambience and Streisand sang the hell out of it. Popular American DJ Kasey Kasem claimed that the note Streisand held for 10 seconds mid-song was the longest unaltered note held by a soloist in a No.1 song. He was wrong—Aussies Air Supply were among a select group who'd bettered Babs—but that didn't make her vocal any less stunning.

Barry and Robin's efforts weren't overlooked, either; they collected the prestigious British Academy of Songwriters and Authors' Ivor Novello Award for Best Song Musically and Lyrically, a huge accolade. As for Streisand, the song was a smash, her fifth

*Billboard* Hot 100 No.1 and one of her biggest-ever sellers. It also topped the UK chart for three weeks in October.

That was only the start of the *Guilty* onslaught. Just as 'Woman in Love' was certified a gold record, the album's title track, a heavy-breathing, soulful duet with Barry—with a hefty serving of high harmonising from the Gibbs—exploded onto the charts and airwaves. It reached the US Top 10 by Christmas, making it a stellar year for Barry, without him even having to step onto a stage. A whole new chapter in his career was in motion.

*Guilty* was unashamedly commercial, a massive hit for both Streisand and Barry (and co-writer Robin). It would go on to sell 15 million-plus copies worldwide, Bee Gees-like numbers, including almost half a million copies in Australia. The title track would score Streisand a Grammy for Best Pop Vocal Performance by a Duo or Group. She was nominated for three others, including Album of the Year.

Intriguingly, long after *Guilty*'s success, Barry felt that his role in its creation had been downplayed; not by Babs, but in the spirit of peace-keeping. '[Barbra and I] won a Grammy,' Barry said in 2003, 'but I was not allowed to mention that Grammy during [Bee Gees] interviews.' He didn't make it known, however, who stopped him speaking about his win, although behind the scenes there'd been major conflict with Stigwood's company RSO regarding the project, which would soon reach a costly and messy flashpoint.

The one person notable by his absence from the *Guilty* success story was Mo. His only credit was as part of a brotherly co-write on the title track. Nothing more. Maurice's boozing had now reached a dangerous level. Barry would eventually come clean. 'The reason the Streisand *Guilty* album doesn't really involve Maurice on more than one song was because at that point Maurice had reached the razor's edge.'

Throughout the *Guilty* sessions, Barry and everyone else who knew the truth about Mo were in denial. 'Let's just keep working, Mo will be fine,' they all agreed. But Mo wouldn't be fine; he was in freefall. And in the wake of *Guilty*, Barry and Robin were fielding more freelance requests, while they were also toying with the idea of a new Bee Gees record, their first of the 1980s. They needed Mo.

Action was required. With the agreement of Hugh and Barbara, Barry, Robin and Yvonne, Mo's second wife, staged an intervention session at Barry's house. When it was Yvonne's turn to confront Mo, she issued him with an ultimatum. He had to stop drinking; he had to enter rehab. He had no option. They had a new baby, Samantha, who'd been born on 2 July 1980, their second child after Adam, and Maurice had responsibilities that extended beyond the Bee Gees. 'Mo,' Yvonne told him, 'it ends now'—the drinking, that is—'or it ends forever.'

Mo duly began his first stint in rehab, ironically enough in a Santa Barbara clinic, interrupted by back surgery, and the brothers slowly eased themselves back into music-making.

Perhaps inspired by the mega success of Barry's duet with Streisand on 'Guilty', lovebirds Andy Gibb nd Victoria Principal agreed to cut a single together. And it's likely there was also a nod to his famous brothers in their choice of song, the Everly Brothers' 'All I Have to Do is Dream'; the Everlys, of course, being a huge early influence on the Bee Gees. The single, which emerged in August 1981, wasn't a hit, but that hardly mattered. They sang together in public, snogged openly and posed for portraits and paparazzi shots, looking every inch the happy-loving couple. They began talking about marriage.

When Principal guested on *Solid Gold*, Andy introduced her as 'not only a beautiful and talented actress, but a special friend'. Radiant in gold and black, Principal walked onto the set and confessed to being 'a little nervous today'. Andy asked her why; she was on TV every week, after all. Starring on *Dallas* was different to singing a love song, Principal said, 'but all depending on who I'm singing it with'. Gushy chat over, the lovebirds linked hands, locked eyes and sang as if they were the only two people in the world.

But within months, there was trouble in paradise. Andy had been tapped for an LA production of Gilbert and Sullivan's *Pirates of Penzance*, with Pam Dawber, of *Mork and Mindy* fame, his co-star. But Andy wasn't a natural fit; his soft voice didn't quite have the necessary oomph to project to a packed theatre. And Andy continued to lack confidence; he still felt that he lived in the huge shadow cast by his older brothers. He continued snorting line after line of coke—one tabloid report had him working his way through a thousand dollars' worth of marching powder a day. The reviews for *Penzance* were fair, but Andy was soon let go. He was just too big a liability.

In March 1982, Principal gave him a choice: her love or his drugs. Andy chose the latter and Hollywood's hottest couple broke up in a very public and messy fashion. One magazine flashed a photo of a distraught Andy beneath a headline that screamed: 'I wanted to commit suicide. Nothing mattered after Victoria left.' And another read: 'My trip to hell and back.' Andy may have no longer been able to sell records, but he could sell tabloids.

'Our breakup was preceded and precipitated by Andy's use of drugs,' Principal told a reporter from *People*, point blank. 'I did everything I could to help him. But then I told him he would have to choose between me and his problem.'

In another interview—with rumoured Gibb girlfriend Marie Osmond, no less—Principal expressed her desperation. 'I really tried every last thing. When it ended, it was a matter of there not being one more thing I could do to save Andy. I knew I had to leave in order to save myself.'

'When we broke up,' Andy told a reporter from *Good Morning America*, 'I gave up everything. I didn't care about life.'

Soon after the split, Andy agreed to appear on *The Tonight Show*, hosted by acid-tongued comic Joan Rivers. He arrived wearing a glittery black jacket and a warm smile, anticipating a convivial chat about his career. After all, he was still the co-host of *Solid Gold*, a very high-profile gig. But what ensued was nothing like he'd expected.

Within minutes, Rivers turned on him. 'How did you know you were breaking up?' she demanded.

'We started to argue a lot at the end,' Andy replied, before screeching to a halt. For perhaps the first time in a public place, a dark cloud descended over golden boy Andy Gibb. He seemed genuinely annoyed with Rivers; he'd been shanghaied. 'I don't want to talk about this,' he said through a forced smile. 'Come on!'

'I don't want to discuss it any more, either,' Rivers insisted. But she continued, regardless, pressing him for more details.

'I was pretty bad for a while [after the split],' Andy confessed, 'very depressed. I missed her for quite a while.'

'Because you were in love,' chimed in Rivers.

'That's right.'

And what about their break-up: how did that play out? According to Andy, 'At the end it wasn't mutual.'

In another interview, Andy opened up even more. When asked what went wrong, he gave the impression Principal shut him out. 'What hurt me,' Andy said, 'is that she didn't seem to go through any pain at all. I felt strange being the man and feeling the pain and the weakness. It really was hell for me. I had a nervous breakdown.'

And drugs—did they still figure in his life? No, no, he insisted. Drugs were all in the past. Yet another tabloid 'reported' he went on a month-long coke bender when he and Principal split. It was becoming increasingly hard to separate fact from Hollywood whispers.

Back on the set of *Solid Gold*, Andy appeared to be settling into a comfortable groove with new host Marilyn McCoo. Andy gave the impression he had the role down pat, so much so that he was introduced as 'the host of *Solid Gold*', while former Fifth Dimension singer McCoo was billed as *his* co-star. And while they didn't seem perfectly matched on-screen—McCoo's height only exaggerated Andy's lack thereof, and she seemed more poised and stylish than Gibb—over time they locked into a perfectly presentable rapport, the cheese laid on extra thick. But at times you had to wonder whether Andy's personal problems had derailed his self-respect, judging by the following typical on-set exchange.

'Good evening and welcome to TV's most exciting hour of contemporary music,' ran the usual Andy intro, as he and McCoo did a gentle boogaloo, before cutting to a song from the 'Godfather of Funk' James Brown.

'You know, Marilyn,' Andy said on their return, 'I can't think of a more exciting way to start off *Solid Gold* than with a living legend like James Brown.'

'I agree,' cooed McCoo. 'And he'll be back a little later to talk with Madam.' (Madam was *Solid Gold*'s surly septuagenarian hand puppet, the show's answer to Miss Piggy.)

Andy rolled his eyes in response, a move he may well have picked up from Bob Hope. 'What a terrible thing to do to a living legend.'

'Well, you can't become a living legend without some suffering.'

Talk then turned to their next guest, Sheena Easton. McCoo said she enjoyed listening to Easton's records; Andy confessed he enjoyed 'watching them'. McCoo was puzzled—how do you watch a record?

'Well, what you have to understand, Marilyn, is that when a beautiful woman is singing, a man's imagination becomes very active. I can almost see her now ...'

When Andy and McCoo weren't warbling 'I Just Want to Be Your Everything', hamming up 'Why Do Fools Fall in Love?' with a little help from the *Solid Gold* dancers, or intro'ing their weekly guests, Andy was duetting with such stars of the moment as Marie Osmond and Crystal Gayle. But then, true to form, Andy started to unravel. Over time, he developed a dubious reputation with his fellow cast and crew. It was rumoured that as Andy became increasingly unreliable, two versions of *Solid Gold* would be prepared each week—one if Andy showed up to film the episode, the other if he didn't. The cause was likely the same problem—drug binges, essentially—that had destroyed his love match with Principal. Gibb was eventually let go after one full season as co-host.

In late 1982, Andy was hired for the lead in a production of *Joseph and the Amazing Technicolor Dreamcoat.* He appeared on TV in the lead-up to the Broadway debut and couldn't have been more excited. 'Broadway,' he exulted, 'that's the peak of theatre, everyone's dream.' It was also the last roll of the dice for Andy's career.

When asked about the lively couple of years when he first broke big, Andy admitted that success came with its in-built problems. 'It certainly made me spoiled,' he said. 'I thought it was always going to be that way, No.1 records and stuff. I'd be foolish to deny you get an ego. It's been a pretty wild rollercoaster ride.' Once again, the talk drifted to his legendary siblings; Andy claimed they helped keep him together.

But even during the show's pre-Broadway run in Philadelphia, the same problems arose with No Show Andy. He missed several performances in Philly, then, when the show did open on Broadway on 1 December—to mainly positive notices—he skipped dress rehearsals and at least a dozen performances soon after the show launched. He was hired to give eight performances a week, but it was all too much for the 24-year-old. 'When Andy was at the theatre, he was a joy,' said producer Zev Bufman. 'But he wasn't there enough. It wasn't fair to the audience.'

'Andy loved being in the show,' insisted his publicist Michael Sterling, 'he loved the company of other actors. [But] he just took on something he couldn't handle.'

To his credit, Gibb was generous. He handed out impressive Christmas gifts to everyone in the show and invited cast members to share his shiny black, chauffeur-driven limo. But after missing every one of the holiday week shows, Bufman had a little chat with his wayward star. 'Andy,' he said, 'you just can't keep missing shows. Missing performances is reserved for the dying.' He cited Elizabeth Taylor taking the stage in *The Little Foxes* while she was wheelchair-bound. The show must go on, he instructed Andy.

Gibb agreed and said that if he missed another performance, he'd quit. It didn't quite work out that way—after going AWOL yet again, when *Joseph* was six weeks into its Broadway run, he was fired.

While it's possible he was still working his way through a mountain of cocaine, Andy's cast members felt he 'suffered from an overdose of fear', chronic stage-fright. One actor was quoted by *People* magazine: 'I guess he was frightened and insecure. That's what happens when you're the baby brother of the Bee Gees.' Andy spent much of his time off-stage slumped in a chair, staring at a TV screen, just like big brother Barry in London when the Bee Gees fell apart in 1970.

Upon his sacking, Andy flew back to a home he kept in Malibu, mother Barbara at his side. Now, *sans* high-profile girlfriend, record label deal, management and TV gig, Andy was again adrift.

Yet he still had some true believers. An agent named Jeff Witjas offered to represent him, convinced that Andy still had the necessary charisma to rebuild his career. Andy agreed, and together they built a Las Vegas-style stage show, which they took to Atlantic City and Bally's Casino in Vegas, and then on the road. But even though Andy's career seemed back on track, his deep insecurity was never far away.

After one particularly well-received show, Andy sat in the dressing room, dejected. Witjas asked him if he had a problem. 'I gave a terrible performance,' insisted Andy.

Witjas was flummoxed. 'But everyone loved you.'

After a long silence, Andy raised his sad eyes to his manager. 'Did you see that girl in the second row? She was practically falling asleep.'

Witjas simply didn't know what to say. There must have been a thousand people in the room, loving the show—and Andy had zeroed in on the one person who wasn't having the night of her life. What *could* he say?

Dionne Warwick, who'd worked with Andy on *Solid Gold*, was the next big star to reach out to the Gibbs to help revitalise their career. Warwick had experienced a dream run in the 1960s, cutting 'Do You Know the Way to San Jose?', 'Message to Michael' and 'Walk on By', among others, legendary songs culled from the platinum-plated songbook of Hal David and Burt Bacharach. But in the wake of Bacharach and David's split, Warwick had only bothered the charts twice in the 1970s, with '74's 'Then Came You' and, five years later, 'I'll Never Love This Way Again'. And neither captured the same magic as her signature Bacharach-David songs.

Warwick's specialty, in the words of *Rolling Stone*, was 'her delivery—cool, swinging and unerring'. She needed to find some of that cool if she was to reclaim her role in the pop mainstream.

What Warwick had in mind was essentially what Streisand and Barry had achieved with *Guilty*: a slick, modern pop record. She teamed with Barry between April and May 1982, at the Gibbs' base,

Middle Ear Studio in Miami Beach. Just as he'd done with Streisand, Barry roughed out a sketch of a song with producer Albhy Galuten, in February, before he and Warwick started work, with Mo also helping. The song was 'Heartbreaker'.

On his way home from the studio, Mo, a huge Warwick fan, had second thoughts about 'Heartbreaker'. The Bee Gees hadn't charted since 1979—a 'comeback' record, 1981's polished *Living Eyes*, the first-ever album manufactured on CD for demonstration purposes, had not caused much of a stir—and now 'Heartbreaker', destined for Warwick, was an obvious hit if he'd ever heard one. '*We* should be doing this,' Mo thought to himself. '*We should be doing this!*'

But it was too late; the deal was set in stone. Yet even then Warwick needed convincing that the song was right for her. Eventually she accepted that the Gibbs knew best. 'It's going to be a smash,' they assured her. Warwick later joked that she 'cried all the way to the bank'. Mo could take some solace in his co-writing credit.

'Heartbreaker' came out in September 1982, just as Aussies Air Supply ('Even the Nights Are Better') and Men at Work ('Who Can It Be Now?') were charting high in the US. Come January 1983 and 'Heartbreaker' had cracked open the US Top 10 and was well on its way to becoming Warwick's biggest hit since the late 1960s—and her best-performing single of the new decade. The core of the *Heartbreaker* album, which surfaced in late September 1982, featured the Midas touch of the three Gibbs, who co-wrote six of the 10 tracks. Barry co-wrote three others with Galuten. The album would sell around three million copies worldwide, proving that the Gibbs' success with Streisand was no fluke. It seemed that they'd invented a whole new line of work for themselves, tunesmiths for hire, resurrecting the careers of fading stars.

Streisand and Warwick's success, as it turned out, was just the beginning. Barry had sketched out another song, 'Islands in the Stream', once again while working at home in Miami. The name was borrowed from a novel by Ernest Hemingway—Mo had chanced upon it and mentioned that it would make a great song title. 'We knew we had a monster song,' Barry said, 'but we just didn't know who was going to record it.'

Their original target was maverick soulman Marvin Gaye, perhaps even Diana Ross, but then veteran country crooner Kenny Rogers reached out to the Gibbs. The 40-something Rogers, greying, whiskery and avuncular, was in a similar position to Dionne Warwick: his career had started with a volley of hits ('Ruby, Don't Take Your Love to Town' in 1969 and more recently, 'Coward of the County'), but he needed a reboot, a song that would make him more than a country superstar. Rogers was keen to record 'Islands' but Barry dug in, insisting that, like Warwick and Streisand before him, Rogers had to commit to an entire album. He agreed.

Rogers worked with Barry, Galuten and Richardson at Inner Ear, but wasn't happy with the first version of 'Islands in the Stream'. A close listen indicated that Rogers was playing it safe, sticking very closely to the Barry demo; his vocal had the same softness as Barry's. It was good but not great. Everything changed when Dolly Parton was brought into the production.

The Tennessee-born Parton, then in her late 30s, had started to 'cross-over' from pure country to pop in the late 1970s, thanks to such hits as 'Here You Come Again', which won her a Grammy in 1978. But her career exploded when she co-starred in the office comedy movie *9 to 5* and sang the title track. In February 1981, '9 to 5' achieved a rare double crown for Parton, topping the pop and country charts at the same time. The film, meanwhile, grossed $103 million in America alone.

With the addition of Parton's rhinestone-studded starpower, 'Islands in the Stream' rocketed into the charts, reaching No.1 in late October 1983. The single went on to sell several million copies, one of the biggest country-pop hits of all time, and a signature song for both artists to this day. *Eyes That See in the Dark*, the album Rogers agreed to record with Barry and his team, was another massive hit, the biggest of Rogers' lengthy career, selling millions of copies worldwide. Yet again, the Gibbs had a hefty slice of the songwriting pie, contributing to each of the LP's 10 tracks.

'Islands' and *Eyes That See in the Dark* were the third instalment in a remarkable hot streak for the Gibbs, in particular Barry. The slight twangy flavour of this project must have also stirred memories for the eldest Gibb, who'd tried to make a country-flavoured solo record of his own, *The Kid's No Good*, when the Bee Gees first came unstuck after their '60s' heyday.

The 1980s were proving as lucrative as the *Fever* era for the Gibbs—and this time around they had no need to don the satin and bling. Barry and Linda purchased a new Miami mansion in 1981, at Biscayne Bay, the jewel in the crown of a range of Gibb properties, which also included a 36.4-hectare estate near London. Over time, his real estate portfolio alone would be worth around US$20 million.

Andy, meanwhile, was desperately trying to salvage his ailing career—and search for his own identity. He was spending more time in LA in an attempt to go it alone and not be just another famous Gibb from Miami. In September 1983, Andy signed on for a cameo in the popular NBC sitcom *Gimme a Break*. Although lightweight, the show was a magnet for high-profile guest stars: Whitney Houston, Sammy Davis Jr, Milton Berle and Don Rickles had all appeared on *Gimme a Break*.

Perky, blonde, 21-year-old actress Kari Michaelsen, who played Katie in the show, was perhaps the biggest Andy Gibb fan on the planet. When it was revealed that Andy would be their next big cameo, the rest of the cast teased her relentlessly: her Gibb crush was no secret. On the first day of his guest spot, Andy joined the cast for a script read-through. Everyone sat around a table, reading their lines, the usual practice. But it seemed as though Andy read all his lines directly to Michaelsen. Clearly, something was happening. As she would recall, 'It was an immediate attraction between the two of us. There was just something there—a chemistry.'

Over lunch, and throughout the week when he was on the set, that spark ignited. While Andy and Michaelsen didn't share a scene, they couldn't be prised apart off-camera. Andy's final love affair was underway.

It seemed that Andy had learned a lot from his very public romance with Victoria Principal. For their first date, rather than treading a red carpet, he and Michaelsen visited his parents, Hugh and Barbara, and snuggled together on the family couch while watching a movie. The new couple kept well under the radar, spending quiet nights at his house, avoiding the Hollywood paparazzi. Then Andy's demons returned. Weeks would pass between calls to Michaelsen, and then when he did get in contact, he'd push her away.

'I don't want you to see me this way,' he told her, without going into any detail of his condition or whereabouts.

Ever since the runaway success of 1977's *Saturday Night Fever*—which earned almost $100 million at the box office and, with a lot of help from the Bee Gees, generated the most successful soundtrack album of all time to date—Robert Stigwood had been planning a sequel. Finally in 1983 John Travolta agreed to resurrect his role as disco king Tony Manero, now six years down the line. The 25-year-old Manero had left Brooklyn for Manhattan, living in a dump while he waited tables and worked as a dance instructor, his gaze fixed on Broadway. In between trying to juggle women and advance his career, Manero returned briefly to Brooklyn—only to discover that his former hangout, Odyssey, was now a gay nightclub. Disco was well and truly dead. Stayin' Alive? Hardly.

Stiggy, of course, knew that Travolta was only one part of the equation—he also needed his boys, the Gibbs, to provide the soundtrack to the movie. In February and March 1983, the three Gibbs convened in Middle Ear, cutting five new tracks—'The Woman in You', 'I Love You Too Much', 'Breakout', 'Someone Belonging to Someone' and 'Life Goes On'—as well as dusting off 'Stayin' Alive', which would be the film's signature song, a flashback to the era of mirror balls and wide, wide lapels. The new songs were slick and solid, but apart from the heartfelt ballad 'Someone', lacked the magic touch of the *Fever* hits. The same could be said for the movie. Interestingly, the flipside of the soundtrack LP comprised songs written by Frank Stallone, whose A-list brother Sylvester, fresh from his Rocky successes, directed the film. Frank Stallone was also cast in the film.

Released in June 1983, the *Staying Alive* soundtrack was a modest success by *Saturday Night Fever* standards, selling 4.5 million copies worldwide. Although these seemed reasonable numbers given the

Gibbs' time out of the spotlight, when stacked up against the 15 million-plus copies *Fever* sold in North America alone, *Staying Alive* was a failure. The film fared better, despite mediocre notices, roughly tripling its $20 million budget at the box office. But it simply wasn't the same as *Fever*; this was no zeitgeist moment, just another predictable Hollywood sequel.

Mo, Robin and Barry set out to promote both soundtrack album and film, but as was the case throughout the Gibbs' shadowy '80s— and the rest of their later lives and careers, for that matter—talk always seemed to return to former glories. Even while discussing *Staying Alive*, *Saturday Night Fever* remained the key topic of interest. Their shared past seemed far more tantalising than the present. 'It was a marriage of music and movie,' figured Mo, when he and his brothers talked about *Fever* with the host of TV's *Good Morning Britain*. 'There were all these elements. The country needed to dance.'

The subject shifted to Barry's discovery of his falsetto voice during the recordings with Arif Mardin, that pivotal moment when the producer asked, 'Can any of you scream in tune?'

Looking at Barry, Mo joked, 'And we gave you a swift kick.'

'That sound can be looked upon as very feminine,' said Barry, sounding very much like a man who's been called on to regularly defend his masculinity, 'so we had to be careful. But then we looked at other groups like the Stylistics, who had an enormous amount of success with that sound, so we just went for it.'

Promotional duties done, and with no interest in going back on the road, the three Gibbs returned to what they did best in the 1980s: writing hits for others.

Diana Ross was yet another superstar in desperate need of a boost. As leading lady of the Supremes, Ross had, erm, reigned supreme during the 1960s, recording such Motown hits as 'Love Child', 'Baby Love' and 'Stop! In the Name of Love'. Ross' 1970s, however, had been less productive, with only the occasional hit single, such as 1975's 'Theme from Mahogany'—a film in which Ross starred—and the disco-tinged 'Love Hangover'. It had been almost five years since her last bona-fide hit single, and even then it was a recycled oldie, a remake of 'Why Do Fools Fall in Love?' Like all those others before her, it seemed that Ross knew that the phone number to call in her hour of need was that of the Bee Gees.

When the prospect of writing for Ross was mooted, Barry immediately set to work, tailoring something for the 41-year-old. When he shared 'Chain Reaction' with Robin and Mo, Barry feared he might have been a little too successful. 'It was so Tamla Motown-ish,' he admitted, 'we were scared of playing it to her. We thought she wouldn't want to go back there.' (All of Barry's original demos, including the songs for Streisand, Warwick, Ross and Kenny Rogers, were later released under such names as *The Guilty Demos*, *The Heartbreaker Demos*, and so on.)

Despite a little resistance, Ross recognised the song as an homage to her stellar work with the Supremes, and cut the single. Oddly, 'Chain Reaction' charted poorly in the US, but became her second solo No.1 single in the UK. The record, which would be Ross's final appearance on the single charts, also topped the charts in Australia, becoming 1986's biggest-selling single. Once again, 'Chain Reaction' was part of a larger package, the Gibbs contributing to all 10 songs on Ross' album *Eaten Alive*, which was released in September 1985.

While his brothers were busy building their very own house of hits, Andy finally accepted the hopelessness of his situation, and checked into the Palm Springs Betty Ford Clinic in April 1985. Barbara Gibb accompanied Andy to rehab, and on his request, called Kari Michaelsen. 'Andy's asking for you,' Barbara told her. 'Will you come and see him?'

Michaelsen still loved Andy, despite his recklessness, and agreed in a heartbeat. She brought a guitar and encouraged Andy to write and play some music, rebuild his sense of worth. 'I watched him come back,' she said, 'a little bit more, every single week.'

Andy talked a lot about Peta to Kari, and how he'd like to build some bridges with his estranged daughter. Sadly, that would never happen.

On his release from Betty Ford, Andy knew he had to make changes. He moved out of his Malibu house—too many bad memories—and entered Alcoholics Anonymous, following its 12-step program. But he continued to relapse and blew any chance of reconciling with Michaelsen. And work was almost impossible to secure; Andy was just too unreliable. A few years earlier he'd been the host of a top-rating TV show and had three straight No.1 pop hits, earning millions, driving a Porsche, living the high life, flying only on private planes, snorting away $1000 a day on coke. Now in 1985, Andy struggled to earn $500 a week. That sum would diminish further over time; eventually he'd file for bankruptcy.

In an attempt to put a positive spin on his broken career, Andy agreed to a Lifetime TV network interview in 1985, recorded at his new digs in LA. Father Hugh hovered in the background, clearly concerned for his damaged son.

The Lifetime interviewer began with the usual soft question about the role his brothers played in his career. 'I don't honestly think I'd be here now if it wasn't for them,' Andy conceded. 'Who knows how it would have worked out?'

The conversation then ranged from family downtime in Miami— apparently the Gibb clan liked to stay in, plunk away on guitars, drink tea and watch the telly, just like regular superstars—and his fallout with Principal. 'It was so intense, our relationship,' a forlorn Andy admitted.

Once again, he owned up to suffering a nervous breakdown, hardly reassuring news for any potential employer.

What about drugs, he was asked. Who knew about your problems and what did they do about it? Andy admitted that he tried to keep his coke problem to himself, but his family finally intervened, which led to his six-week stretch at Betty Ford. 'It got to the point of danger,' said Andy, who believed he'd 'never be cured'. The best he could do, in recovery speak, was to take things 'one day at a time'.

As the interview wound up, Andy made a frank admission. 'I've failed a lot. I've let a lot of people down. Life to death is all one big lesson, that's what I think. I'm just not going to get hurt like I did before; I don't want to go through that again. No way.'

Andy had spoken with Barry about possibly returning to the studio. He also had a Royal Command Performance coming up, where he would headline an all-Aussie line-up that included singers John Farnham and Glenn Shorrock, performing for Princess Anne. 'Though I'd rather be performing for Lady Di,' Andy laughed.

Andy now seemed to spend more time explaining himself and his behaviour, and talking up his future, than singing or performing.


Years had passed since the last Bee Gees record, 1981's *Living Eyes*, time they'd devoted to cranking out hits for superstars, and in which Robin had quietly released a trio of solo records: *How Old Are You?*, *Secret Agent* and *Walls Have Eyes*. But by 1987, the brothers felt that enough time had elapsed since the *Fever* phenom for them to record again. It was a chance for them to be judged by the music they would make, rather than the music they'd previously made, or the craze they'd help nurture.

The Bee Gees signed with a new record label, Warner Bros. Fellow Stiggy client, Eric Clapton, had just shifted his business to Warner and achieved success with the albums *Money and Cigarettes* and *Behind the Sun*, surely a good omen. It was Clapton, after all, who tipped them off to Miami—and look what came out of that. The brothers had known Mo Ostin, the label's chairman and Frank Sinatra's former right-hand man, for many years, and trusted him. They also needed to put some distance between themselves and Stigwood; the Gibbs' estrangement with their mentor had continued to grow since the problems with the *Guilty* project.

'[Ostin's] always believed in what we were doing,' said Barry.

Barry remained a prolific songwriter, the type of obsessive who kept a dictaphone beside his bed for those moments when the muse might descend on him without warning. One morning in 1987, he was jolted awake at 4 a.m., a melody and lyric stuck inside his head, something along the lines of 'you win again'. He groggily hit the record button, but discovered there was no tape in the machine. Barry was now awake and in a mild panic. He dashed about the house, trying to find a tape, capture the moment. To his relief he finally got it down. He called Robin early the next day. 'What do you think?' Barry asked, playing his brother a sketch of 'You Win Again'.

'It's great. Let's cut it.'

Mo had set up a basic recording studio in his garage, where they set to work on a demo. The song, at this stage, had no drums; nor were there any in Mo's studio. So the brothers improvised, finding anything that made some kind of percussive noise—bins, whatever— and flailed away. They backed this up with some heavy foot stomps, which would become the rhythmic core of the song.

But there was a problem. When they got to New York to start officially recording 'You Win Again', the Gibbs thought they were to start from scratch, fashion a new song using the demo recording as a blueprint, as with most studio sessions. But their programmer, Rhett Lawrence, asked, 'Have you got the stomps?'

The brothers hadn't thought to bring along the Miami demo.

'You've got to get the stomps,' said Lawrence. 'They make the record.'

The Gibbs flew back to their southern base, where they'd 'sampled' the stomps on a drum machine, which they then burned onto a disk and sent to New York.

Yet when 'You Win Again' was premiered to the staff at Warners, not everyone was sold on the stomping, the tsunami of sound that gave the song real muscle. For once, the Gibbs dug in. 'They stay.'

The Bee Gees were proved right. As comebacks go, 'You Win Again' was hard to beat. While no great hit in America, this defiant pop anthem topped the UK chart late in 1987, their first smash of the decade. It also established an impressive landmark for the Bee Gees: they'd now had UK chart toppers in the 1960s, '70s and '80s, the first group to do so. 'You Win Again' claimed another coveted Ivor Novello award—it was even Lady Diana's favourite song, according to Mo.

As for the stomps, they became desirable property. One day, Phil Collins spotted Mo in an airport and rushed over. 'Can you give me a copy of the stomps?' Collins pleaded.


Perfect-haired *MTV* Australia host Richard Wilkins caught up with the Bee Gees in 1987, soon after 'You Win Again' began to climb the charts. The 1980s might have been a period of change for the Gibbs, but as the camera rolled, Barry's appearance—hirsute, sun-kissed—and his role as group leader and big brother remained unchanged. Florida was now very much the Gibbs' home. Everything about the place suited them, including the climate ('It reminds us very much of Queensland,' noted Barry) and the geography—it was close enough to showbiz centres such as New York and LA and not too far on Concorde from London. 'It's nice to get up in the morning and get some sun before going into the studio,' added Maurice. 'Relax *and* work.'

The Bee Gees' recently released album *E.S.P.*, a reunion with producer Arif Mardin, their first collaboration since 1975, was a success. But their audience had shifted; now the UK and Europe was where things were happening for them. Their American popularity was fading. *E.S.P.* had sold 30,000 copies in the UK in one day, much on the strength of 'You Win Again'—not quite *Fever* numbers, admittedly, but not a bad bounce-back.

Each of the brothers had an explanation for the group's commercial slide in America. Robin blamed a pop culture that was now 'very video-obsessed, image-obsessed', an unconvincing logic given how visual and image-obsessed disco had been. Barry talked about the 'saturation situation' that had occurred in the wake of *Fever*. There'd simply been too much Bee Gees. 'The question,' declared Barry, 'was who was going to allow us to forget the *Fever* thing', and let the group move on.

'You Win Again' failed to crack the US Top 20 and *E.S.P.* reached only No.96 in the *Billboard* Hot 200 album chart. Yet in the UK and Europe, where the group had been out of hits since 1979, the *E.S.P.* album went on to sell more than a million copies.

'[But] I don't think America is the most important,' Barry stressed. 'Wherever the heat is, that's important to us. Europe has given us back the respect we had before *Fever*, which is very special to us. We're trying to prove that the Bee Gees are as good as they ever were, just six years later.'

So where had they been, asked Wilkins. Six years was a long time between albums. The one thing left unsaid, of course, was Mo's drinking problem, but that was deftly sidestepped—with a joke, naturally. 'For the past six years,' Barry explained, 'life has been relatively quiet. We've been bringing up our kids, being normal people for a while—which is especially difficult in Robin's case.

'We really tried to broaden our songwriting,' he continued, 'not be the Bee Gees for a little while. In doing that, we decided to write

for other artists and produce them. It's worked very well for us …
whether Streisand, Kenny Rogers, Dolly Parton, Dionne Warwick,
Diana Ross—we have an unbroken record. But I think probably one
of the highest moments was [Ross'] "Chain Reaction". It's nice to
see it do well in Australia.' The single had topped the Oz charts in
March 1986.

Working with Barbra Streisand was, Barry told Wilkins, another
big moment. After all, he actually got to sing on his own song, 'Guilty',
which won a Grammy. 'It certainly wasn't the Barbra Streisand we
expected to work with,' he said. 'You know, a bit of ego … Barbra
turned out to be the opposite.'

As was their way, however, whenever an interview took a reflective
turn, the brothers managed to change the topic. In this case, Barry
directed the conversation with Wilkins to Michael Jackson and his
hit *Thriller*, and how video-driven that monster was. Barry wasn't so
sure that the rise of video—*MTV* was still just three years old—was
a good thing for musicians and songwriters. 'A video director comes
along and makes a video that has no relation whatsoever to the song,'
noted Barry, 'and you don't have much control. You're so far down the
line, you might be 200 grand down … It can get out of your control.'

Control was key to the Gibbs as they settled into the third phase
of their career. They were no longer working with Stigwood; they'd
changed labels. Everything was new. Next up was a world tour, starting
in Europe in May, then Australia in July and America after that.

So, asked Wilkins, did they have a 10-year plan?

'We can't see ourselves being the Bee Gees in our 50s,' Barry
admitted with more candour than usual. 'We'd like to make films.'

'That and doing Polaroids for *Hustler* on the weekend,' added
Robin, clearly tiring of the interview.

The brothers' fallout with Robert Stigwood, the Bee Gees' patron saint, had been some years in the making, dating back to time of the Streisand project. RSO, Stigwood's label and the then recording home of the group, had initially forbidden Barry to undertake the work without its consent. Soon after, the Bee Gees, clearly unimpressed by RSO's edict, sued for release from all ties with Stiggy, claiming a conflict of interest on his part—he was, after all, their label head, manager and music publisher. Had been for years. The Gibbs also commissioned an audit of RSO's accounts and claimed Stigwood had withheld millions of dollars in royalties. They wanted out of their RSO contract and were seeking something like $75 million compensation, along with the return of all their master recordings and copyrights. The empire, in short.

Stiggy, holed up in Bermuda, shot back that he was 'angry, dismayed, revolted' by the goings-on. Finally, having digested the Gibbs' claims, he responded with a whopping $310 million suit of his own, claiming that the brothers had libelled him; he also accused them of extortion and breach of contract. Stigwood also let it be known that they had history, saying, with some validity, that he'd transformed the Gibbs from 'penniless youths into multi-millionaires'.

Regardless of who was 'right'—if indeed anyone was—it was a messy chapter in a relationship that was closer than family. Without Stigwood's enthusiasm back in 1967, the Gibbs may as well have jumped back onto the *Fairsky* and returned to Australia.

An out-of-court settlement was finally reached between the warring parties, but even then the Gibbs felt it necessary in mid-1981 to take out a full-page ad-cum-declaration of independence in both *Variety* and *Rolling Stone*. It was also a rebuke to some fighting words expressed to *Rolling Stone* by Freddie Gershon, the head of RSO.

Gershon said that the Gibbs had dropped their suit because they'd decided it simply wasn't worth the hassle; litigation, in Gershon's view, may well have shown them 'that Stigwood has always treated them fairly and correctly … They dropped the suit and went away with their tail between their legs.'

'First and foremost,' read the group's terse response, 'the Bee Gees have never "apologised" to Robert Stigwood or RSO; this has never been the case, nor will it ever be the case, no matter what any other press article may claim.'

*Living Eyes* was their final release for RSO, the 1981 album completing their contractual obligations with the label.

Mo's boozing notwithstanding, it's little wonder that the Gibbs continued as songwriters-for-hire through much of the 1980s. The fallout from the clash with Stigwood was toxic. However, Dick Ashby, a stalwart from the NEMS days, continued working with the group as their personal manager.

Around the time of the *E.S.P.* album, Barry, Mo and Robin tried to help Andy, who'd recently declared bankruptcy, owing former manager Stigwood $1 million. Barry, always the closest to his youngest brother, spent time with him in Miami, playing tennis and hanging out. But Barry knew Andy's health was poor. He sometimes had trouble breathing and suffered intense chest pains. Andy was hospitalised. He was diagnosed with myocarditis, an infection of the heart. He'd have to curb his lifestyle, immediately. A stimulant such as cocaine was dangerous at the best of times, but for someone with Andy's condition it could be fatal.

Andy found himself feeling well enough to return to the Gibbs'

Inner Ear studio to cut four new tracks with Barry. On playback, both believed that Andy's spark had returned—one song in particular stood out, 'Man On Fire'. A new recording deal was discussed with UK-based Island Records, the label of choice for acts as diverse as Traffic, reggae star Jimmy Cliff and folkies Fairport Convention. The meeting had been set in place by Barry. Andy shifted base to the UK in January 1988, staying next door to Robin, who was living in his Oxfordshire manor house with his second wife, Dwina Murphy, an artist with a keen interest in Druidism. The brothers ensured Andy had pocket money, giving him $200 a week to get by. Robin told a reporter that Andy's health had improved and he was ready to record again. The future looked bright.

Andy's 30th birthday, on 5 March, was fast approaching. Mo called Andy to wish him many happy returns. Instead, a distressed Robin answered the phone.

'Where's Andy?' Mo asked.

'He can't come to the phone,' Robin said. 'He's out of his skull.'

Robin revealed that Andy had been slipping away to the off-licence and binging heavily. Again. He was a mess. Robin suspected that Andy was in the grip of a major depression. His old insecurities had resurfaced: he was unsure if had real talent or was just a product of his famous surname.

This was all too much for Mo, who knew a fair bit about the perils of overindulgence. 'Well, tell him to sod off!' Mo barked, before hanging up the phone with a thud.

'How could he?' Mo asked Yvonne soon after. 'When will he learn?'

That night, Mo dreamed Andy died. 'It scared the hell out of me,' he said afterwards.

Big brother Barry had a similar situation. He managed to get Andy on the phone, but the conversation was fiery. 'You've got to get your act together,' Barry snapped. 'Now!' Then he too hung up, angry and disappointed at Andy's relapse.

Barry's tough love didn't work. After celebrating his 30th birthday in London, Andy suffered further chest pains and was taken to John Radcliffe Hospital in Oxford. On 10 March, Mo's phone rang. It was one of Robin's staff. 'Andy's dead.' Mo dropped the phone.

Andy's myocarditis had killed him, a diagnosis confirmed by Beverly Hills cardiologist William Shell, who had recently treated him, and backed up by a statement from John Radcliffe Hospital, which also read: 'There is no evidence that his death is related to drink or drugs.' But there's little dispute that his excessive lifestyle didn't help his condition, although an overdose death, which some tabloids hinted at, just wasn't the case. One rag blared: 'Cocaine Kills Andy Gibb.' His brothers asked questions that were beyond their ability to answer: What if we'd made him a Bee Gee—would that have helped? Did we do enough for Andy? They thought about the nights on the 'Spirits Having Flown' tour, when Andy would join them for 'You Should Be Dancing'. He'd never seemed happier.

Barry said that Andy's death was the 'saddest moment of my life'. He regretted encouraging Andy's showbiz career; Barry had bought him his first guitar, for Andy's 12th birthday. 'He would have been better off finding something else.'

Robert Stigwood was as devastated as Barry, Mo and Robin. He had helped launch Andy's career and tried hard to guide and support him. 'One mustn't think he was some dope who let himself go on drugs,' said Stiggy. 'So many artists have been through that drug scene. It was his weak heart—he couldn't afford the stress of the lifestyle he'd adopted.'

Andy's body was flown to the US, where he was interred at Hollywood's Forest Lawn Memorial Park, the final resting place of Lucille Ball, Liberace and Bette Davis. His headstone bore a simple message: 'Andy Gibb … March 5, 1958—March 10, 1988 … An Everlasting Love'. His mourners, which included all the Gibbs and close friends such as Olivia Newton-John, were overwhelmed by grief. No one could believe he was dead. He was just so young.

Mo, in particular, felt huge despair, flashing back to his final, aborted call to Andy only a few days earlier. As Mo and the others drove away from the cemetery, Andy's coffin was being readied to be placed inside the Forest Lawn mausoleum. At that moment, Mo looked out the rear window of the limo and saw Andy's not-yet-interred casket. He'd never seen such a lonely sight. He was tempted to tell the driver to turn back. 'There was no one else there,' Mo would recall, 'just his coffin, resting against this wall. I felt like he'd been abandoned.'

Andy Gibb had sold 15 million records by age 21 and his first three singles had all reached No.1 in America, an unprecedented achievement. But just like his health, his career had been in decline for several years. As *People* magazine reported after his death, 'In a way, Andy Gibb's story ended a long time ago, and whether it could have had a fresh beginning we will never know.'

Mo, Robin and Barry felt that the best way for them to mourn was to write music together. A week after Andy's death, they gathered in the studio, thinking it would be the best way to both grieve and refocus. But it simply didn't work; their sense of loss was just too much. All three Gibb brothers broke down in tears and went home.

The brothers' grieving was long. Their hearts had never been heavier. A song in honour of Andy did eventually come together, 'Wish You Were Here', centrepiece of their new album, *One*, which dropped mid-1989. Finally, after an absence of 10 years, the Bee Gees went back on the road, having recently returned to performing with such high-profile one-offs as a concert for Nelson Mandela, a 40th anniversary celebration of Atlantic Records, and the Prince's Trust 30th Birthday Concert. They now had a reason to tour again, to mourn their lost brother.

The 'One for All' tour—its name a nod to a proposed but never fulfilled tour with Andy that had been slated for 1989—kicked off in Germany on 3 May, before setting down in 19 different European cities. Their crowd-pulling power hadn't diminished; at one show in Hanover they drew 50,000 fans, the mood in the stadium so upbeat that the brothers managed to drag Hugh out on stage. In Hamburg they dedicated 'You Win Again' to a glowing Steffi Graf, champion tennis player, who was looking on from the stands. In the US, boosted by the hype of their first tour since *Spirits Having Flown*, *One* made a surprise appearance in the Top 10.

During the usual round of press conferences, Barry still came across a tad defensive, especially when the madness of the *Fever*-era was discussed. He'd heard way too much talk of discos and big flares and John Travolta striking poses and pointing at the ceiling. The Bee Gees had been making music for 30 years, he wanted to remind people, there was much more to them than *Saturday Night* Bloody *Fever*. 'I want to see the Bee Gees where they are not made fun of,' said Barry. 'It may never happen, but I don't care. I'm prepared for the fight.'

Barry went even further in an interview with *Rolling Stone*, when asked specifically about the song 'Stayin' Alive'. 'We'd like to dress it up in a white suit and gold chains and set it on fire.' It was quite the statement from the typically cautious Gibb.

Still, the Gibbs remained crowd-pleasers, padding their set with 'Jive Talkin'', 'Nights on Broadway', 'How Deep Is Your Love'—usually dedicated to Andy—'Stayin' Alive' and 'You Should Be Dancing', along with newer material from *One* and a bevy of 1960s standards. Their setlist was a Bee Gees all-sorts, spanning three decades of music-making, a stark reminder they were much more than the *Fever* guys. They knew their fans wanted the hits and nothing but and served them up accordingly. The brothers also reclaimed the hits they'd recently written for others, strumming their way through a medley of 'Heartbreaker' and 'Islands In the Stream'.

The lengthy world tour neared its end, fittingly, with a run of sold-out shows in Australia. In Oz their dates were co-promoted by David Trew, who'd been the promoter for their early 1970s tours and even earlier, winning their trust forever by once plying the teenage brothers with pies and soft drink after a far-flung country show. Throughout November 1989 the Gibbs played to full houses in Canberra, then Adelaide, followed by two gigs apiece in Perth, Melbourne and Brisbane, with three shows in Sydney. The demand was huge—not surprisingly, really, given that they hadn't toured Australia during the heady *Spirits-Fever* days.

The Australian shows struck just the right balance of showbiz and musicality, big hair and stadium-sized production. The garish outfits of *Fever* were gone, replaced by up-scale street clothes: blue jeans, black shirts, a tailored suit jacket for Robin, who stood centrestage, and a slick leather number for Mo, who shuffled between keyboards and guitar. They were all in fine voice, too, chiming together on the set opener 'Ordinary Lives' as if they'd spent every night of the past 10 years on stage.

Barry, despite the physical restrictions brought on by recent back problems—the pain was so bad he'd started talking about surgery, and he winced frequently—still looked every inch the leader, the big brother, his swept-back hair shining as brightly as his perfect teeth. But he and his brothers gladly shared the spotlight with their razor-sharp backing band which cut loose on lesser-known numbers such as 'Giving Up the Ghost' and 'It's My Neighbourhood', songs that simply screamed 'contemporary pop', with their sleek synths, glacial grooves and cool vocals. There were no pyros, mirror balls, white suits or eruptions of blinding lights—the brothers' voices, and their vast catalogue of songs, were front and centre.

'Let's go back a few years,' Barry announced in Melbourne with one of his awkward giggles, 'and a few more, and a few more …' as they eased into the still glorious 'To Love Somebody', 'and a few more, and a few more …' Though in pain, Barry hadn't forgotten the whereabouts of his funny bone. The crowd erupted for the first of many times, a common occurrence in Australia, where there was a palpable sense of communion every night. A rockier, dynamic 'Gotta Get a Message to You' followed, Robin's hand clutched tight to his left ear, struggling to hear himself over the powerful band and the eager, full-throated audience who sang along. 'Words' was another early-set highlight, Barry moving to centrestage, illuminated by a single spot, pouring out his heart and soul, urging the crowd to help him out during the 'la-la-la-la-la' part of the chorus, then goofing it up with Mo when the room's collective roar drowned out his singing.

Sure, there was more than a whiff of Vegas, and it was a tad schmaltzy, but the connection between the Gibbs and their fans was very, very real. The crowd even leapt to their feet at the end of Robin's showpiece, the aching-hearted 'I Started a Joke', and at the end their applause was long and generous.

Then the brothers gathered around a single microphone, harmonising on 'New York Mining Disaster', their voices inter-twining sweetly. For a flash it was as though the Gibbs were back in the front room at Keppel Road, or on the flatbed barrelling around the Redcliffe Speedway, catching the flying pennies flung their way, their young lives full of possibilities.

'Spicks and Specks', a song that meant the world to their Australian fans, being the Bee Gees' first big hit at home, also brought the house down. Any resentment Barry may have felt about their 'rejection', having endured flop after flop in the 1960s, was long gone, washed away by the good vibes. In 'Holiday', Mo darted off stage and returned with one of the TV cameras being used to film their show, dashing about the stage like a starstruck fan, lightening the mood, distracting his brothers. Always the joker in the pack.

Even during the Bee Gees' well-received return to the stage and the charts, and his ever-chirpy on-stage demeanour, Mo's battle with the bottle continued. During one weekend at home in Miami, not long after Andy's death, with Yvonne and the kids out of town, Mo claimed to have put away four bottles of whisky, two bottles of brandy and eight gallons of Guinness—way more than a skinful. It eventually led to a second stint in rehab in the early 1990s.

Maurice agreed to sit down with British actress Lynn Redgrave to discuss his troubles. The result was the unsettling 1992 BBC program *Maurice Gibb: Fighting Back*. The interview was staged in Mo's stately, whitewashed mansion on Miami's Biscayne Bay, Redgrave disembarking from a boat at his private jetty. Mo greeted Redgrave in what had become his trademark look over the past decade: designer jeans, open shirt, black hat, tinted shades, dazzling smile, sculpted stubble. He looked every bit the successful man moving into middle age.

Yet the opening voice-over was in stark contrast to the peaceful, easy setting: 'A personal tragedy was in the making, as Maurice slid into the depths of alcoholism.' It was clear where this show was headed, despite the presence of the highly credible Redgrave.

Maurice was candid, opening up about his early encounters with booze—uncorking the old story about his idol John Lennon, the Speakeasy club in London and the scotch and Coke—and his never-ending party lifestyle while married to pop princess Lulu. As Mo recalled, they shared a life of 'no responsibilities—we'd party, we were never at home'.

Yet Mo's boozing continued even when he met and married Yvonne. He became a sly drunk, sneaking a scotch and Coke before breakfast, then drinking in secret. Mo kept 'back-up bottles' stashed throughout the house. 'Everyone knew I drank,' he told Redgrave, 'but not how much I drank. I didn't want anyone to know.'

Mo revealed to Redgrave that it was the post-*Fever* period when his musical deficiencies appeared. His bass parts would often be re-recorded by session players; sometimes he missed sessions altogether. Then there'd be the times on tour when Mo was so sloshed 'he had to feel his way along the wall to the stage'. Robin, in his separate interview with Redgrave, admitted to feeling more concerned for Mo's wellbeing than the group's performance.

As Mo's drinking intensified, his health suffered: he had problems with his liver, the curse of every career boozer. He'd wake up most mornings hugging the toilet bowl, vomiting copiously, before downing his first drink of the day. His state of mind was in bad shape, too. 'I was verbally abusive, arrogant, obnoxious, belligerent.' He somehow managed to be a good father to Samantha and Adam, but at the same time 'it was all me, me, me,' he confessed to Redgrave. 'I would always put myself before my wife and my children, which is what the disease [of alcoholism] does to you.'

Maurice's alcohol-induced issues came to a head soon after he returned from the group's 1991 tour of Europe. The tour was a huge success, an experience Mo shared with Yvonne who was on the road with him. But once he was back in Miami, his mood darkened. Mo was bored out of his mind, suffering from a classic case of post-tour comedown, with nothing to do but reflect on past and recent glories. There were no immediate Bee Gees plans. One day he jumped in his car and drove to the local supermarket, where he bought a bottle of brandy. So began a month-long bender.

Every day, Yvonne would ask Mo if he'd been drinking, but he was in extreme denial. 'Don't be a silly cow,' he'd snap at her, 'how dare you.'

Then Mo would head downstairs to his studio and down another brandy. He was now drinking straight brandy, no mixer, no ice. Almost every day he'd be driving into town to stock up. 'I didn't get drunk, I didn't get merry,' Mo admitted. 'I just got sicker and sicker.'

Mo kept a gun in the house—Barry did, too, as had Andy on his boat when he stayed in Miami. As Mo's drinking intensified, and after yet another row with Yvonne and the kids, she came downstairs and Mo, leglessly drunk, was holding the gun, a malevolent gleam in his eyes. 'Oh my gosh,' Adam thought, 'he's going to shoot us.'

Yvonne bolted upstairs, threw some essentials into a bag, grabbed the kids and raced out the door to Barry's house nearby. Once inside, Yvonne insisted that Barry lock the door. She had no idea what Maurice might do with that gun. 'I was determined,' Yvonne admitted, 'this time I wasn't coming back until he did something [about his drinking].'

After a couple of days, perhaps the bleakest time of their married life, Yvonne went back to the house to collect a few more things. Mo was in tears. 'I'm so sorry,' he sobbed. 'I know I have to do something about this.'

Barry summoned the family, *sans* Mo, to his house, isolating his brother. 'He needed to bottom out. He needed to realise that everyone around him was no longer going to support what he was doing. We just turned into a brick wall.'

It was one of the hardest things Barry had ever had to do, to tell his beloved brother, 'You no longer have our support.' But he knew it was necessary to save Mo's life.

Eventually, Mo, in his own estimation, 'just surrendered'. He accepted that he'd become a monster, someone who badly needed help. He approached his daughter Samantha and insisted that she throw the unloaded gun into the bay, which she did without a moment's thought. That was the first step. But Mo really needed to go back to rehab, to get straight, this time for good.

He already had a sponsor from his previous attempt to dry-out, a man named Louis. Louis passed along a number for a program called the New Life Substance Abuse Centre. The in-house addiction expert was 60-year-old Dr Jules Trop, a former GP at Miami's Mt Sinai Hospital. He'd recently retired from the hospital to run New Life full time.

Mo called the centre and was asked to an interview at four that afternoon. Although he was still woozy from his final binge the night before, he agreed. Mo was in deep emotional pain, right on the edge. He needed help, and fast. He packed a bag and got a ride to New Life.

It wasn't the five-star lifestyle he'd become used to. Upon arrival, an assistant named George greeted him gruffly, and asked Mo to hand over his bag. George emptied the contents on the floor, going through everything in case Mo had stashed away some booze. 'I took great offence to this,' said Mo.

His anger intensified when George insisted on strip-searching him. Now in a serious huff—how dare they treat me like this!—Mo packed up his bag and headed for the communal coffee room. He was seriously thinking about leaving. In the coffee room, the other New Life clients were very interested in the celebrity in their midst and started firing questions at Mo.

'What's it like, being a star?' 'Do you know Barbra Streisand—what's she like?' As these people gathered around him, Mo came to a shocking realisation: Wherever he went, he was, inescapably, a Bee Gee. He wondered if he even had an identity away from the group. 'I realised as I was talking,' said Mo, 'that this was such a mask. A façade.'

His anger subsiding, Mo agreed to the 28-day program. In one of his first sessions with Dr Trop, the doctor said something that resonated deeply with Mo.

'You can play the game,' Trop told him, *just don't become the game.'*

Just don't become the game. Mo liked that a lot.

He realised that for much of his life he'd indeed 'become the game'; he'd bought totally into the idea that he was privileged and untouchable—a star. But none of that mattered inside New Life. Mo stayed in a small, bland room, with cream-coloured walls, a single lamp, dull brown carpet, a small bedside drawer. No superstar trappings.

During one of his first days there, he was informed that volleyball was at three o'clock. 'Volleyball?' Mo thought. '*Moi?* I've never played volleyball in my life.' He reluctantly sat courtside, silently fuming, wondering why he'd put himself in such a place.

'Group'—where all the clients got together and talked things through—was a part of daily life. During one session, a man named Si told his story, which hit Mo hard. Si had alienated his wife, his children, his family, everything. 'That's *me,*' Mo realised. He burst into tears.

Si reached over and grabbed Mo's hand. 'You know you've been an arsehole, don't you?'

Mo knew it was true. That night, still teary, he called Yvonne and told her he was willing to make big changes in his life, in their life. 'There was a method behind the madness of what they were doing [at New Life],' said Mo. 'They wanted to see if you could take suggestions, if you were willing to listen to somebody.'

Mo saw it as life-saving stuff. He also came to understand, over time, that he'd felt his success with the Bee Gees was a fluke, that he was somehow 'unworthy' of all the acclaim. He was full of self-loathing. Like brother Andy, he was experiencing insecurities and fears. 'You can't love anyone else,' Mo reasoned, 'if you can't love yourself.'

Yet Mo's role in the group, that of the man in the middle—he actually wrote a song with that title—was essential, and this was one of many things he'd have to learn to accept when he finally checked out of New Life and into a halfway house named Transitions, the next step in his recovery. At Transitions, he was holed up in yet another bland, nondescript room, this time sharing with three other men. It was a further step down for Mo, most of whose life had been spent in one gilded cage after another. Now he was hanging out with a fellow recoveree named Dave, jamming 'Not Fade Away' with him on a couple of battered acoustic guitars. But Mo got into the spirit of campus-like Transitions—to him, it was the college days he'd never experienced.

Eventually, however, Mo had to return to a normal, post-booze existence with Yvonne and the kids. It wasn't easy, but over time he won back Yvonne's trust, so much so that in 1992 they renewed their wedding vows, in a big-hearted ceremony staged at their home, surrounded by family and friends.

As Mo looked into Yvonne's eyes and said, 'I, Maurice, take thee, Yvonne, my beloved wife …' the strains of 'How Deep Is Your Love' swelled and seemed to linger in the air. The ballad now had a more profound meaning in Mo's life than ever before. Mo, true to character, messed up a vow or two, playing to the audience, lightening the mood.

Mo gradually built a new network of friends, non-drinkers,

some from the program. They were his role models. Together they conducted 'rap' sessions every Saturday. Yvonne also helped out at the centre. Like pretty much everything in Mo's life, recovery was a family affair.

While Mo was in treatment, Barry and Robin understood that Mo still needed them, and the group, to continue with his life. The BBC cameras caught the trio together, working on a new song called 'Size Isn't Everything'. 'It's nice to go into the studio and know you don't have to replace the parts you did the night before,' smiled Mo, a whole new chapter of his life opening up before his eyes.

The year 1992 was full of mixed emotions for the extended Gibb family. Mo passed through rehab to recovery, and Barry and Linda welcomed a baby girl, Alexandra, Barry's fifth child. But then, on 6 March, Hugh Gibb passed away aged 76, one day after what would have been Andy's 34th birthday. The Gibb paterfamilias died from internal bleeding.

Barry believed that Andy's sudden, tragic end hastened his father's death. '[Hugh] stopped living when Andy died,' added Mo. 'I think he died of a broken heart.' Hugh was buried alongside Andy at Forest Lawn, in the Court of Remembrance.

The album that the brothers were slowly piecing together, called *High Civilisation*, had been released in 1991, but didn't even chart in America, and in the UK it only reached No.24, despite a charting hit named 'Secret Love'. They only played three dates to promote the record in the UK, followed by a tour of Europe. It seemed right that in the wake of so much loss—near-loss in Mo's case—that they step away from the limelight, again.

There was an album in 1993, the cheekily-titled *Size Isn't Everything*, which did produce a UK top five in 'For Whom the Bell Tolls'—another Hemingway title—but they didn't tour the record. They had no interest in going back on the road. It really wasn't until 1997, with the release of the *Still Waters* album that the brothers publicly reunited. And it was on 6 May of that year that the Bee Gees were given an accolade that truly acknowledged their remarkable career.

The 12th annual Rock and Roll Hall of Fame awards were held for the first time at the award's spiritual home, the Hall of Fame itself in Cleveland, Ohio. The new inductees included Parliament-Funkadelic—16 members of the ever-changing line-up shared a stage—along with Crosby, Stills and Nash, singer-songwriter Joni Mitchell, the Young Rascals and the Jackson 5. But the biggest moment of the night was reserved for that other family band, the Bee Gees. As their name was announced, a video montage, with voiceovers, flashed on the screen, depicting their long and winding road to the top, intercut with songs and clips from their many phases and stages: child stars, Beatles devotees, disco innovators and, more recently, pop statesmen.

Brian Wilson stepped up to the dais. He recalled how when he and his brothers Carl and Dennis were kids in California, perfecting three part harmonies, the three Gibbs were doing likewise on the other side of the world. 'I love the Bee Gees and whenever one of their songs comes on the radio I definitely stop what I'm doing and listen,' continued Wilson, sounding less like a man dependent on the autocue and more like a fan.

'The magic of the Bee Gees,' he added, 'is in their songwriting and their lyrics . . . but the real secret is, they're a family, they're brothers. There's nothing more important than spiritual love in music and the Bee Gees have been giving us that spiritual love for 30 years.'

As 'Nights on Broadway' played, Mo, Robin and Barry stepped onto the Hall of Fame stage and the crowd rose to their feet. Not for the first time that night, as it so happened. The years had taken their toll—Robin's hair was all but gone, his face was lined, tinted shades hid his eyes; Mo's ever-present hat was firmly in place; even Barry's mane had thinned a little. But the brothers did look undeniably dapper in their dark suits. As they strode to the podium, Barry stepped forward to speak on their behalf.

'We should be speechless,' chuckled Barry from behind his glasses, 'but we're not. First of all, we should thank our Mum and Dad.' Barry asked mother Barbara to stand up and take a bow, along with their wives, Yvonne, Linda and Dwina, who were all seated together.

'We are in fact the enigma with the stigma, we know this,' Barry went on, referring to the frequent denouncing of the group's worth, the party line among critics that they were merely disco automatons and/or Beatles clones. 'We've lived with it. But tonight I hope I don't sound too corny when I say I think we've come home. I thank you very much for this honour.

'Do we play now?' Barry asked, and then he, Mo and Robin did just that, stepping up for a million-dollar medley of 'Massachusetts', 'Words', 'How Deep Is Your Love', 'Jive Talkin'', 'Stayin' Alive'— and by the time they sang 'You Should Be Dancing', the finale, the usually staid Hall of Fame crowd were up and out of their seats. It was party time in Cleveland.

As big moments went, this was hard to top. They'd sold records by the warehouse load, filled arenas, earned millions of dollars, set all kinds of commercial benchmarks, but finally they were being acknowledged as peers by the cream of the music industry.

On the strength of the success of their new *Still Waters* album, which eventually sold more than four million copies and hit No.11 in the US and No.2 in the UK—their highest chart placing there since 1979—the brothers agreed to a one-off show in Las Vegas, at the MGM Grand Garden Arena on 14 November 1997. They were loath to undertake a lengthy tour; Barry had been experiencing worsening back pain which, with his arthritis, threatened his ability to play. His 51-year-old body just wasn't up to the rigours of touring.

The Vegas show, and its accompanying CD, was called *One Night Only*, and for good reason: as far as the Gibbs were concerned, it was the final show of their stellar career. Forty years on the road, more or less, were plenty.

However, they hadn't anticipated the commercial success of the *One Night Only* CD, which sold five million copies. The album went platinum, or better, in the US, the UK, Australia, Austria, Canada, New Zealand, Norway and Switzerland. The brothers Gibb remained a global phenomenon. What began as a one-night stand in Vegas grew into a handful of *One Night Only* gigs, reluctantly agreed upon by Barry. At London's Wembley Stadium they played to 56,000 people on 5 September 1998; there was a Sydney show scheduled for six months later.

Their Sydney concert at the new Olympic Stadium in Homebush, on 27 March, opened with fireworks synched to *Bandstand*-era images of the trio followed by a montage of their entire history—40-plus years in a matter of minutes, all to the backdrop of 'You Should Be Dancing'. Why leave the party-starters to the end, seemed to be their mindset, when you can open with a little friendly bump'n'grind?

Their on-stage look was different to the street spirit of '89.

Leather ruled—all three sported shiny leather coats; full length in Mo's case, matched with leather duds in Barry's. They could have passed for pop storm troopers. Robin's receding hair was now offset by what had to be a hairpiece; it looked a little too neat for a man whose hair hadn't seemed quite ... right for some time. Shades hid his eyes. Mo opted for his signature black felt hat, now matched with prescription glasses. Barry still looked the goods, the archetypal glowing middle-aged pop star, a blinding smile fixed to his dial.

The balance of the Gibbs' set changed this time around—'Stayin' Alive', a set-ending roof-raiser in the past, came and went within the first 10 minutes. 'Night Fever', which segued into 'More Than a Woman', continued the funky mood, and much of the audience was up and on their feet before their seats were warm. So what if Barry's falsetto sometimes wobbled when he reached for those tricky top notes? The crowd was up for a party. Even Barry, despite his chronic back problems and the imposition of a brace, managed a little swivel of his hips. And their set design was a bit more cutting-edge, seemingly millions of lights flashing in all directions, a huge video screen pulling the 72,000 crowd into the action, even those way up in the nosebleeds. The more recent 'You Win Again' was another favourite, bringing on a massive singalong, thousands of voices echoing around the vast concrete bunker.

Fully aware that the Gibbs' confidante Olivia Newton-John was in the front row, they eased into a smooth take of 'Grease', which Barry had written for the hit film way back in the Stiggy days. Images of John Travolta and ONJ from the movie flickered on the screen behind the group. Then it was time for the first of many golden oldies, a gentle rework of 'To Love Somebody', arguably still the best song the Bee Gees ever recorded, recognised as a stone-cold, blue-eyed-soul classic. Finally.

Andy, 'who lived here for a quite a few years ... who would have loved to have seen a crowd like this', in Barry's words, was remembered with the understated '(Our Love) Don't Throw It All Away' and an accompanying video montage: Andy as a kid at the suburban pool with Barbara, Andy riding a jet-ski in Florida, on the beach, then getting married to Kim, chilling with Stiggy backstage somewhere, and soaking up the madness during the Bee Gees' '79 *Spirits Having Flown* frenzy. They even used an Andy vocal, their lost soul of a brother singing along from beyond the grave. It was a touching, fitting and very public farewell to their dead sibling.

Yet as the applause continued for what seemed forever on that magical night, it would have been unimaginable to anybody in that arena that the Bee Gees would never play together in Australia again. Five decades down the line, the end was drawing near for the Gibbs.

The Gibbs surfaced with a new record, *This Is Where I Came In*, in April 2001. This time they shared the creative load: Robin and Barry only co-wrote three of the dozen tracks, the other nine were shared between Barry (four), Robin (three) and there were two songs from Mo, who finally stated publicly with his song 'Man In the Middle' what everyone close to the brothers had known for years. That was his role in the group, the middle man, the cheery soul who acted as a buffer between the volatile Robin and group leader Barry.

Even without the support of a tour—they played just one show, a *Live by Request* spot on American cable network A&E—the album generated a Top 20 hit in the US, with 'This Is Where I Came In', supported by a quirky, offbeat video that briefly rewound time way back to Redcliffe and the 1950s, seemingly a nod to their Aussie roots. (Who'd have ever imagined the Gibbs consenting to filming a scene where they shared a beaten-up Kombi, let alone a bed.) The album reached the Top 20 in the UK and US. There was another one-off show, at the Love and Hope Ball in 2002, but that was it. The brothers dropped out of sight, again, until tragedy reunited them centrestage.

In early January 2003, on a Wednesday evening, Maurice collapsed at his home in Miami and was rushed to nearby Mt Sinai Medical Center. He was diagnosed with an intestinal blockage and was scheduled for surgery. The plan was to remove a part of his stomach; his doctors said it was possible that his intestines had been blocked for many years. But then Mo suffered a heart attack. The medical staff decided to operate, but Maurice died soon after, at 1 a.m. on 13 January. He'd only recently turned 53.

Everyone was stunned: Barry, Yvonne and Mo's children, Adam and Samantha, and Robin, who'd just flown in from the UK to be at his twin's bedside. Their grief was virtually bottomless. It was only in the past decade that Mo really turned his life around, got off the booze—he didn't deserve this. It was simply wrong. How could Mo, someone so full of life, suddenly be dead?

Barry and Robin questioned the doctors; should they have operated after Mo's heart attack? No one knew for sure.

'It is with great sadness and sorrow that we regretfully announce the passing of Maurice Gibb,' read the official Gibb family statement. 'His love and enthusiasm and energy for life remain an inspiration to all of us. We will all deeply miss him.'

Barry spoke to the press after the news broke.

'None of the sequence of events have made sense to us,' he said, brushing tears from his eyes.

Privately, Barry had to deal with the additional trauma of knowing that he and Mo weren't getting along at the time of his death. They'd had a falling out and never found the chance to remedy things.

'I can't come to terms with it,' said a devastated Robin. 'It's like a nightmare ... it's going to take a long time even just for it to sink in.'

Michael Jackson, godfather to one of Barry's children and a long-time Gibb family friend, was one of hundreds at Mo's funeral, along with Eric Clapton. Every mourner was in shock.

Soon after, Robin spoke with *Mojo* magazine. 'We spent the whole of our lives together ... I can't accept that he's dead. I just imagine he's alive somewhere else.'

Within a month of Mo's death, the Bee Gees, 'the enigma with the stigma', were acknowledged at the Grammy Legends awards. With Tony Bennett, Elvis Costello and John Mayer clapping them onto the stage, Barry and Robin accepted their gong with the usual reverence, but they were both shattered men. 'It was incredible to receive [the award],' Barry said afterwards, 'but we were sort of numb. If Mo had been there with us, it would have been the cream on the cake.' Robin felt the night was bittersweet. 'Mo wasn't there,' he said simply.

Barry kept a brave face after Mo's tragic death—the band would go on, he insisted, if for no reason other than reminding people about Maurice, his brother, the group's in-house court jester, a guy who brought any room to life as soon as he entered. There will still be a Bee Gees, Barry insisted.

But that proved to be wishful thinking. In an interview in late

January, Robin revealed that the Bee Gees' name was to be 'retired', despite Barry's intentions to keep going.

'The Bee Gees, to us, was the three brothers,' Robin said. 'In Maurice's name, we would respect that and not be the Bee Gees anymore. Anything [Barry and I] do, we will do together, but it'll be as brothers and not under the name of the Bee Gees. We don't want to be the Bee Gees again.'

And that was it. The Bee Gees' odyssey was officially over.

Barry and Robin had different ways of dealing with Mo's death, but his loss pulled them apart. Robin spoke of 'an emotional vacuum' that opened between he and his brother. 'Barry had a way of dealing with it, I had mine.' There was talk of a tribute concert in Mo's honour, but the two surviving Gibbs couldn't agree on the details. Barry and Robin drifted, not speaking for a year or more. 'Robin and I functioned musically, but we never functioned in any other way,' Barry confessed in 2014. 'We were brothers, but we weren't really friends.'

When Robin released a new solo album, *Magnet*, in February 2003, Barry was as surprised as anyone: he had no inkling that Robin had been recording new music. Nor did he know that Robin had re-recorded 'Wish You Were Here', their sad tribute to Andy, and included the song on *Magnet*. According to a 2003 report in the *New York Times*, that decision left Barry 'devastated'. That was *their* song, *their* valentine to Andy, not Robin's alone.

Then there were some business moves that split the pair. In 2001, Barry had severed his ties with British lawyer Michael Eaton, who'd represented the Bee Gees for more than 30 years, and hired John

Branca, a Hollywood music lawyer, and John Cousins, a British accountant. Mo and Robin continued to work with Eaton—although Branca, at least for a time, thought that he was representing all three Gibbs. In 2002, Barry had also shifted his publishing to Warner/ Chappell Music, while Mo and Robin stayed with long-time music publisher BMG. In 2003, Barry ascribed these changes to a 'midlife crisis', but the real reason for his decisions was that he didn't like how his finances were being handled. Nor did he like the way the group's music was being promoted; he didn't believe the Bee Gees were being well treated by their publisher in this new, lucrative age of 'synching', where popular songs were used in everything from cell phone ring tones to computer game soundtracks. The big money was now being made in a world beyond record sales, and the Bee Gees weren't cashing in, according to Barry.

By May 2003, Barry insisted that any troubles between he and Robin had been resolved, but it was a new world order for a family group who'd taken the 'one in, all in' approach throughout their career. And the stakes were high: the Bee Gees' publishing catalogue was valued at somewhere around $150 million.

The one thing that seemed certain was that the Bee Gees were no longer a living, breathing entity, despite Barry's initial intention to honour Mo by keeping the group alive. Stiggy, in a rare public announcement, had said he could imagine the brothers 'in wheelchairs, still recording'. That didn't seem likely now.

While Barry and Linda and various other Gibbs remained in Florida, Robin spent most of his time with his second wife Dwina in a 13th-century mansion in Thame, Oxfordshire. They shared a 40.5-hectare spread with some history—it was a former monastery mentioned in the *Domesday Book* that had once been visited by Henry VIII and his wife Anne Boleyn. Photos of Robin and his brothers with seemingly every celebrity on the planet lined the walls of his stately home, alongside gold and platinum records marking their many and varied sales landmarks. A bust of Winston Churchill, one of Robin's heroes, rested alongside a suit of armour. Expensive oil paintings covered the walls. It was the kind of home expected of a man whose estimated worth was in the vicinity of £140 million.

At night, Robin would quietly retire to his music room, noodling away on a piano, working on music that he wasn't sure should ever be recorded. Dwina would lie in bed and hear his soft, high voice drift up from downstairs.

Their marriage had always been an 'open' affair, but Robin had really tested the boundaries when he started an eight-year affair with their live-in housekeeper, Claire Yang, who was in her early 30s. A baby girl, Snow Evelyn Robin Juliet, was born to Claire and Robin in 2009. When a reporter asked 56-year-old Dwina how she dealt with a budding romance under her own roof, she admitted to never being a 'jealous person—my attitude has always been live and let live. People who are creative are very different, I think, from conventional couples.'

Barry and Robin supported various charities, and it was this charity work that finally drew them back together. On 20 February 2006, they shared a stage for the first time since Mo's death, at a fundraiser for diabetes research at the University of Miami in Florida. Three months later, there was a much larger event, the Prince's Trust 30th Birthday Concert, staged at the Tower of London.

'Evening all,' Barry said nonchalantly as he and Robin, both wearing suits and looking more like businessmen than pop stars, took the stage. Still, the poignancy of the moment was lost on nobody. The brothers sang 'Jive Talkin'' and a slowed-down, haunting 'To Love Somebody'. In the stands, looking on, Princes Charles, Harry and William jiggled a little in their seats. The Gibb brothers could still be pretty funky for middle-aged white guys.

It was the last time Barry and Robin would share a stage.

Robin continued as a solo act, appearing at some unlikely places—the Miss World pageant in Warsaw, a convention for NuSkin Enterprises in Salt Lake City, at the National Palace of Culture in Sofia, Bulgaria, as a guest mentor on the Australian TV version of *The X Factor*—but as he moved into his late 50s, 'Bodding' appeared even more gaunt, his face drawn, his frame pencil-thin, his health failing. He worked on a new solo album, *50 St Catherine's Drive*, the address of the Gibbs' house on the Isle of Man.

On 14 August 2010, while performing in Belgium, Robin experienced abdominal pains. Eight days later he underwent surgery at an Oxford hospital for a blocked intestine, the condition that hastened Mo's death. Robin recovered and continued making sporadic appearances, but a string of events—a planned tour of Brazil, a Paris concert in October 2011, a charity appearance in London—were cancelled due to his ill health. There was talk of a tour with Barry, perhaps even a Steven Spielberg-produced Bee Gees biopic, but nothing transpired.

In late October 2011, looking distressingly drawn and thin, Robin assured a reporter that he felt 'absolutely great', but Robin was dying. In November, he was diagnosed with colorectal cancer, which had spread to his liver. He underwent chemotherapy to battle the disease. Barry visited Robin in the hospital. 'I love you,'

Robin told him. Barry tenderly kissed his brother's forehead, not saying a word.

In January of the new year Robin was still talking tough, saying that his London Clinic doctor, Peter Harper, had told him the results of his chemotherapy were 'spectacular'.

'I am not and have never been at "death's door",' Robin insisted. He talked up the health benefits of Dwina's herbal tea. 'I've mostly felt great,' he stressed.

On 21 February, Barry played his first-ever solo show, at the Seminole Hard Rock in Fort Lauderdale, Florida, his son Stephen alongside him, playing guitar and singing. 'Say a little prayer for Rob,' Barry told his fans from the stage. Come March and Robin was hospitalised again for further surgery. In April, Robin contracted pneumonia and lapsed into a coma, from which he briefly emerged. But his cancer had advanced, and on 20 May Robin Gibb died from liver and kidney failure. He was 62.

The Robin Gibb memorials were many and varied: Who belter Roger Daltrey talked up Robin's oft-overlooked talents as a vocalist; John Travolta remembered him as 'gifted, generous, a real friend to everyone he knew'. Dionne Warwick called Robin 'wonderful, a jokester ... fun to be around'. Elton John, Peter Frampton, Ronan Keating, Liam Gallagher and dozens of other peers and friends paid tributes to Robin Hugh Gibb.

The final word on Robin, however, was left to Barry, his big brother, musical collaborator and occasional sparring partner for the past 62 years. In a touching sound and vision montage simply called 'Bodding', incorporating behind-the-scenes Bee Gees footage and home movies, Barry assembled a heartfelt online tribute to his brother, all the way from Redcliffe to the top of the charts, set to the strains of the Bee Gees' 'Heart Like Mine'. Music was the best way for Barry to express his terrible pain. Unfortunately for Barry, Robin's passing had jarring echoes of Mo and Andy's death: he wasn't getting along with any of his brothers when they died. 'A few more good times would have been wonderful,' Barry said not long after Robin's death.

A white horse-drawn carriage took Robin's body to the burial ground at the Church of St Mary the Virgin, near his home at Thame. A lone bagpiper played a mournful solo as the procession moved slowly through the streets. Barry solemnly walked alongside the carriage with Dwina. His hair was now snowy white and the strain of the past 10 years showed on his face. His remaining family surrounded him, but Barry was very much alone. He was the Bee Gees' sole survivor. The last man standing.

# epilogue

'*You know, the more I look at Mo, and Robin and Andy, the more I realise we were just the reincarnation of the Marx Brothers.*' BARRY GIBB

February 2013. For one of the few times in his life, Barry Gibb seemed lost centrestage. He'd spent much of his 50 years in the entertainment biz surrounded by his brothers, Maurice and Robin, but now they were gone. The stage could look cramped when three brothers sang together—four, occasionally, when Andy joined them—but now it looked vast and empty, cavernous. Barry could sense that, too. This was going to be tough.

Tonight in Brisbane was one of the earliest dates on his 'Mythology' tour, supporting a release of the Bee Gees' hits of the same name, but it was also one of the most significant. Brisbane, the Gibbs' surrogate hometown, was as much a part of their journey as Manchester, the Isle of Man and Miami. And this was the first time Barry had played there since the death of the twins. This was the city where the brothers had met Johnny O'Keefe and Col Joye, who'd advised them to head down to Sydney, the 'big smoke', to try to build a career. It was also where they'd connect with the two Bills, Goode and Gates, who each played key roles in getting their journey underway. To Barry, this Australian visit, his first as a solo act, was a 'sentimental journey'.

'It's been a shocking decade,' Barry said just prior to the tour, reflecting on the harrowing loss of his brothers. 'It's tough for Mum; she sheds a tear nearly every day. I feel for her. But, as I say, the windows are opening, the fresh air's coming in—and life must go on.'

There was no financial need for Barry to tour. Even a conservative estimate of his worth meant that something like $5 million hit his bank account every year on the strength of music publishing revenue and record sales alone. He had sizeable properties in Miami, England and elsewhere. He was a wealthy, successful man with a bad back and arthritis, zeroing in on 70. Barry could have chosen to slip quietly into his twilight years, but felt he had to pay tribute to his siblings in the way he knew best: through music. He also came to understand that it was his responsibility to keep his family's music alive. 'That's my job now,' he said.

Two other people influenced his decision to get back on the road. One day, at home in Miami's Millionaires Row, Linda grew tired of seeing Barry sprawled on the couch, channel surfing.

'You can't just sit here and die with everybody else,' she told him, point blank. 'Get on with your life.'

Soon after, Barry met up with former Beatle Paul McCartney in New York and they discussed career longevity.

'I'm not sure I can keep doing this,' Barry admitted.

'What else are you going to do?' McCartney asked him.

'Fair enough,' Barry thought to himself. 'OK then. Time to get back to work.'

His brothers were gone, but Barry still made the tour a family affair. Maurice's daughter Samantha and Barry's eldest son Stephen were among his backing band; the latter joined Barry for a potent rendition of Robin's 'I've Gotta Get a Message to You'. Off-stage, Barry's daughter Ally worked the teleprompter, while Linda, Barry's wife of 40-plus years, looked on from the wings. If someone stuffed up, it was likely their surname was Gibb.

The absence of his brothers really became apparent during 'New York Mining Disaster', which Barry strummed alone on an acoustic guitar. It brought the house down, applause resounding in the hall for two minutes. Seated on a stool to prop up his aching back, Barry wiped the tears from his eyes, briefly turning away from the audience, clearly distressed. This wasn't showbiz; his feelings were real and sincere and deeply, deeply felt.

After a long, long pause, Barry said, 'What about this fantastic band?', doing his best to get on with things.

Later on, deep into the show, he slowed things down. The image of an eternally youthful, bare-chested Andy briefly flickered on the video screen behind him. 'OK,' Barry whispered, taking a deep breath, sipping from a cup he held in his hand. 'I want to say a quick few words about my brothers. You know, the more I look at Mo, and Robin and Andy, the more I realise we were just the reincarnation of the Marx Brothers.' The crowd laughed along with him.

'Andy was our kid brother, he wanted to be a pop star, he wanted to be like his older brothers. And Andy became a pop star. He succeeded. He was a bright spark and we love him and he left us well before his time. Andy.'

An image of Mo was next on the big screen as applause rang out into the night. Barry took another deep breath and continued. 'Mo was special. He was very extroverted, outgoing, he was the guy who was always out there trying to help other people. He did magic tricks; he'd make coins come out of your ears. That was Mo. I miss him and I love him. He'll always be right here,' Barry said, touching his heart. A corny gesture, yes, but totally sincere.

'And then of course there's Robin,' Barry continued, as the image behind him changed. 'Robin was an absolute dichotomy: he was two extremes. He could be the funniest man you've ever known, or the saddest man you've ever known. That was his gift; some of the great songs he came up with came from this sadness.'

Then another pause.

'I think he knew long before any of us did that it wasn't going to be a long life. He just knew. I didn't know why he was that way, but I admired it. So here's to Rob, the guy who would dye his hair the same colour as his dog.' A photo flashed on the screen to back that up—it was harder to tell whose hair was more rust-coloured, that of Robin or his pooch.

Barry raised his cup as a family portrait now showed on the screen. His sister Lesley didn't make the shot. She was still alive, living in Oz with eight kids; Barry had just visited her during a rare day off.

'It's been a fantastic experience all down the line, from Redcliffe, where the music began for us, to now, where we come full circle.'

After another pause, Barry and the band eased their way into the song 'Immortality', tears in his eyes, his voice wobbly with emotion. Barry then waved wildly to the crowd, shouted a heartfelt 'Goodnight!' and disappeared into the wings.

The house lights came up.

Barry Gibb's long journey back to where it all began, almost 50 years earlier, was over.

# bibliography

ABC TV Australia: Interview with the Bee Gees, July 1974

Anon: *Australian Women's Weekly*, 29 January 1960

Anon: *Australian Women's Weekly*, 13 March 1963

Anon: *Australian Women's Weekly*, 7 August 1963

Anon: *Australian Women's Weekly*, 6 November 1963

Anon: 'Bee Gees raise questions over death of Maurice'; *Daily Mail Australia*, 21 September 2012

Anon: Bob Hope's All-Star Comedy Revue USO Special, NBC, May 1980

Anon: 'The Bee Gees 35 Years of Music', *Billboard*, 24 March 2001

Anon: *Canberra Times*, 27 December 1967

Anon: The Bee Gees, *Everybody's*, 13 October 1965

Anon: Popping the Question, *Everybody's*, 27 July 1966

Anon: *Everybody's*, 3 August 1966

Anon: *Go-Set*, 25 January, 1967, p. 12

Anon: *Go-Set*, 24 May 1967, p. 1

Anon: *Go-Set*, 31 May, 1967, p. 3

Anon: *Go-Set*, 9 August 1967, p. 3

Anon: *Go-Set*, July 1974 review of Bee Gees in Australia

Anon: www.rollingstone.com/movies/pictures/play-the-album-burn-the-film-20-great-soundtracks-from-bad-movies-20140630/saturday-night-fever-1978-0723560#ixzz3HrOefzSU

Anon: www.rollingstone.com/movies/lists/the-25-greatest-soundtracks-of-all-time-20130829/saturday-night-fever-1977-19691231#ixzz3HrOB1Xl6

Anon: 'The Two Lives of Colin Petersen', *The Hinterland Times*, 9 May 2011

Apter, Jeff: *Up From Down Under: How Australian Music Changed the World*, The Five Mile Press, 2013

Bakker, Tiffany: 'Life Must Go On', interview with Barry Gibb, *Sunday* magazine, 13–19 January 2013

BBC: 'Maurice Gibb: Fighting Back', BBC TV, 1992

Bernstein, Fred: 'The Bee Gee and Sandy', *People*, 21 April 1980

Bilyeu, Melinda, Cook, Hector and Hughes, Andrew Môn: *The Ultimate Biography of the Bee Gees—Tales of the Brothers Gibb*, Omnibus Press, 2001

Brennan, Joseph: 'Gibb Songs', www.columbia.edu/~brennan/beegees

Casey, Bill: 'The One Eyed Fan in the Butcher's Storeroom', http://lmg.hurstville.nsw.gov.au/Ossie-Byrne-and-The-Bee-Gees.html

Casey, Bill: 'Mr Can-Do Meets Mr Make-Do', http://lmg.hurstville.nsw.gov.au/Nat-Kipner-and-The-Bee-Gees.html

Cohn, Nik: 'Tribal Rites of the New Saturday Night', *New York* magazine, 7 June 1976

D'Angelo, Joe: 'Bee Gees Name to be retired, Robin Gibb says', MTV News, 22 January 2003

DeCurtis, Anthony and Henke, James (editors): *The Rolling Stone Album Guide*, Virgin Books 1992

Dede, Mehmet: 'Jive Talkin' with Arif Mardin Man of the Year 2001'; www.lightmillennium.org/summer_fall_01/mdede_arifmardin.html

Diliberto, Gioia: 'AWOL from Broadway Once Too Often, Andy Gibb is Ordered to turn in his dreamcoat', *People*, 31 January 1983

Eagle Rock Entertainment: *This Is Where I Came In: The Official Story of the Bee Gees* DVD, June 1991

Eagle Rock Entertainment: *The Bee Gees: One Night Only 1997* DVD, August 2010

Eagle Rock Entertainment: *The Bee Gees In Our Own Time* DVD, November 2010

Eells, Josh: 'Barry Gibb: The Last Brother', *Rolling Stone*, 4 July 2014

Elder, Bruce: Various Bee Gees album reviews, www.allmusic.com

Fabrikant, Geraldine: 'Talking Money with Barry Gibb: Harmony on the Stage, Solo at the Bank', *New York Times*, 11 May 2003

*Good Morning Britain*: 1983 interview with Barry, Maurice and Robin Gibb

Gibb, Barry, Maurice and Robin: *The Bee Gees: The Authorised Biography*, *Telegraph-Herald*, 22 July 1979

Holden, Stephen: 'Arif Mardin, Music Producer for Pop Notables, Dies at 74', *New York Times,* 27 June 2006

Holden, Stephen: *Main Course* review, *Rolling Stone*, 17 July 1975

Hugus, Jennifer K: 'Tai Babilonia: Story of Survival On and Off the Ice'; *The Los Angeles Beat*, 5 February 2014

Kent, David: *Australian Chart Book 1970–1992*, Ambassador Press, 1993

Levin, Eric: 'Death of a Golden Child—For a Few Shining Moments, Andy Gibb Seemed to Light Up the Sky, Then he Found a Potent Distraction', *People*, 28 March 1988

Maslin, Janet: *Saturday Night Fever* movie review, *New York Times*, 16 December 1977

McFarlane, Ian: *The Encyclopedia of Australian Rock and Pop*, Allen & Unwin, 1999

McGrath, Noel: *Australian Encyclopedia of Rock*, Outback Press, 1978

Meyer, David N: *The Bee Gees The Biography*, Random House, 2013

National Film & Sound Archive of Australia: Bee Gees in Canberra 1974: www.nfsa.gov.au/collection/television/highlights/stories-from-the-capital-television-news/bee-gees-in-canberra-1974/

NBC @ 5: Interview with Andy Gibb, 1983

Neil, Beth: 'Bitter Bust-ups Led the Band to Split', *The Mirror*, 3 November 2009

Osmond, *The Donny and Marie Talk Show*: Interview with Victoria Principal, 22 September 1999

Pareles, Jon: 'Solid Gold Countdown: The 1985 Hit Parade', *New York Times*, 25 February 1986

Payne, Will: 'Lulu: Why I had to Dump Bee Gee Husband Maurice Gibb Over His Drinking, *The Mirror*, 13 May 2012

Polygram video: *Keppel Road: The Life and Music of the Bee Gees* DVD, June 1997

Sandoval, Andrew: *Bee Gees The Day-By-Day Story 1945–1972*, Retrofuture, 2012

Scott, Paul: 'The Bee Gee Who Hired a Hitman to Bump Off His Wife: FBI Files Reveal the Raging Jealousy and Drug-Fuelled Paranoia Behind Robin Gibb's Astonishingly Toxic Divorce', *Daily Mail Australia*, 21 September 2012

Tresca, Amber J: 'Maurice Gibb Dies at 53', http://ibdcrohns.about.com/cs/news/a/aa011303a.htm

Universal Studios: *Sgt. Pepper's Lonely Hearts Club Band* DVD, 2003

*The Warner Guide to UK & US Hit Singles*, Carlton Books, 1994

Various: *Billboard Tribute to the Bee Gees*, 24 March 2001

Weaver, Blue: www.blueweaver.com

# discography

## BEE GEES STUDIO ALBUMS

*The Bee Gees Sing and Play 14 Barry Gibb Songs* (November 1965)
I Was a Lover, a Leader of Men / I Don't Think It's Funny / How Love Was True / To Be or Not to Be / Timber / Claustrophobia / Could It Be / And the Children Laughing / Wine and Women / Don't Say Goodbye / Peace Of Mind / Take Hold of That Star / You Wouldn't Know / Follow The Wind

*Spicks and Specks* (November 1966)
Monday's Rain / How Many Birds / Playdown / Second Hand People / I Don't Know Why I Bother with Myself / Big Chance / Spicks and Specks / Jingle Jangle / Tint of Blue / Where Are You / Born a Man / Glass House

*Bee Gees 1st* (July 1967)
Turn of the Century / Holiday / Red Chair, Fade Away / One Minute Woman / In My Own Time / Every Christian Lion Hearted Man Will Show You / Craise Finton Kirk Royal Academy of Arts / New York Mining Disaster 1941 / Cucumber Castle / To Love Somebody / I Close My Eyes / I Can't See Nobody / Please Read Me / Close Another Door

*Horizontal* (February 1968)
World / And the Sun Will Shine / Lemons Never Forget / Really and Sincerely / Birdie Told Me / With the Sun in My Eyes / Massachusetts / Harry Braff / Daytime Girl / The Earnest of Being George / The Change is Made / Horizontal

*Idea* (August 1968)
Let There Be Love / Kitty Can / In the Summer of His Years / Indian Gin and Whisky Dry / Down to Earth / Such a Shame / I've Gotta Get a Message to You / Idea / When the Swallows Fly / I Have Decided to Join the Air Force / I Started a Joke / Kilburn Towers / Swan Song

*Odessa* (March 1969)
Odessa (City on the Black Sea) / You'll Never See My Face Again / Black Diamond / Marley Purt Drive / Edison / Melody Fair / Suddenly / Whisper Whisper / Lamplight / Sound of Love / Give Your Best / Seven Seas Symphony / With All Nations (International Anthem) / I Laugh in Your Face / Never Say Never Again / First of May / The British Opera

*Cucumber Castle* (April 1970)
If I Only Had My Mind on Something Else / I.O.I.O. / Then You Left Me / The Lord / I Was the Child / I Lay Down and Die / Sweetheart / Bury Me Down by the River / My Thing / The Chance of Love / Turning Tide / Don't Forget to Remember

*2 Years On* (December 1970)
2 Years On / Portrait of Louise / Man For All Seasons / Sincere Relation / Back Home / The First Mistake I Made / Lonely Days / Alone Again / Tell Me Why / Lay It on Me / Every Second, Every Minute / I'm Weeping

*Trafalgar* (September 1971)
How Can You Mend a Broken Heart? / Israel / The Greatest Man in the World / It's Just the Way / Remembering / Somebody Stop the Music / Trafalgar / Don't Wanna Live Inside Myself / When Do I / Dearest / Lion in Winter / Walking Back to Waterloo

*To Whom It May Concern* (October 1972)
Run to Me / We Lost the Road / Never Been Alone / Paper Mache, Cabbages and Kings / I Can Bring Love / I Held a Party / Please Don't Turn Out the Lights / Sea of Smiling Faces / Bad Bad Dreams / You Know It's For You / Alive / Road to Alaska / Sweet Song of Summer

*Life in a Tin Can* (January 1973)
Saw a New Morning / I Don't Wanna Be the One / South Dakota Morning / Living in Chicago / While I Play / My Life Has Been a Song / Come Home Johnny Bridie / Method to My Madness

*Mr Natural* (May 1974)
Charade / Throw a Penny / Down the Road / Voices / Give a Hand, Take a Hand / Dogs / Mr. Natural / Lost in Your Love / I Can't Let You Go / Heavy Breathing / Had a Lot of Love Last Night

*Main Course* (June 1975)
Nights on Broadway / Jive Talkin' / Wind of Change / Songbird / Fanny (Be Tender With My Love) / All This Making Love / Country Lanes / Come on Over / Edge of the Universe / Baby as You Turn Away

*Children of the World* (September 1976)
You Should Be Dancing / You Stepped Into My Life / Love So Right / Lovers / Can't Keep a Good Man Down / Boogie Child / Love Me / Subway / The Way it Was / Children of the World

*Saturday Night Fever* (November 1977)
Stayin' Alive / How Deep Is Your Love / Night Fever / More than a Woman / Jive Talkin' / You Should Be Dancing [all other songs on album not recorded by the Bee Gees]

*Sgt Peppers's Lonely Hearts Club Band*
(July 1978)
Sgt Pepper's Lonely Hearts Club Band

(with Paul Nicholas) / With a Little Help From My Friends (with Peter Frampton) / Getting Better (with Peter Frampton) / I Want You (She's So Heavy) / Good Morning Good Morning (with Paul Nicholas) / She's Leaving Home (with Steven Tyler) / Oh! Darling (Robin Gibb) / Rise To Stardom Suite [all other songs on soundtrack album not recorded by the Bee Gees]

*Spirits Having Flown* (February 1979)
Tragedy / Too Much Heaven / Love You Inside Out / Reaching Out / Spirits (Having Flown) / Search, Find / Stop (Think Again) / Living Together / I'm Satisfied / Until

*Living Eyes* (October 1981)
Living Eyes / He's a Liar / Paradise / Don't Fall in Love With Me / Soldiers / I Still Love You / Wildflower / Nothing Could Be Good / Cryin' Everyday/ Be Who You Are

*Staying Alive* (July 1983)
The Woman in You / I Love You Too Much / Breakout / Someone Belonging to Someone / Life Goes On / Stayin' Alive (edited version) [all other songs on soundtrack album not recorded by the Bee Gees]

*E.S.P.* (September 1987)
E.S.P. / You Win Again / Live or Die (Hold Me Like a Child) / Giving up the Ghost / The Longest Night / This is Your Life / Angela / Overnight / Crazy for Your Love / Backtafunk / E.S.P. (Vocal Reprise)

*One* (April 1989)
Ordinary Lives / One / Bodyguard / It's My Neighbourhood / Tears / Tokyo Nights / Flesh and Blood / Wish You Were Here / House of Shame / Will You Ever Let Me / Wing and a Prayer

*High Civilization* (April 1991)
High Civilization / Secret Love / When He's Gone / Happy Ever After / Party

with No Name / Ghost Train / Dimensions / The Only Love / Human Sacrifice / True Confessions / Evolution

*Size Isn't Everything* (September 1993)
Paying the Price of Love / Kiss of Life / How To Fall in Love (Part One) / Omega Man / Haunted House / Heart Like Mine / Anything For You / Blue Island / Above and Beyond / For Whom the Bell Tolls / Fallen Angel / Decadence

*Still Waters* (March 1997)
Alone / I Surrender / I Could Not Love You More / My Lover's Prayer / With My Eyes Closed / Irresistible Force / Closer than Close / I Will / Obsessions / Miracles Happen / Smoke and Mirrors

*This Is Where I Came In* (April 2001)
This Is Where I Came In / She Keeps On Coming / Sacred Trust / Wedding Day / Man in the Middle / Déjà Vu / Technicolor Dreams / Walking on Air / Loose Talk Costs Lives / Embrace / The Extra Mile / Voice in the Wilderness / Just in Case / Promise the Earth

## ANDY GIBB SOLO ALBUMS

*Flowing Rivers* (September 1977)
I Just Want to Be Your Everything / Words and Music / Dance To the Light of the Morning / Too Many Looks in Your Eyes / Starlight / (Love is) Thicker Than Water / Flowing Rivers / Come Home For the Winter / Let It Be Me / In the End

*Shadow Dancing* (April 1978)
Shadow Dancing / Why / Fool For a Night / An Everlasting Love / (Our Love) Don't Throw It All Away / One More Look At the night / Melody / I Go For You / Good Feeling / Waiting For You

*After Dark* (February 1980)
After Dark / Desire / Wherever You Are / Warm Ride / Rest Your Love On Me / I Can't Help It / One Love / Someone I Ain't / Falling in Love With You / Dreamin' On

## ROBIN GIBB SOLO ALBUMS

*Robin's Reign* (February 1970)
August October / Gone Gone Gone / The Worst Girl In This Town / Give Me A Smile / Down Came the Sun / Mother and Jack / Saved by the Bell / Weekend / Farmer Ferdinand Hudson / Lord Bless All / Most of My Life / One Million Years

*How Old Are You?* (May 1983)
Juliet / How Old Are You? / In and Out of Love / Kathy's Gone / Don't Stop the Night / Another Lonely Night in New York / Danger / He Can't Love You / Hearts On Fire / I Believe in Miracles

*Secret Agent* (June 1984)
Boys Do Fall in Love / In Your Diary / Robot / Rebecca / Secret Agent / Living in Another World / X-ray Eyes / King of Fools / Diamonds

*Walls Have Eyes* (November 1985)
You Don't Say Us Anymore / Like a Fool / Heartbeat in Exile / Remedy / Toys / Someone to Believe In / Gone With the Wind / These Walls Have Eyes / Possession / Do You Love Her?

*Magnet* (February 2003)
Please / Wait Forever / Wish You Were Here / No Doubt / Special / Inseparable / Don't Rush / Watching You / Earth Angel / Another Lonely Night in New York / Love Hurts

*50 St Catherine's Drive* (September 2014)
Days of Wine and Roses / Instant Love

/ Alan Freeman Days / Wherever You Go / I Am the World / Mother of Love / Anniversary / Sorry / Cherish / Don't Cry Alone / Avalanche / One Way Love / Broken Wings / Sanctuary / Solid / All We Have is Now / Sydney

## MAURICE GIBB SOLO ALBUMS

*The Loner* (November 1970, unreleased)
Journey to the Misty Mountains / The Loner / Please Lock Me Away / I've Come Back / Soldier Johnny / She's the One You Love / Railroad / Laughing Child / Something's Blowing / Silly Little Girl / Insight

*A Breed Apart* (1984, soundtrack, unreleased)
Hold Her In Your Hand / A Breed Apart / Jim's Theme / Solitude / The Intruders / On Time / Mike and the Mountain / Adam's Dream / A Touch Apart / The Breed Ending / Hold Her in Your Hand (instrumental)

## BARRY GIBB SOLO ALBUM

*Now Voyager* (September 1984)
I Am Your Driver / Fine Line / Face to Face / Shatterproof / Shine, Shine / Lesson in Love / Only Night (for Lovers) / Stay Alone / Temptation / She Says / The Hunter

## BEE GEES HIT SINGLES IN AUSTRALIA

Spicks and Specks (October 1966)
New York Mining Disaster (May 1967)
To Love Somebody (August 1967)
Massachusetts (October 1967)
World (December 1967)
I've Gotta Get a Message to You (September 1968)
I Started a Joke (January 1969)

Don't Forget to Remember (October 1969)
Lonely days (February 1971)
How Can You Mend a Broken Heart? (July 1971)
My World (January 1972)
Run to Me (August 1972)
Mr Natural (October 1974)
Jive Talkin' (August 1975)
How Deep Is Your Love (December 1977)
Stayin' Alive (February 1978 )
Night Fever (May 1978)
Too Much Heaven (December 1978)
Tragedy (February 1979)
You Win Again (October 1987)

Sources: *Noel McGrath's Australian Encyclopedia of Rock / Australian Chart Book 1970–1992*, compiled by David Kent

## BEE GEES HIT SINGLES IN NORTH AMERICA

Massachusetts (December 1967)
I've Gotta Get a Message To You (September 1968)
I Started a Joke (January 1969)
Lonely Days (January 1971)
How Can You Mend a Broken Heart (July 1971)
Jive Talkin' (July 1975)
Nights on Broadway (November 1975)
Fanny (Be Tender With My Love) (March 1976)
You Should Be Dancing (August 1976)
Love So Right (October 1976)
Boogie Child (March 1977)
How Deep Is Your Love (November 1977)
Stayin' Alive (January 1978)
Night Fever (February 1978)
Too Much Heaven (December 1978)
Tragedy (February 1979)
Love You Inside Out (May 1979)
One (September 1989)

Source: *The Warner Guide to US & UK Hit Singles*, compiled by Dave McAleer

279

## BEE GEES HIT SINGLES IN THE UK

New York Mining Disaster (May 1967)
Massachusetts (October 1967)
World (December 1967)
Words (February 1968)
I've Gotta Get a Message to You (August 1968)
First of May (March 1969)
Don't Forget to Remember (September 1969)
Run to Me (August 1972)
Jive Talkin' (July 1975)
You Should Be Dancing (August 1976)
How Deep Is Your Love (November 1977)
Stayin' Alive (March 1978)
Night Fever (April 1978)
Too Much Heaven (December 1978)
Tragedy (February 1979)
Love You Inside Out (May 1979)
You Win Again (October 1987)
Secret Love (March 1991)
For Whom the Bell Tolls (December 1993)
Alone (1997)
This Is Where I Came In (2001)

Source: *The Warner Guide to US & UK Hit Singles*, compiled by Dave McAleer

## AUTHOR'S TOP 20

With the rise of such apps as Spotify, it's easy to compile your own wishlist/playlist for the Gibbs, but here's my personal Top 20. Admittedly, it changes frequently:

Claustrophobia
Spicks and Specks
To Love Somebody
Every Christian Lion Hearted Man Will Show You
World
Edison
Lamplight
Trafalgar
Paper Mache, Cabbages & Kings
Mr Natural
Throw a Penny
Wind of Change
Fanny (Be Tender With My Love)
Country Lanes
Love is (Thicker Than Water) (Andy Gibb)
Guilty (Barry Gibb with Barbara Streisand)
For Whom the Bell Tolls
You Win Again
This is Where I Came In
Alan Freeman Days (Robin Gibb)

# index

# acknowledgements

Julia Taylor and Kay Scarlett and all at Echo Publishing/The Five Mile Press deserve a stadium-sized shout out for their support during what turned out to be a longer-than-anticipated writing process. I sincerely hope *Tragedy* was worth the wait. I'd like to thank Pippa Masson at Curtis Brown for putting together the pieces of *Tragedy* and also thank her for seven years of lively, supportive guidance. Larry Writer did a wonderful edit, yet again; I can't thank him enough for his sage advice and deft touch. Here's to many more, Larry. And thanks to Tom Seabrook at Jawbone Press for putting together this new UK/US edition.

Like many of my recent projects, *Tragedy* was a book that required the type of digging typically only found among archaeologists. There's so much on the record about the Gibbs that I needed to scratch away, dig a little deeper, in the search of that magic morsel of information. Accordingly, thanks to Simon Drake, Clare Norton and Kathryn McLeod at the National Film and Sound Archive and Peter Cox at the Powerhouse Museum for their support, patience and advice. Likewise Gemma Beswick at the Hurstville City Library.

My heartfelt thanks also goes out to Philip Morris, Steve Kipner, Eleanor Leamonth, Rick Pointon, Bob King, Blue Weaver, Barry Plummer, Chris Walter and Marion Adriaensen.

There were a couple of key items among the many, many books, docos, articles and artefacts that document the Gibbs' life and music. The documentaries *This Is Where I Came In* and *Keppel Road* both showed that candour—and the odd imaginative embellishment—was as natural to the Gibbs as high harmonies. The recently updated book, *Tales of the Brothers Gibb: The Ultimate Biography of the Bee Gees*, originally published by Omnibus Press in 2001, is, as the title says, the ultimate guide to all things Gibb. And I mean all things. The book's a monster.

As ever, my family—my wife Diana and my children Elizabeth and Christian—were with me for the ride, always understanding that even though my study door may be shut, it's never really closed. To them at least.

## PICTURE CREDITS

The photographs used in this book come from the following sources: **jacket front** Jan Persson/Redferns/Getty Images; **145** *1963 promo* GAB Archive/Getty Images; *Liverpool* Bentley Archive/Popperphoto/Getty Images; **146** Barry Plummer; **147** *Robin* Chris Walter/Photofeatures; *Sydney* Philip Morris; *Isle of Man* Chris Walter/Photofeatures; **148** *Andy* Philip Morris; *TOTP* Barry Plummer; *'Spirits' tour* Chris Walter/Photofeatures; **149** *Billboard Awards*, *Maurice* Chris Walter/Photofeatures; **150–1** *live, backstage* Barry Plummer; **152** *Miami* Michael Brennan/Getty Images.

# ALSO AVAILABLE IN PRINT AND EBOOK EDITIONS FROM JAWBONE PRESS